The fishing boats carrying the basketball team back to Lanai moved slowly into the channel. Danny and Bernard went to sit out on the bow of Teru's boat, looking over the water at the heights of Haleakala, the gigantic extinct volcano of Maui. Several miles out at sea, they felt a sound that vibrated the boat itself.

"Dat big kohola, humpback whale," Teru said. "He like sing on such nice day."

There was some commotion from the boys at the back of the boat. "It's moving! It's moving!" somebody shouted. All of a sudden, the humpback breached, hurling its fifty-ton body almost entirely out of the water. The backwash from the splash rocked the boat. Teru cut the motor.

"I've never seen anything like that," said Danny excitedly.

Teru put his finger to his lips and pointed in the direction of a smooth patch of water. "Humpback footprint," he said. He continued to point. Then gently, slowly, the snout of the huge humpback parted the water right next to the boat. It rose higher and higher until an eye the size of a cantaloupe stared at them. The boys pressed themselves against the opposite side of the boat. Teru laughed. "Him spyhop. Him like see da team win big game wid Lahainaluna last night. No scared, eh? Dis Teru friend."

CROSS
CURRENTS

CROSS CURRENTS

LEE G. CANTWELL

Deseret Book Company
Salt Lake City

Library of Congress Catalog Card Number: 93–12389

ISBN 0–87579–672–9

Printed in the United States of America

10   9   8   7   6   5   4   3   2   1

To Karen,
my wife, my editor,
my sweetheart, and my friend

Acknowledgments

Writing a book is a lonely task, but it is not without help. My thanks to Amy Fuchigami Wilson and Rose Abinosa Ernstrom for the loan of certain materials and for help with research; to my son Steve for reading and editing the various drafts; to Richard Tice, who did the final editing and supervised the publication process; and to my good friend Jack Lyon, who urged me to write the novel and gave me encouragement when I needed it most.

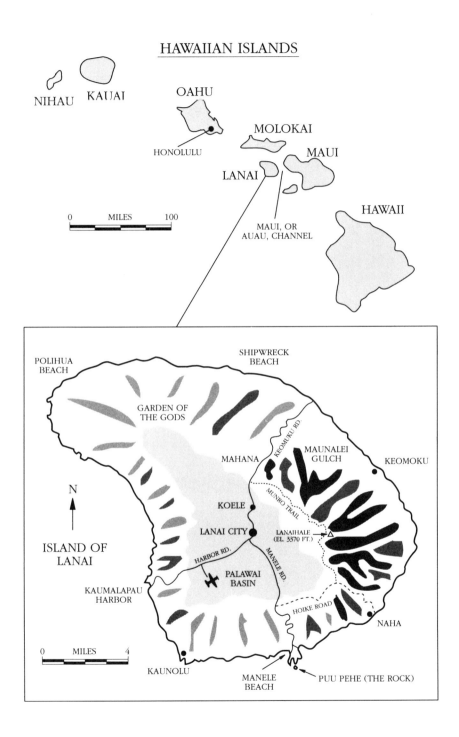

HAWAIIAN ISLANDS

NIHAU   KAUAI

OAHU

HONOLULU

MOLOKAI

MAUI

LANAI

MAUI, OR
AUAU, CHANNEL

HAWAII

0   MILES   100

POLIHUA
BEACH

SHIPWRECK
BEACH

GARDEN OF
THE GODS

MAHANA

KEOMUKU RD.

MAUNALEI
GULCH

KEOMOKU

N

ISLAND OF
LANAI

KOELE

MUNRO TRAIL

LANAI CITY

LANAIHALE
(EL. 3370 FT.)

HARBOR RD.

KAUMALAPAU
HARBOR

PALAWAI
BASIN

MANELE RD.

HOIKE ROAD

NAHA

0   MILES   4

KAUNOLU

MANELE
BEACH

PUU PEHE (THE ROCK)

Chapter
1

As Danny jogged across the park and up the street toward home, his mind filled with questions. Why had Nori refused to come to the party? The excuse she had given was just that, an excuse. Why had she been so uncomfortable? Was it because the party was to be in a Mormon chapel? Nori was a Buddhist, but other Buddhists would be there tonight. Was she not allowed to date? Maybe that was it! Maybe her father wouldn't let her date in high school. Maybe she was embarrassed about his old-fashioned ideas and ashamed to tell Danny about them. Maybe she just didn't want to go with him. Maybe she liked him as a friend but wasn't interested in him as a boyfriend.

None of it made any sense. This wasn't the first time Nori had come up with an excuse to avoid going on a date with him. He had asked her three times in the past few months, and each time she had come up with an excuse not to go. She hadn't said, "No, I won't go!" but she had always given some compelling reason why she couldn't. Her cousin was being married in Honolulu. She was spending the New Year's holiday with her aunt in Lahaina. She was a volunteer at the hospital and was on duty that night.

Danny stopped at the gate in front of his home and looked

at the little boxlike house where he had lived for eighteen years. He looked up and down the street. The houses were different colors, but otherwise as alike as the houses in a Monopoly game, all with corrugated metal roofs and compact yards. In Honolulu, houses were as different as the many nationalities who lived in them. Here on Lanai, they looked as though they had been made on an assembly line. Nori's house was different, but she lived on "Snob Hill" with her father and all the other plantation bigwigs. Danny's house was a light purple color. Maybe Nori promised her mother on her deathbed that she would never go out with a guy who lived in a lavender house. It was an amusing thought, but Danny didn't feel like laughing just then. He pushed open the gate and went in.

His father was busy in the kitchen when Danny came through the door. There was the noise of something dropping to the floor, followed by a burst of Filipino swear words that sounded like someone banging a wooden spoon on some old pots and pans. Benito Tolentino appeared in the kitchen doorway, smiling broadly. "You no mo' practice tonight, Danny? Maybe so, Coach Manning t'ink no need fo' practice after such plenty fine game last night, eh? You guys play too good. Dat Hana team get no chance wid you."

"He let us off early, but we practiced," Danny said. "He didn't want us to be away from basketball for three full days. I was afraid he might call a practice for tomorrow. Bernard and Podogi and I have been planning to go to Manele beach to poke fish. Looks like we can go now."

"Too good, boy! I hope you poke plenty. Since you all time play basketball, I get hungry fo' eat fish. When da season over, maybe so we go down Keomuku side, catch any kind big ulua, eh?"

Benito Tolentino was sixty-two years old, but his face looked older. The sunlight reflecting off the surface of the harbor where he worked had combined with the sun's direct rays to dry and tan his skin like old leather. His shirt was open at the neck. A deep V of tanned skin stood out like a brand against the lighter protected skin of his chest. The lines in his face betrayed his optimistic nature and naturally outlined the whimsical smile he wore most of the time. Benito was slightly vain about his full head of black hair. It was not unlike Danny's own, and until recently it had carried no trace of gray. Danny had caught him at the mirror plucking out the few white hairs that had dared to make their appearance. He was a wiry little man who worked hard and seemed to enjoy it. His heart had starting acting up a couple of years before, so the doctor had given him a supply of nitroglycerin tablets, which he carried in a small brown bottle in his pocket. He had always thought of himself as a specimen of good health, so this crutch embarrassed him a little. He was always careful not to let anyone see him taking one.

"Dat game last night too good, Danny. By 'n' by you come 1954 Maui District champs. I hope so!"

"We played well, but we were lucky too, Pop. Their best player had a pulled muscle and sat out most of the game."

Though Danny often spoke Pidgin when he was with his friends, he rarely used it when speaking to his father. It seemed disrespectful somehow, like pretending to limp around a crippled person. He also hoped that by speaking good English to him, he could help his father's English improve. Danny wished he could speak Tagalog, his father's native language, like his older brother and sister. They could rattle on like native Filipinos.

Danny's sister, Precious, had insisted that the family speak

English in their home after Danny was born. It had helped Danny but had been hard on his mother. Her English had not even been as good as Benito's since she spent most of her time at home and rarely had an opportunity to practice. Her halting, broken, Pidgin English made her sound ignorant and unrefined. At night when they thought Danny was asleep, Rosvena and Benito had lapsed into their native tongue. Sometimes Danny would lie quietly in his bed and listen. The language sounded so beautiful when they spoke it. His mother's voice was low-pitched and musical. In Tagalog, her words gushed forth like water from a flowing well, now quiet and secretive, now excited and full of mischief. Sometimes Benito laughed out loud, then spoke quickly in a warning tone, only to soften and dissolve into laughter again. When they were speaking Tagalog, they were like completely different people, strangers that Danny could never really know and appreciate properly.

"Dinner be ready plenty quick, you bet. Try take rest, eh?"

"I'm really not too hungry, Pop," Danny said quietly.

"No hungry after basketball practice? You must be sick. What-sa-matter, Danny?"

"Don't worry about me, Pop. I'm fine, really. Maybe I'm a little tired from the game and practice tonight. I think I will take a short nap before dinner." Danny started toward his room.

"Danny, you like tell your pop what kind problem you got?"

There was no fooling Benito. He could always tell when Danny was troubled. They had few secrets. Living alone together for the past eight years had brought them very close. Benito had confided things to his son that no other living person knew. They had an unspoken pact between them to face problems together. Danny returned to the kitchen.

"The Mormon kids are throwing a party for the team on

Saturday night, in the recreation hall at the church. The team members can bring dates if they want to. I happened to see Nori Satō in the park just now, and I asked her to go with me. Her aunt's visiting this weekend, so she can't go." Danny tried to water down the importance of the incident with Nori, but his father saw at once that he was crushed.

Benito's eyes flashed. "You every time ask her go any place wid you; she every time say, I no can go! How come you no shame?" He blinked his eyes rapidly and spoke in short bursts. "Plenty nice Pilipino girl t'ink you some fine guy, Chinee girl too. Even dat haole girl from mainland, she look to you wid big eyes, eh?" Benito rarely spoke sharply to his grown-up son. When he did, Danny listened with respect.

"What-sa-matter your brain, Danny? Forget Japanee girl. Her poppa real big potatoe in da plantation. Already he not so much like Pilipino. By 'n' by he find out you try make date wid Nori, come huhu, all mad, cause any kind trouble." Benito reached out and put his hands on Danny's shoulders. His voice was soft now, almost pleading. "No make trouble, Danny. Play ball, poke fish wid spear, look to another girl. Maybe so mo' better you forget girl for litty bit while! Plenty time for find girl when you go school Honolulu."

"Maybe you're right, Pop," Danny said softly. "Maybe I should just stick to basketball and spearfishing and forget about girls for a while." He walked over to where the older man was sitting and patted him gently on the shoulder. "There are plenty of girls in Honolulu, like you say." Danny walked to his room, went in, closed the door behind him, and then added, "But I won't be going to school in Honolulu anytime soon." The best scholarships went to the high schools in Honolulu, like Punahou, Iolani, and Kamehameha. Lanai High offered three scholarships to graduating seniors. They were all based on academic excellence. Bernard Ōta would get the best one; the Tam twins, Ronald and Connie, would get the other two. Danny was a good student, but not really in the same league with those three.

He lay down on his bed and folded his arms across his eyes. I know Pop plans to give me money for school, but I won't take it. For all those years, he sent money to his folks and mom's folks back in the Philippines. He needs every bit of the little he's been able to save for his retirement. Precious and Carlos need the money they make for their own families. I've got to make it on my own. I'll go to school, but maybe I'll have to wait a little while. It's okay, I have plenty of time. He thought of his father's advice concerning Nori. Pop means well, but he just doesn't understand. Maybe if Mother were still alive . . .

Danny's mother had died when he was only ten years old, but he remembered her very well. She was rather tall for a Filipino, with features that suggested a strong Spanish influence somewhere back in her lineage. Her face was attractive, with a well-formed nose and a generous mouth that displayed beautiful white teeth when she smiled, which was often. Danny had inherited her ready smile and Hispanic features; all his father's friends commented on the resemblance. "Look like da mama dis one, all same face, all same smile, all same teeth. Some good-lookin' fella he gonna come. Girl look to him every time when he come big."

Danny's mother, Rosvena Samonte, had been a picture bride. Relatives in the Philippines had arranged everything. Benito Tolentino sent a picture of himself that had been taken several years before. His family represented him as being much younger than his twenty-nine years. Rosvena had looked just like her picture when she stepped off the boat in Honolulu. If she was disappointed in Benito, she never showed it.

Danny thought of the old joke about the Filipino bachelor who had fallen in love with a beautiful blonde in a red dress in the Sears catalog. He had ordered her immediately and was terribly disappointed when "only da dress come."

Benito and Rosvena were married in a Catholic church in Honolulu with several other couples who had met for the first time that day. By evening they were on their way to Lanai on a pineapple barge. With the exception of a short trip to Honolulu to attend their daughter's wedding and a few trips by small fishing boats — sampan — to Maui, they had never left the tiny island of Lanai. They had a baby girl a year after their marriage and named her Precious. The next year they had a healthy boy and named him Carlos after Rosvena's father back in the Philippines. The next fourteen years were filled with heartbreak and disappointment for Benito and Rosvena, who had dreamed of having a large family. There were long periods between Rosvena's pregnancies, and each one had ended in a miscarriage.

When Danny was delivered full term and vigorous, they were jubilant. They determined to be happy with the wonderful children they had and agonized no more about having a larger family. When Danny was four years old, his brother, Carlos, joined the navy. That same year, Precious, who had gone to Honolulu to work, married a haole sailor from the midwest. They moved to the mainland when he was transferred to San Diego shortly after the wedding. Visits from the older children were few and far between. They seemed more like an aunt and an uncle to Danny than a sister and brother; he wished he could have known them better.

When Danny was ten years old, his mother became very

ill. The doctor diagonosed acute appendicitis and operated immediately, but the appendix had burst, and peritonitis set in. After forty-eight hours of fighting for her life, Rosvena died. Some people blamed the doctor, who was young and inexperienced, but Benito was not among them. "He try everyt'ing for save Rosvena," he said. "Some good dis one doctor. He stay wid her for da whole night. He no sleeping; he no eating, only watch Rosvena. He cry too when she die, jus' like me. He no can help, eh?"

Danny's father was broken-hearted. He could not sleep for many nights. Precious came home and stayed for a couple of weeks. Carlos was on shipboard, and they could not contact him until he got into port. After the funeral, Benito tried to put aside his grief and turned to the task of raising Danny.

In those years immediately following Rosvena's death, Danny went everywhere with his father. They often went fishing together at Keomuku. After Benito cast his line into the surf, they would sit back, watch the waves crash in, and listen for the jingle of the little bell attached to the pole that signaled a strike. They caught papio and the big ulua that sometimes weighed forty or fifty pounds. When the fish weren't biting, they would look out across the water at the islands of Maui and Molokai and "talk story." Danny was considered part of his father's team when they went to the bowling alley on Thursday nights. Sometimes Danny even tagged along when his father went to the cock fights. Cock fights were betting affairs, and feelings ran high. If things got out of hand, the two of them would leave. Some said that there were fewer arguments when Danny was there. No one wanted to be the cause of Benito having to leave.

As Danny grew up and began to be more involved with his friends, he and his father spent less time together, but if an activity involved parents, Benito was there. He seldom missed a home basketball game for any reason. His loyal support for Danny and the team emanated from his face like the beam from a lighthouse. Benito was remarkably perceptive in matters that affected Danny. He always seemed to know when Danny was disturbed. He took time to listen to Danny's problems and sometimes offered advice. Usually his advice was good. Danny valued his opinion, but forget Nori Satō? Danny wasn't sure he could do that.

How could he forget Nori? Nori with the ready smile and sparkling eyes, Nori with the slender body and quiet grace. It sounded foolish, but he knew it was true: he had fallen in love with Nori when he was six years old. The teacher had seated the children alphabetically the first day of school, and Danny Tolentino had ended up right behind Nori Satō. They had kept that seating arrangement all the way through elementary school, and she had been his inspiration from that very first day.

Nori was a model student. When the teacher gave an assignment, Nori bent to the task, hardly looking up until it was completed. Danny admired her ability to concentrate and tried to emulate it. When they started to read, Danny saw the level of books she was reading and tried to read them too. Nori was right there in front of him every day. He loved to watch her, loved the way her hair lay in soft curls on the back of her neck. He loved the way she talked to him and listened when he answered her. She made him feel important and capable. She gave him confidence and a motivation to try his best.

After his mother died, Danny became quiet and withdrawn. He was irritable and defensive with his classmates. After several rebuffs, some of his friends began to avoid him. Only Nori, who had lost her own mother a few months before, understood.

She saw him sitting alone in the playground behind the school one night and came and sat down beside him. At first Danny seemed not to notice that she was there. When he finally looked up, Nori could see that he had been crying. Tears formed in Nori's eyes too, and for what seemed like a long time, they sat in silence. Finally Nori spoke, "When my mother died last summer, I felt like I wanted to die too. If you want to talk to me about your mom, it's okay." They talked for over an hour, and their shared pain created a bond between them that was unique for a boy and girl of ten. Through the difficult times that followed, Danny never allowed his bitterness to affect his relationship with Nori.

Danny translated his deep sense of loss into feelings of anger. The natural, carefree manner of his classmates seemed like sacrilege: his world had been turned upside down, and they laughed and played as if nothing had happened. He mis-understood their well-meaning efforts to involve him in their games. They were just trying to be friendly, but to Danny they seemed callous and unfeeling. He became overly sensitive and defensive; any jokes about the Filipino race made him bristle. He had some fights in the school yard and began to get a reputation as a trouble-maker. The older boys baited him by talking "Pilipino Pidgin," then laughed at his efforts to fight back. He was a real scrapper and usually was able to do some damage to his tormentor, but that just made the older boy angry and made Danny's punishment worse. Many nights he went home with a bloody nose or some scratches and scrapes. Benito worried about him constantly.

One night there was a particularly bad scene in which the enraged Danny found himself charging back and forth between two large, teasing boys who were singing a song they knew Danny hated. Sung to the tune, "Polly Wolly Doodle All the

Day," it made fun of all the strange foods that the people of the islands ate. It started out innocently enough with verses like

> You come my house; you eat daikon.
> Dat's da Japanese style. . . .
> You come my house; you eat raw fish.
> Dat's da Hawaiian style.

In some of the later verses, the needle got in a little too deep. The verse about the haoles—the whites—bothered Danny.

> You come my house; you steal my wife.
> Dat's da haole style.

The chorus was worse.

> Haole pilau! Haole pilau!
> All da haoles are pilau.

Pilau meant rotten and vile. The Mormon missionaries who went from house to house trying to teach people about Jesus were haoles. Were they all rotten and vile? Then there was the Filipino verse:

> You come my house, you eat bagoong.
> Dat's da Pilipino style.

For some reason it was worse when they imitated the Filipino tendency to reverse *f*s and *p*s. Many of the first generation Filipinos said "Pilipino," but when someone else said it that way, it sounded like a slam. Bagoong was a Filipino fish sauce that Danny's father loved but that looked and smelled offensive to other races. The Filipino chorus was short and infuriating:

Pilipino, Pilipino, poke knife.

They sometimes repeated it several times. It made all Filipinos seem primitive and hot-headed, solving their problems with knife fights.

On this particular night, the rowdy boys sang the Filipino verse over and over, enjoying the rage it put Danny into. Frustrated at trying unsuccessfully to hit them with his fists, he finally picked up some rocks and began to hurl them at the bullies. They left the scene quickly but called out threats from a safe distance. They would get him the next day.

As Danny started home, he saw Nori sitting on a bench nearby, crying. Danny rushed to her side. "Did somebody hurt you, Nori?" he shouted. "I'll step their necks; I'll broke their heads!" He was shaking with rage.

"Oh, Danny," Nori said, looking up through her tears. "You can't fight the whole world. What's happened to you? You didn't used to be like this. When you fight like you did tonight, I feel so ashamed. Please don't do it anymore, Danny. Please!" She continued to sob quietly, while Danny stood helplessly by. Then she dried her tears with her handkerchief and stood up. She looked into Danny's eyes and tried to smile. "I'm sorry, Danny; I know it isn't any of my business, but I just couldn't help it." Then she walked away leaving him standing alone.

Danny never fought again. The baiting continued for a while, but it was no fun without Danny's furious response. There were times when his temper flared, but always with the anger came the image of Nori's tear-stained face and the echo of her words, "When you fight . . . I feel so ashamed." About that time Danny became interested in sports and discovered that he was a natural athlete; he also began to grow. His enemies soon evaporated, and in their place he found good friends.

He and Nori had worked together as members of the executive council during their sophomore and junior years. Now, as a senior, Danny was president of the student body, and Nori was vice-president. Nori spoke clear, correct English in school. She could speak Pidgin also, and she did with the kids at the beach or at a ball game, but it was definitely a second language to her and not a dialect that she was trapped into. Danny's best English was as good as Nori's, but he loved the casual freedom of Pidgin and lapsed into it often, even when speaking to the student body in an assembly program.

Danny took his arms away from his eyes and stared up at the ceiling. Forget Nori? he thought. It would be like trying to forget a part of myself.

"Danny! Danny come quick! Dis food jus' right now."

Danny smiled. Benito didn't like to let his home-cooked meals get cold before they were eaten. Danny sat up on the edge of the bed for a moment, shook his head, then stood up and went into the other room to join his father.

Chapter

2

When Nori left Danny in the park, she didn't go directly home. Instead, she walked up to the hospital and checked the schedule to see when she was expected again as a volunteer. She already knew the schedule, but it was a good excuse to avoid going home right then. The waiting room was empty, so she picked up a magazine and pretended to read it while she gathered her thoughts.

Danny knew I was just making another excuse, Nori mused. I know he did. He was hurt—I could see it in his eyes. If only things were different—if Daddy was different—it would be fine. I'd love to go on dates with Danny. But Daddy will never change, never in a million years. Oh, Danny, why do we have to date? Why can't we just be friends like we've always been? She wished they were just finishing their first year in high school instead of their last. Everything had been perfect, too perfect to last.

She kept picking up one magazine after another and leafing through them, page by page, seeing nothing. "There comes a time when a boy and girl can't be 'pals' anymore," Nori said half aloud. The sound of her voice echoed in the empty room, and she looked up to see if anyone had heard her. No one was around. She looked down at the stack of magazines in front of her and then up at the clock on the wall. "Oh my gosh, it's almost dinner time." She jumped up, arranged the magazines in a fan shape on the table, and left.

When Nori arrived home, she found her father sitting in his favorite chair by the window. He had a bottle of beer in his hand, and an empty bottle stood on the table beside him. He seemed to be drinking more lately, and it worried her. His sister, Mitsuko, didn't like it, and for him to be drinking when she was visiting worried Nori even more.

"How long have you been home, Daddy?" Nori said. "Where's Aunt Mitsy?"

Hiromi looked up from his magazine and smiled. "I've been home for nearly an hour, and your Aunt Mitsy is in the kitchen, helping Annie with dinner. Any other questions?"

"Sorry I'm late. I'll go in and help them," Nori said, heading for the kitchen.

"They don't need you. Sit down and talk to me."

Nori sat down in a chair near her father and waited for him to speak. He seemed unsure how to bring up the subject that was on his mind. Finally Nori spoke. "What did you think of the game last night, Daddy?"

"Good game," Hiromi said without feeling. He was still thinking of something else.

"I heard some people say that Danny plays like you did when you were a boy."

Hiromi smiled, obviously pleased at the comparison. "Danny plays very well; I have to admit that." The smile faded quickly, and Hiromi glanced away from Nori to the window that looked down over Lanai City. He cleared his throat and continued. "By the way, wasn't that Danny you were walking with in the park a little while ago? What's up, student-body business? Don't you have time at school to take care of all that?"

Nori blushed at her father's mention of the incident. "We were just talking," she said, trying to sound casual.

"I'm sure you didn't think anything about it, Nori, but this is a very small island. It's better to be with groups of friends. You start spending time alone with one boy and pretty soon . . . well, people misunderstand. Even the boy can misunderstand. Now Danny's a good kid; he's a heck of a basketball player, but . . . "

Aunt Mitsy pushed the door open with her hip and entered the room, carrying two large dishes of steaming tempura. "Get the sauce, will you, Nori?" she said, nodding toward the kitchen. "I sent Annie home early. We can clean up after dinner by ourselves, can't we?"

"Sure Aunt Mitsy; I'll get the sauce." Nori hurried into the kitchen, glad to have the conversation with her father cut short.

Hiromi dived right into the tempura and helped himself to a heaping bowl of steaming rice. "You always know what I like," he said as he used his chopsticks to half-scoop some rice into his mouth from the bowl in his hand. "Even your rice tastes better than anybody else's. If Kenji ever starts beating you, come and live with us." All three of them laughed at the idea of gentle, soft-spoken Kenji manhandling his spunky little wife.

"You of all people should know there's no danger of that," Mitsy said. "Remember when I saved you from the Okamura boys? They were going to tie you to a tree at school and leave you overnight."

"You should have seen her Nori," Hiromi said, laughing out loud. "She was like an angry grizzly bear protecting her cub. Those Okamura boys never knew what hit them. They didn't come back to school for two days."

After dinner, Hiromi left to attend a plantation management meeting, leaving Mitsy and Nori to do the dishes and clean up the kitchen.

"I'll wash, you dry," Mitsy said with finality and plunged her hands into the sink filled with dishes and soap suds.

"Tell me about the grandkids," Nori said with a wink. She knew Mitsy was dying to talk about them. Mitsy launched into a review of her grandchildren's antics that kept Nori laughing during most of the cleanup.

"I love it when you come to visit, Aunt Mitsy," Nori said, as they were putting away the last of the dishes. "Daddy is so much happier. I wish you could live with us all the time."

"Your Uncle Kenji would probably complain if I left him for good, but I think he enjoys these little visits. It's probably more peaceful with me gone. He knows it's important for me to come and help out here once in a while. Even with Annie coming in for a few hours each day, you carry a pretty big load for a high school girl."

"I don't mind," said Nori. "But I have to admit I feel relieved when you're here. You just take over everything, and I turn into a worthless teenager for a few days." They both laughed.

"It'll be interesting to see how your father gets along when you go away to school next year. I wonder if he appreciates the responsibility you take for running the house. Annie's a good hard worker, but I'm smart enough to know that you do the meal planning and a lot of the cleaning. By the way, when did you start paying the bills?"

"Oh, I just make sure the bills are correct and write the checks. Daddy reviews everything and signs them. He's so busy;

I thought it might help him for me to get things together for him."

"He was 'reviewing' the household bills this morning," Mitsy said, chuckling. "He never looked at a one. He just signed the checks as fast as he could write and left them for you to mail. He trusts you and depends on you more than he realizes." Nori blushed a little and said nothing.

They hung up their aprons and went into the living room. Mitsy settled into a corner of the couch and began some mending she was doing for Hiromi. "You were the first child in your family too, weren't you, Aunt Mitsy?" Nori asked as she sat down beside her.

"The first and only one for ten years, then your father came along and broke the spell. Your Uncle Shigeo was born four years after that, then the three youngest boys in the next six years. Your grandmother was forty-four years old when she had the last one."

"You were the only one for ten years? I guess you know what it feels like to be an only child," Nori said.

"Enough to know there are good and bad sides to it. I got a lot of attention during those first ten years that I didn't get after the boys started coming, but it's kind of lonely, isn't it?"

"At least Grandfather finally got some sons; Daddy probably never will. Do you think he wishes sometimes that I were a boy?" Nori asked. "If I were, we'd be going fishing together every week, and he'd be watching me play basketball and cussing the coach for not letting me play more. It would be great."

"I used to wonder about the same things, before the boys came along. After that I felt kind of special," Mitsy said with a smile. "I was glad for all those brothers. Girls weren't always welcome in a Japanese family back then. Some of the older people still thought of girls as liabilities, someone to take care of for years and then pay a big dowry to get rid of. Boys meant strength and security, someone to help the parents financially when they were old. A boy could carry on the name, maybe take over the family business."

Nori nodded. "After mother died, I felt like Daddy needed me, like he counted on me to be here with him. We used to sit and talk for hours, like two adults. The past few years we seemed to have grown apart, though, and I think I'm more of a worry to him than anything else. I'm so concerned that I might do something he doesn't like, or embarrass him somehow. Sometimes I feel all tied up in knots. I don't dare live my life. Remember what you said about the old Japanese families thinking of their daughters as problems?"

Mitsy nodded.

"You'll probably laugh at me, but sometimes it seems like Daddy feels that way about me."

"Why do you say that?" Mitsy asked.

Nori took a deep breath, let it out slowly, and continued. "Daddy was so affectionate with me when I was little. He'd hold me on his lap and hug me, and he always kissed me goodnight. Sometimes when he was late coming home from a meeting, and I was already in bed, he'd slip in and just stand there looking at me. Often I'd only be half-asleep, and I'd see him there or feel him tuck me in and kiss me on the cheek."

"Maybe he felt like you needed that extra attention when you were little," Mitsy said. "You're pretty grown up now for lap-sitting."

"Oh, I don't expect him to hold me on his lap and rock me to sleep or anything, but he hardly ever touches me anymore. Aunt Mitsy, he treats me almost like a stranger sometimes.

If he'd just give me a hug once in a while . . ." Nori's voice quavered, and her eyes filled with tears.

"Baby daughters are soft, fun to cuddle, and more inclined to it than boys. Fathers love all that attention and closeness, and they can be very loving to their little girls. When those little girls start to grow up into beautiful women like you, some fathers become uncomfortable around them."

"Why?" Nori asked.

"I don't know, but I think your Uncle Kenji was a little uneasy when our Naomi started growing up; it seemed to happen overnight."

"How did he act?" Nori asked.

"Oh, he just became a little strict and formal with her," Mitsy said laughing. "It was like he was trying to find reasons to keep her at a distance. It didn't last long, and I never noticed it with the younger girls."

"It sounds just like Daddy," Nori said. "But, with us, it has lasted for years now. What can I do? I feel like it's my fault."

"You can only try to understand. You haven't done anything wrong. I'm sure your father still loves you as much as he ever did. Maybe he just doesn't know how to show his love to this beautiful woman who has replaced his baby daughter."

"Sometimes I wish I hadn't grown up. It causes all kinds of problems," Nori said sadly.

"Like boys wanting to be alone with you?" Mitsy asked. "I overheard part of that conversation you were having with your father. That's why I rushed in with dinner so fast."

"It's embarrassing, Aunt Mitsy," Nori said. "I'm nearly eighteen years old, and he talks to me like I was twelve."

"Have you ever been on a date?"

"Not really."

"Has anybody asked you out?"

"Danny has asked me a few times. He asked me tonight."

"Danny Tolentino?" Mitsy shook her head. "I'm afraid Hiromi wouldn't like to see his only daughter dating a Filipino boy. Has anybody else asked you for a date?"

"I don't want to go with anyone else," Nori said. "Aunt Mitsy, why does Daddy hate Filipinos?"

"I don't know if hate is the right word," Mitsy said, "but he is prejudiced against them; I know that."

"What did they ever do to him to make him feel like he does?"

Mitsy didn't answer at once, she seemed reluctant to speak. Finally she looked up from her sewing and began. "In 1941, your grandfather was sixty-two years old. He had been in charge of the Lanai Plantation for over twenty years. He had taken an inefficient operation and turned it into a smooth-running machine that made lots of money for Dole Pineapple. He had earned and been promised a position on the board of directors of the company. The position included stock options and a salary increase that would have made him a wealthy man in a few years. Everything depended on that promotion. His appointment to the board was to have been announced at year end.

"On December 7, 1941, the Japanese bombed Pearl Harbor, and the United States was dragged into World War II. Suddenly, Americans everywhere hated the Japanese. Since we had Japanese names and looked Japanese, many people hated us too. Your grandfather's promotion was never mentioned again. Matsuo Satō was a loyal American. Before the war was over, three of his five sons saw action, but because he was of Japanese ancestry, he was denied a position that was rightfully his. A Filipino named Balderas got the promotion instead. Your grandfather had worked with Balderas at the Dole plantation in Wahiawa years before and knew him to be an imcompetent yes-man.

"Father accepted the lost opportunity without a word, but when he heard about Balderas, something in him snapped. He just quit trying. If it hadn't been for Hiromi covering for him, he probably would have been replaced. He retired with a small pension in 1944, and by then the Americans of Japanese ancestry had made such a name for themselves fighting in Italy that everyone was feeling a little ashamed of the way they'd treated us. They put Hiromi in charge of operations here on Lanai, replacing Father.

"Your grandfather died two years later. He was delirious at the end. He kept saying 'Balderas . . . Balderas' over and over again. I think that did something to Hiromi. It doesn't make sense, I know, but maybe it will help you understand."

"I feel awful about the way Grandfather was treated, but it wasn't the Filipino's fault, was it?" Nori asked.

"Like I said, it doesn't make any sense; prejudice never does. I haven't helped you much, have I? Maybe I've just confused you more." Mitsy put down her mending, took Nori in her arms, and held her for a long, long time.

Chapter

3

When Danny's alarm went off on Saturday morning, he buried his head deeper into his pillow and fumbled about on the bedside table for the clock. He felt grumpy and out of sorts, and by the time he found the turnoff switch, he remembered why. He had spent most of the night trying to find a comfortable position in the bed, and trying to shut out the mental replays of his conversation with Nori the previous day.

He suddenly remembered the spearfishing trip he had planned with Bernard and Podogi. His eyes popped open, and he turned to look at the clock: 5:35, and the guys would be picking him up at 6:00. He threw the covers back and sat up quickly, shaking the sleep from his still sluggish brain. Soon he was rushing around gathering up his gear and foraging in the kitchen cupboards and refrigerator for something to eat. The activity lifted his spirits, and he started thinking of the beach and all the fish he would spear.

He put some cold cereal in a bowl, poured milk over it, and picked up his spoon. He heard a familiar vehicle driving down the street, then the squeal of its brakes as it skidded to a stop in front of his house. The horn honked; it honked again. Danny chuckled and continued spooning cereal into his mouth.

He glanced at the kitchen clock. They're two minutes early, he thought. Let 'em wait.

"Danny, Danny," they called together in a sweet pleading tone like that used to wake a child for school. They dissolved into laughter, then Podogi began gunning the motor, which caused the ancient jeep to backfire; more laughter followed by more soft pleading. Danny started to laugh too. He lifted his bowl to his mouth and drained it at a gulp, then grabbed his spearfishing gear and ran out the door.

"Hey, Danny, what-sa-matter you, you no can hear?" Bernard said.

"Sleep, sleep, sleep, all time sleep, by 'n' by no mo' time for poke fish!" Podogi taunted Danny as he ran down the steps and jumped into the front seat.

"Talk, talk, talk, you all time talk. You scare fish at Manele; they hear you loud talking from Lanai City. Mo' better you drive; no more talking, eh?" Danny punched Podogi in the ribs and turned to ruffle Bernard's hair. The diminutive Bernard always sat in the back seat. He was under five feet tall and needed very little leg room.

Podogi took his race-car driver position, bending low over the steering wheel as if to cut down wind resistance. He shifted into first gear and let out the clutch abruptly, without pressing down on the accelerator. The car lurched forward in little jumps. With exaggerated precision, he shifted quickly into second and then third gear. Soon the ancient jeep was coughing and chugging down the street, belching blue exhaust but just barely moving.

Danny pounded Podogi on the back, choking with laughter. "No play! I like poke fish today, not next week, eh?"

Podogi shifted down and the jeep moved swiftly through the deserted streets. Light was just starting to spread over the island, and most of Lanai was still sleeping. They saw Mr. Okimoto entering his grocery store through a rear door. Saturday was a busy day for him, and he started early. As they left town, Danny automatically looked up to Snob Hill where Nori lived. There was a light burning in her bedroom window, which surprised him. What could she be doing up this early? He jerked his head back and stared down the road before him, angry that he hadn't been able to keep himself from looking up at her house and thinking of her.

They turned on to Kaumalapau Highway, then took a sharp left to Manele Road. Manele Road crossed the fertile Palawai Valley, ten thousand acres of rich red soil that filled a once-active volcano crater. The entire crater was planted in a geometric pattern of pineapple fields. The plants nearest the roads were covered with a thick layer of the red dust that permeated everything in the valley, swirled in little wind devils above the fields, and even gave the black asphalt a reddish cast.

"You like eat pine?" Podogi asked. Bernard and Danny shook their heads. Without warning, Podogi turned the speeding jeep up a side road between the pineapple fields. Stopping in a cloud of dust, he reached under the seat and pulled out a small machete, then bounded from the jeep. He alternately flipped his finger against the back of his hand and then against one pineapple after another, trying to find one that sounded the same as the back of his hand, a sure-fire test for ripeness. Finally satisfied, he picked the pineapple and cut the green top into the shape of a handle. Then holding the pineapple by that handle, he exposed the juicy, golden fruit with deft strokes of his knife, turning it into a huge popsicle-like delicacy. He ran back to the jeep, gave the pineapple to Bernard to hold, pulled his tee shirt off, and tossed it to Danny. He replaced the knife under the seat, then drove back to the highway.

Bernard handed him the pineapple, and he immediately began taking large bites of the ripe fruit. The sweet, sticky juice ran down his chin and dropped onto his bare chest.

"Pine juice on chest make fish come close," he said with a laugh. He offered a bite to Danny who shook his head. "I no breakfast," Podogi continued. "Poking fish hard work."

They reached the edge of the crater and began their descent down the winding road toward the white crescent beach just visible at the end of the island. Kahoolawe floated in the blue ocean about fifteen miles away to the southeast, and off in the purple distance Mauna Loa and Mauna Kea towered indistinctly above low-lying clouds that obscured the island of Hawaii.

Nori turned the lamp on near her bed and started to read. She decided that it was no use trying to sleep anymore. Saturday mornings were usually her mornings to sleep in, especially when Aunt Mitsy was there to keep her father from waking her up. The night had seemed to last forever as she drifted in and out of consciousness, thinking about how she had hurt Danny and trying to understand her father's prejudice against Filipinos.

She heard a sound like a gun going off, then a little later the sound of a jeep threading its way through the sleeping city. She stepped to the window and caught sight of the ancient jeep, hand-painted a bright yellow, rumbling noisily down the road to the harbor. She recognized it at once as Podogi's. She knew Danny and Bernard would be with him, and she wasn't surprised when they turned left on Manele Road and headed for the beach. As usual, Podogi cut the corner too short and raised a billowing cloud of red dust as he made the turn. Good, they were going spearfishing, a sport they loved more than anything else except basketball. Danny loved the beach; he said it calmed him and made him feel peaceful. Maybe it would take his mind off their conversation of the night before.

Nori decided to try to take her mind off it too, and grabbing her robe, she headed for the bathroom to take a shower. I'll make pancakes with coconut syrup and surprise Daddy, she thought.

As she reached for the bathroom door handle, the door opened and Hiromi came out, clad only in his underwear. He was obviously surprised and embarrassed. He hurriedly stepped back into the bathroom. "What are you doing up?" he demanded from behind the half-opened door. "You never get up this early on Saturday morning."

His eyes were swollen, and there was pain in them. Nori could tell that he had been drinking. "Go back to your room and give me a chance to get dressed before you start strolling around the halls."

Nori went back into her room and sat down on the bed. That's not Daddy talking, she thought; it's somebody else, somebody I don't know at all.

Suddenly Podogi skidded to a stop, and standing up in the jeep, he pointed with his half-eaten pineapple at the white crescent of sand in the distance. "Manele Beach!" he shouted. "Close by da bay where any kind huge fish live who gonna die today and end up in Podogi's opu." He gestured at his bare abdomen, which he had distended to make it look as if he had already eaten them. "Watch out, you fishes, swim out to sea! By 'n' by da great Podogi take aim wid his spear gun an' . . . " He tossed his pineapple away and, taking aim with an imaginary spear gun, followed the unlikely course of an imaginary fish swimming around the jeep in loops and curlicues. Then he made the sound of the spear slashing through the water and striking the target. "Swishhhh-pock! Perfeck shot, like always," he boasted. Podogi pretended to reel in the twine attached to the spear, hand over hand, grimacing at the effort of dragging this monster of the deep through the water.

Bernard stifled a yawn. "You like eat pretend fish, okay wid me. How about Danny and me borrow your jeep and go down and poke some real ones, eh?"

Podogi pretended to pout, turned off the jeep, and sat with his arms folded on his chest. He stared straight ahead as he waited for an apology. Bernard assumed the same posture in the back seat and said nothing. Danny looked over at his two best friends, frozen in their silly poses. Podogi's real name was Keaka Kanahele. It sounded pure Hawaiian, but he was three-quarters Portuguese so they called him "Podogi." He was tall and handsome, with reddish brown hair and blue-grey eyes. He looked like a haole with a great tan. Bernard was pure Japanese and looked it. His hair was straight and black, and his eyes almost disappeared when he smiled.

Danny reached over, turned on the key, and started the jeep, then he pounded Podogi on the back and pointed toward the beach. "Today!" he shouted in Podogi's ear. "I like spearfish today!"

Podogi and Bernard burst into laughter, and soon the jeep was roaring down the winding road at high speed. They parked in the shade of the Kiawe trees that rimmed the beach area. The ground was littered with long brown pods from the trees. The three carried their gear toward the rocks at the far end. The tide was out, and the surf was low. The waves broke gently, washed up the slope of unblemished sand, then retraced their paths with a soft hiss, gaining momentum until they collided with the next breaking wave. Swells moved slowly in from the sea at regular intervals, waiting their turn to make a rush at the shore.

Danny looked out to sea. He wondered where the swells came from. There was no land he knew of between this little island and the east coast of China. These swells had crossed the great Pacific Ocean, only to become three-foot waves lapping at the sand of Manele Beach. If they had been sixty-five miles north, they might have carried a surfer into Waikiki or Makaha. Double that, and they would have passed through the Kauai Channel, missed the islands completely, and rolled all the way to Mexico.

At the far end of the beach, the boys left the sand and began to walk on the rough lava shelf that would carry them around the rocky point to the little inlet where they liked to fish. "Look," cried Bernard. "Puhi!" Several Moray eels had been trapped in a tide pool by the receding water. They were churning the surface of the pool in their efforts to escape. The sight of their intertwining bodies sent a shiver down Danny's spine. The eel's open mouths and movement of the water through the holes on each side of their necks made them look like they were blowing. *Puhi* is a Hawaiian word that means to blow.

"You ever spear puhi?" Danny asked Bernard.

"Not anymore," he answered. "I speared one down deep once and lost the spear."

"What happened?"

"The spear didn't kill him, and I couldn't pull him out of his hole. I pulled as hard as I could, but he wouldn't let go. I think he swelled his body up inside the coral; he wouldn't budge."

"Was he a big one?"

"No. That's what was so strange. He was smaller than these."

Podogi had been watching in silence. He spoke finally in a quiet, serious voice. "I heard one guy try catch lobster. He reach in hole, puhi grab finger. He had sharp fish knife, but he no can pull eel out far enough fo' poke."

"What did he do?" Bernard asked.

"He cut off finger." Podogi answered. "I stay away from puhi, big or small." He turned and continued on around the point. Danny and Bernard followed.

The gentle surf splashed fine spray and foam into the tide pools that rimmed the rocky point. Soon the little bay where they were headed came into view.

" . . . And beyond this lovely little bay is famous Black Sand Beach of Lanai," Bernard said as though he was a tour guide showing the island to a group for the first time. "White sand, black sand, Lanai has it all." Others cursed the smallness of the little island and called it "dis rock." But Bernard loved every inch of it, from the heights of Lanaihale, which cast its shadow over Lanai City, to the secluded white sands of remote Polihua beach, where giant sea turtles had once hatched their eggs.

"How come you so crazy for dis rock, Bernard?" Podogi asked. "I like go Honolulu; I like go Mainland! Lanai no mo' nothing! One teeny tiny little dot on da map. I like drive car sixty, seventy miles an hour fo' two, three, maybe four hours; no stopping, just drive. You no can do dat Lanai; fifteen minutes you run out of island!"

Bernard smiled. "Fo' what you like drive so fast, so long?"

"I like room fo' breathe," Podogi said, spreading his arms wide.

Danny smiled as he put on his fins and goggles, picked up his spear gun, and slipped down among the rocks at the water's edge. "See you out at the rock," he called over his shoulder.

Slowly he worked his way down into the water, being careful to hold onto the larger rocks to avoid being dragged through them by the surf. He found an opening, and when a wave came in that was large enough, he pushed off through it, kicking his legs vigorously to propel himself out beyond the breakers and into the quiet water of the bay. He looked back and saw Bernard and Podogi still quarreling as they put on their gear. Podogi finally put his fingers in his ears. Bernard shook his head and started down toward the water.

Danny swam toward the large rock that stood like a sentinel near the far shore at the entrance of the bay. It was his favorite spot to spear fish. The great rock was honeycombed beneath the surface by air bubbles trapped in the flowing lava that had formed it. When the lava had poured into the sea, some of those bubbles burst, creating concavities of all sizes in its undersea surface. Fish abounded in and around these holes. The rough walls of the rock provided hand-holds that Danny could use to keep himself down deep while he waited for the right fish to come along. A swell covered Danny's snorkle, and he got a mouthful of sea water. He cleared the snorkle by rising to the surface and blowing a blast of air through it. The salty taste persisted, but air filled his lungs, and he swam on.

"Only on Lanai," Nori thought as she saw a teenage boy drive up in front of Okimoto's grocery store and abandon his car in the middle of the street while he ran in to buy something. She pointed it out to Annie, who was standing by her at the checkout counter and both of them laughed.

"Hi, Nori," a familiar voice said from behind her, and Nori turned to see Margie Morita pushing a loaded cart down one of the aisles.

"Margie, where are you going so fast?" Nori called after her.

"I'm feeding the multitudes tonight, remember? Are you coming?" Margie was moving purposefully down the aisle looking for something, and Nori didn't feel like shouting her answer.

Annie saw her plight and smiled. "Why don't you go talk to her, if you can keep up," she laughed. "I'll get one of the Okimoto boys to help me load the groceries in the car, but don't be late for dinner; your Aunt Mitsy has something special planned."

Nori hurried off to find Margie and found her in the produce section. "I guess I won't be able to come tonight, Margie. My Aunt Mitsy is in town, and I have to entertain her. I hate missing it—it sounds like a great party. But I couldn't leave her alone when she's come all the way from Maui to be with me." Nori flushed. Her excuse sounded phony when she said it.

Margie looked up from the avocados she had been squeezing and smiled at Nori. "We're not serving avocados tonight, but I can never resist these big beautiful ones. I just cut them in half, salt them a little, and eat them right out of the rind with a spoon. In fact, that's just what I wish I was doing tonight for dinner instead of making all that hekka." She seemed not to have heard what Nori said, but then she asked a question that made it clear she had. "Do you think Danny will come by himself?"

"Oh, of course he'll come," Nori said. "He wouldn't miss one of your hekka dinners for anything." She laughed nervously. "You'd better make extra. I saw the boys heading for Manele to spearfish this morning, and I'll bet they come back hungry as sharks."

"Is that where they are? That Podogi! He promised me he'd bring me to Okimoto's in his jeep this morning and help me do the shopping. Maybe I'll make less hekka and not give him any." Margie laughed at the picture of Podogi at the party with an empty plate.

"I'm really sorry about missing the party," Nori said.

"There's nothing you can do," Margie said. "It wouldn't be very polite to leave your aunt by herself. There'll be other parties."

"Well, I guess I'd better be going," Nori said and left Margie still searching for the perfect avocado.

Nori felt terrible on the way home. Babysitting Aunt Mitsy was a very thin excuse at best. Margie could have asked her a lot of embarrassing questions: Where is your father going tonight? Couldn't he stay with your aunt for a couple of hours? Does she know about the party? Surely she'd insist on you going if she knew that it was important to you. But Margie wasn't like that; she was a loyal friend who took you at your word. If you said you couldn't leave your aunt, she believed you and tried to understand.

Halfway to the rock, Danny paused to rest and to let Podogi and Bernard catch up. The ocean floor beneath him formed a little valley where a whole community of sea-life flourished. But trying to spearfish there in the open water was hopeless, so he just floated above them and watched. He lay completely still on the surface of the water and soon a school of striped manini passed close to him. Some of the larger ones were eight or nine inches long; the smallest were almost microscopic and had not yet begun to acquire their convict stripes. They moved in concert like a flight of birds. When they were directly in front of him, Danny jabbed his spear gun at them and they fled as one, hardly breaking formation.

He spotted several lauhau with their yellow bodies and horizontal blue stripes and a lauwiliwili, also yellow but with rows of black dots forming vertical lines along the six-inch length of its body. The clear water on this calm day allowed the rays of the sun to penetrate deeply. The light playing on the brightly colored fish accentuated their iridescent hues and remarkable designs. The variety of fishes seemed contrived, as though a tropical fish fancier had bought a few of each kind and released them here to dazzle the swimmers. A blowfish, nearly a foot long, puffed itself out into a spiny ball. It swam away, as Danny drifted near, its pectoral fins fluttering like floppy ears. Two grey nu nu, looking like translucent sticks, passed by unconcerned, followed by a humu humu nuku nuku apua'a about eight inches long. The little humu's tapa-cloth design looked as though an elementary school child had finger-painted it during a very short art class.

As Bernard and Podogi swam up beside him, Danny struck out again for the rock. They swam steadily for several minutes before reaching their goal. As soon as they had caught their breath, they began diving. Bernard got the first one, an eight-inch black mamo, good eating, but not very impressive. Podogi said he was "poking fo' food, not fo' trophy" and soon had three small fish in the net bag he wore tied to his waist.

Danny was more particular. He enjoyed stalking the larger fish that lived down deep and didn't mind coming up empty-handed time after time as he waited for just the right shot. He loved the cool, refreshing feel of deep water, and the salty taste of the mouthpiece of his snorkle was pleasant and familiar. Podogi and Bernard's thrashing had ruined several potential shots for him, so he swam a little ways off from them, well behind the rock, where he was more protected from the breakers coming in from the open sea.

After taking a series of deep breaths he held the last one and dove downward, kicking vigorously. In one hand he held his spear gun. The other hand was at his nose. As the pressure increased, he held his nose and blew against it. He felt a soft pop as the pressure equalized inside his ears. His bamboo goggles pushed into the soft skin of his cheeks, sealing the water out. He reached out and grasped a projecting shelf of lava rock and felt its rough surface bite into his hand slightly as he gripped it to fight against his natural buoyancy. The salt water tingled in his nostrils. He blew out a small amount of air and watched the bubbles rocket skyward. Twenty feet above him, the surface of the water glittered like translucent glass, a barrier that blocked out the sky and the clouds and the seabirds, enclosing him in this silent world.

Above him the surf crashed into the huge rock that sheltered him, and seabirds called to one another in high-pitched shrieks. Down here it was quiet and peaceful. The violent action of the waves on the surface was muted into gentle rhythmic currents that ebbed and flowed almost imperceptibly. The light was diffused, but sufficient for clear vision. Danny felt strangely at home here.

As he held very still, the little community of fish he had disturbed with his thrashing entrance reconvened and went on with their routine. Predators and potential victims swam by together without apparent fear of each other or him. As they passed closer and closer to him, he hoped that he looked like part of the rock he clung to. Then an eighteen-inch kumu headed toward him, and Danny slowly raised his spear gun. As it turned and presented a broadside, he pulled the trigger. The spear hissed through the water and pierced the fish just behind the gill slits. A puff of crimson issued from the hole as the weight of the spear carried the wounded fish downward. Gravity and its feeble fluttering movement carried the dying kumu to the head of the spear where a thin steel wing, hinged to the spear tip, opened to keep the fish from escaping. Danny started to reel in the twine that attached his spear to the gun and realized that he couldn't hold his breath any longer. He released his last bit of air and shot to the surface.

The boys spearfished for nearly two hours, taking breaks now and then to get their breath. Finally they compared their bags of fish, and Danny said "Let's take a rest on the rock and go back. We have plenty of fish to eat and some to take home." Bernard and Podogi quickly agreed.

They waited for a large swell, rode it in, caught hold of an outcropping of lava, and hung on while the wave rebounded off the rock and collided with the next wave. In that few moments, the water level around them dropped briefly, giving them a chance to clamber up on the rock and away from the pounding surf.

Podogi and Bernard threw their gear in a pile and lay back panting from the exertion. Danny sat in his favorite spot on the edge of a natural pool that had been formed by a large bubble in the lava and smoothed by the erosive action of the sea. The pool had been the scene of one of his most exciting experiences. When he was thirteen, he had been sitting exactly as he was now when a large wave had swept over the rock and dropped a thirty-pound ulua in the pool. In a lightning reflex action, Danny had picked up his loaded spear gun and fired from the hip. The spear had pierced the huge fish right through the head. Within seconds another wave crashed in and nearly carried the flailing fish back into the sea, but the heavy twine attached to the spear held, and Danny landed the fish. Ever since then, he took this position when he was on the rock.

Danny had been a hero when he brought that fish home, and his father had proudly tacked its tail on the chicken coop behind their house. Lots of ulua fishermen did that, and many of their tails were larger than Danny's, but they caught theirs with huge rods and reels and heavy test line. Danny had shot his with a homemade spear gun in the few seconds that were available for him to shoot. Opportunities were often like that, it seemed to Danny; a door opened and closed, and if you were not ready, you missed it.

Chapter

4

"What kept you?" Mitsy asked as Nori came in after walking home. She was sitting on the living-room couch, reading a magazine.

"Oh, I ran into Margie at Okimoto's store. She was buying groceries for the party tonight, and I just stopped to talk."

"What did you talk about? You seem kind of glum. Was she upset because you're not coming to the party?"

Nori dropped into a chair, pulled a pillow onto her lap, and began tracing the pattern in it with her finger. "No, nothing like that," she said. "Margie just asked me if Danny was coming without me. I guess I never thought about the possibility that he might decide to stay home too, but that's silly. Of course he'll go. He's the student-body president and captain of the basketball team; he has to be there. And he's a Mormon; he wouldn't miss a party that's being held at the church."

"Are all the other team members bringing dates?" Mitsy asked.

"I think they are," Nori said. "Do you think he might feel a little strange there by himself?"

"Maybe he'll ask someone else," Mitsy said.

The idea of Danny with someone else gave Nori a strange

feeling in the pit of her stomach, but she shrugged it off and tried to answer in an off-handed way. "Yes, sure, maybe he will. That would solve everything, wouldn't it? He wouldn't have any trouble finding a date. There are plenty of girls at Lanai High who would be glad to go with him." Suddenly, Nori didn't want to talk about Danny and the party and who he might take. "Aunt Mitsy, will you excuse me for a few minutes. I've got a little headache, nothing bad, but maybe if I could just take a couple of aspirins and lay down for a little while."

"Go ahead," Mitsy said. "We won't start dinner for an hour or so. I might even take a little nap myself."

Nori didn't take any aspirin, but she did go to her room. She sat at the window and looked out at the pineapple fields that stretched off into the distance. A jeep was speeding along the road that led from the beach. It turned out on the harbor road and headed for the city. It wasn't Podogi's, of course, but it made her think about him and Bernard, and Danny.

Why had she had that sinking feeling when Aunt Mitsy suggested that Danny might take someone else to the party? Of course it was a possibility, but it hadn't occurred to her before that moment. But why shouldn't he get interested in someone else, someone who would be proud to be seen with him, not worried for fear her father might drive by and get the wrong idea. Wouldn't that be best? Danny could have a girl and still be Nori's friend. Nothing serious then, no complications, no feeble excuses, no embarrassing situations. They could just work together in the student council and go to classes together, and be pals like she was with Bernard and Podogi. It would be so perfect, like when they were in grade school.

Nori stood up and walked away from the window and stood in front of the mirror that hung on the wall behind her dressing table. What do you think? she asked the person who looked back at her. Wouldn't it be perfect? Wouldn't it solve all your problems? The image in the mirror nodded. Nori moved closer to the mirror and stared deeply into the troubled brown eyes. If you're so keen on the idea, why does the very thought of Danny with another girl make you sick to your stomach? Oh, Nori, you don't know what you want, do you?

"Hey, brah, you get too much sun, eh?" Danny teased as he pressed his finger against Podogi's chest and noted the reddish mark it made. They were lying in the sand, under the shade of the Kiawe trees, digesting the fish they had just cooked and eaten.

"Try be quiet, I sleeping," Podogi mumbled. Then opening his eyes, he continued. "I get good tan an' Hawaiian blood. Sun no can burn Hawaiian, eh?"

"Sun no can tell you Hawaiian, eh?" Bernard said. "He think you one haole. By 'n' by you go hospital like Elder Ihunui."

"Naa, dat Elder Ihunui real shark bait; he too white, from all time wear suit and tie. I remember dat guy, some burn he get, den by 'n' by come all over blisters. Oh, da big elephant-size blister he get." He spread his hand to show the size.

"What Elder Ihunui's real name?" Podogi asked. "I forget already. Nobody ever call him by his real name."

"Mike Parkinson," Bernard chimed in.

Elder Mike Parkinson had a big nose, not grotesque, but much larger than the Orientals and Filipinos on the island. The Hawaiian word for big nose is ihunui. Someone called him Elder Ihunui as a joke, and the name stuck. Soon nobody called him anything else; he even called himself that.

"He still writes to my brother, Kyoshi, and signs his letters, 'Ihunui,'" Bernard said. "He was one good elder!"

Podogi dozed off again, and Bernard dropped off too. Danny sat stirring the dying fire with a stick and staring out at the surf. Ihunui. He remembered how concerned everybody was when the doctor insisted that he spend the night in the hospital. But the next week he was back at the beach with the kids. By then the blisters had turned to dry skin hanging in patches all over his back. Podogi and Bernard were having a contest to see which one of them could pull off the largest piece of dead skin intact. Nori had been there, and Danny had noticed her shiver as she watched them "skinning" Ihunui. She and Margie had run off down the beach to get away from the sight, and Danny had joined them. It was so simple then. They were just friends playing on the beach, pushing each other into the surf and chasing each other with handfuls of wet sand.

Barnard woke with a start. "Hey, you guys, how about a swim? My hands are all sticky from the fish."

"I like sleep," said Podogi without opening his eyes. "No make noise, eh? I get one nice dream. We beat Lahainaluna in the da big game next Friday; I get fifty points, Danny get no mo' nothing."

"Keep dreaming," Danny said with a short, coughing laugh. "That Lahaina team is plenty tough; nobody's going to get fifty points that night."

"You guys had better get way ahead of them early in the game so the coach will put me in. I'm getting tired of riding that bench."

Podogi opened one eye. "Maybe da coach start you at center and leave me sit da bench."

Bernard pretended to give the idea some consideration. "I tell you wot, Brah. If da coach start me, I work real hard and make plenty points so he no scared to let you play fo' couple minutes in da fourth quarter, eh?"

Podogi jumped up, grabbed Bernard, and poured a handful of sand into the top of his swimming suit, then took off running down to the water and dived in. Bernard was right behind him, and when Podogi surfaced, he pelted him with wet sand. Finally they stopped fighting, swam out beyond the breaking surf, and floated on the gentle swells.

Danny looked out at his two friends, bobbing up and down in the ocean. At this distance, they looked like father and son. George Bernard Ōta, he thought. What a big name for such a little guy. Bernard's mother had heard the name, George Bernard Shaw, thought it sounded very dignified, and named her second son after the Irish author. They had been planning to call him George, but when Dole brought in a heavy-handed luna, or field boss, by the name of George, whom everyone soon learned to hate, the Otas changed their minds and called him by his middle name.

When he introduced himself, Bernard always said his name with a brogue and put the accent on the last syllable of his surname as in O'Toole. "George Bernard O'Ta, at your service," he would say with a bow. He rolled his rs shamelessly and looked for all the world like a little brown leprechaun. Bernard was not just small, he was tiny. His features were delicate and so was his frame. His body was perfectly formed, but formed in miniature. Hours of weight-training and exercise had given definition and strength to his muscles, but they had added little to his bulk.

Bernard loved basketball and had been team manager since he started high school. He had done the laundry and taken care of the equipment, just so he could be near the players. The coach let him do the drills with the team and sometimes even put him in during practice games. He practiced dribbling around the benches in the locker room and became a clever ball-handler. Every year he tried out for the team, and every year he stayed on as manager, but this year, as a senior, he had made the team. Everyone was happy for him, but they suspected that it was a sentimental choice on the part of Coach Manning, who admired Bernard's spirit and dedication to the sport.

There was an outdoor court across the street from Danny's house. Every night, during basketball season, Bernard came to that court and shot one hundred foul shots. Even after he made the team and was attending basketball practice every night after school, he still stopped on his way home and shot his hundred foul shots. Sometimes Danny went over and shagged balls for him so he could stay at the line and develop his shooting rhythm. One night Bernard dropped fifty-seven in a row through the hoop. "How do you do it, Bernard?" Danny had asked. "You hardly ever miss."

"I watched the professionals on television," Bernard answered. "They have a little ritual they go through before shooting a foul shot. They bounce the ball the same number of times, take the same number of breaths, some of them even do a little shuffle with their feet, but it's always the same."

"Do you have a ritual? What is it?"

Bernard took his position at the line. "I plant my right foot on the line. I hold the ball in front of me with both hands. I bounce it twice." He bounced the ball. "Then I bring the ball up to my face and sight over it at the basket. Sometimes I talk to it, like a hunter talking to a falcon." He spoke softly to the ball. "See that hoop, that's where you're going. Then I cock my wrist and let fly." He lofted the ball up toward the basket, his two hands held high over his head in follow through as though still controlling the flight of the ball. The ball dropped into the hoop without touching the rim. "Fifty-eight," Bernard said softly to himself.

Danny looked up in time to see the boys catch a wave and body-surf in to the beach. He motioned to them with his hand and pointed to the watch on his left wrist. "It's time to go," he shouted over the crash of the waves, then he picked up his gear and headed for the jeep.

As the boys pulled into Lanai City, they passed Okimoto's grocery store. Margie Morita was just going in. She spotted them and waved them over. When they came to a stop, she was standing with her hands on her hips looking disgusted. "So, you've been at the beach fishing, eh? Podogi, I thought you were going to help me get the groceries over to the church for the party tonight."

"Dat's right, you bet, here I am, right on time. I even bring Danny and Bernard to help, some good, eh?" Podogi never cracked a smile, but Danny and Bernard couldn't keep straight faces.

Margie gave Podogi's shoulder a shove. "You phony-baloney. You forgot all about your promise. Maybe I'll forget to give you any food tonight. I took most of the stuff over to the church hours ago. I just came back to get a few last-minute things. I could use a ride though. Why don't you drop the boys off and come back and get me." Podogi saluted and roared off down the street toward Danny's house.

Chapter

5

When Danny arrived at the church, he could hear talking and laughter coming from within the little frame building. He stood for a moment and looked at the chapel. The building was supported by specially treated timbers that held it three or four feet above the ground to allow the air to circulate and avoid dry rot. These timbers were masked by a lattice-work of small intersecting strips of wood. Stairs led up to double doors in the front. The porch was flanked by two large windows on either side to provide ventilation on warm summer days. A ragged hibiscus hedge ran the length of the property in the front near the road, but it had no real chance for survival. When the youth of the Lanai Branch decided to leave the road and head for the steps, they took the most direct route available, usually through the hedge. Several varieties of ti leaves were planted around the porch, and poinsettias grew under the windows. These shrubs also fought a losing battle for existence against the bare feet of the Primary children who met there on Wednesday afternoons.

The Lanai Branch was unique in the islands in that almost all its active members were under nineteen years of age. The elders were the only Melchizedek Priesthood bearers on the

46

island. A couple of older women came to the Sunday meetings, but activities like tonight's were usually attended only by the elders and the youth. The current elders were trying to reverse this trend and were spending a lot of their time with the older, inactive members. They were having little success. The older members were unwilling to take positions in the branch and were uncomfortable attending when the youth were in charge. On this particular night, the elders were at a birthday party in the home of one of the members they hoped to reactivate.

Margie Morita passed the door, carrying a tray filled with food, and spotted Danny standing out in front of the chapel. She pushed open the screen door with her elbow and shouted at him. "Hey, Danny, you better hurry. The hekka is going fast!"

Danny shook off his dark mood. As he entered the room, Jerry Tano crossed his arms over his steaming plate and called out through a mouthful of food. "Dis da wrong place, Danny! No chicken hekka here! Mo' better you go saimin shop, eh? Get plenty good food dere. No waste time, eh?" Everybody roared.

Bernard waved Danny over to his table where he was saving a seat. "I don't mind Danny sit by me. He eat too many fish Manele. He no room for hekka, eh?"

Just then Margie came in from the missionary quarters at the back of the building where she had prepared the food in the elder's small kitchen. She was carrying a large serving bowl, and she headed right for Danny. Everyone protested. "Hey, Margie, more hekka, eh?" "No give hekka to Danny; he eat plenty fish at beach; he full already!"

"Would you like some, Danny?" Margie asked, extending the bowl. Danny leaned over the bowl and breathed deeply of the aroma rising off the hot mixture. The smell of the well-browned chunks of chicken mingled with the tangy fragrance of onions cooked in ginger and soy sauce. Carrots and broccoli added color and texture; mushrooms and little squares of tofu swam in the light brown broth. Danny took the bowl from Margie and sat it before him. "Margie, you some good cook, smart too! You bring just right-size bowl for me. Thanks, eh? Hey, Podogi, try pass me da rice, eh?"

The crowd hooted. Podogi stood up and brought the rice around the table. Then he held Danny's arms behind his back while Bernard filled his plate. Bernard helped himself to more and then handed the bowl to Podogi, who took it to the other end of the table.

Danny looked down at his plate. "You greedy guys! Dis all I get? By 'n' by I pass out on da way home."

Margie was shaking with laughter as she retrieved the bowl, now empty after its quick circuit around the table. "No huhu, Danny, no be angry, eh? Get plenty more hekka inside; you no pass out. By 'n' by you come strong, beat Lahainaluna, eh?"

Danny looked around the room. Most of the team members had brought dates: Jerry Tano, Rudy Garcia, even Darrell Fujimoto, the shyest boy on the team. Darrell was all smiles, but Danny could tell that he was feeling a little uncomfortable. Bernard didn't seem to mind being a single. Podogi was there with Margie, but as busy as she was, he might as well have been alone. The other members of the branch who were high school age had been invited, but they were not asked to bring dates. Danny decided that he need not feel self-conscious.

Margie came back with more hekka. She was followed by several of the younger girls in the branch, who were helping serve the meal, carrying bowls of rice and pitchers of water. The girls were dressed to look like cheerleaders and had large, felt *Ls* stitched to the backs of their white T-shirts. Margie, who was a cheerleader at the school, wore her uniform. Margie is really something, thought Danny. What would the Lanai Branch do without her?

Margie Morita was only sixteen years old, but she was the heart and soul of the little branch. Her unbounded enthusiasm and skill at organization were common knowledge. If the elders wanted to have a branch social or plan a trip to the beach, they had only to mention it to Margie, and she would take it from there. Margie was not petite like Nori; she was tall for a girl, and very athletic. Years of ballet and hula lessons had given Margie the legs of a dancer, and she could beat most of the boys in a foot race. Besides all that, she could cook.

Why didn't I fall for Margie? Danny thought. She's pretty, she's smart, she can do anything. She's fun to be with and easy to talk to. I never freeze up when I'm around her; I talk my head off. I can be funny and casual and relax when I'm with her, and I don't feel like I have to prove anything. She's the best "little sister" a guy could have!

Margie stopped beside him and refilled his bowl from the large one she was carrying. "You eat too fast," she said and bumped his head playfully with her elbow as she hurried away.

That's the problem, she's like a little sister, he thought. Sometimes she's more like a big sister. She's so talented and capable it's hard for her to resist taking charge of anything she's involved in. I love the way she organizes things, but I just don't know if I'd want her organizing me. It's probably better that she goes with Podogi; he needs organizing, and doesn't seem to mind being mothered a little.

When they had finished eating, everyone helped with the clean up. "Hey, Margie, how about a recipe for that chicken hekka?" one of the girls called out.

"I don't have a recipe," laughed Margie. "I just throw things together, and it comes out like that."

"Wait a minute," Bernard said, loud enough for everyone to hear. "I saw a recipe once; at least I saw a shopping list."

"No, no, no! Don't you dare tell that old story," Margie said, blushing.

"What old story?" Jerry shouted. "How can be old story, I never hear?"

Bernard was obviously enjoying himself. "One day, Margie sent me to the market to buy groceries for her. She was making hekka for the branch. I got all the way there before I looked at the list." Margie was wagging her finger at him and trying to look threatening.

"What it say?" Jerry asked.

"Chicken — real plenty, onions — plenty, ginger — not so plenty, soy sauce — kinda plenty . . . The lady at Okimoto's grocery store thought I was lolo." Everybody laughed but Bernard. Margie had rushed up behind him, and she was pretending to choke him. Bernard acted like he was strangling.

"No kill Bernard," Podogi said. "He like play Lahainaluna next Friday." Margie finally let go of him, and he slumped on the table as if he were dead.

After the food was cleared away, Margie called on Bernard to introduce the basketball team. The branch members applauded each one and called out "Speech, speech!" until they responded. Podogi was first. "As Kamehameha said" — he struck a pose like the great statue of the old king, an imaginary spear at his side supported by his left hand, his right hand extended, palm up, his gaze off into the distance — "Ua mau ke ea o ka aina i ka pono!"

"What dat mean?" someone called out.

"How do I know?" asked Podogi with a shrug. "I'm a Podogi,

eh? Sound real good though. I think it mean 'Lahainaluna gonna lose da big game next Friday night.' " Everyone cheered.

Danny and most of the the other team members responded briefly, but Jerry Tano made his speech in rambling Filipino Pidgin. After a couple of minutes, Podogi finally clapped his hand over Jerry's mouth and sat him down. Jerry didn't resist, but when Podogi let go of him, he stood back up and continued speaking as if he had never stopped. This happened several times, and the little hall echoed with laughter each time. Jerry finally remained seated and the program continued.

The serving girls did a couple of cheers Margie had taught them. They had all the right moves, but they were a little out of sync and short on confidence. It didn't bother anyone in the audience though; they cheered all the louder. Several of the freshman and sophomore boys left the hall and returned carrying posters they had made. Generally, the art work was primitive, and some of the words were misspelled, but the meaning was clear: Lahainaluna was in big trouble. One poster depicted the Lahaina team as fish being pursued by the Lanai team in spearfishing gear. The caption read: Poke Lahainaluna!

Margie produced a ukulele and called for Jerry to play some favorite solos. Jerry, obviously pleased at the opportunity, pretended to be too shy to perform. "No, no!" he said, holding up his hands in protest. The group began to applaud. "I no mo' good ukulele, try have Bernard play!" He was careful to choose someone who really could not play. Bernard laughed at the joke and began chanting "Jer-ry, Jer-ry" and clapping rhythmically. Jerry stood up and took the ukulele from Margie. The group quieted down, waiting as he strummed idly and checked the tuning. Suddenly he looked up as though he had just thought of something important. "I just remember; my agent say I no can play for nothing no more. You get money fo' pay me?" The kids laughed derisively. Jerry shrugged his shoulders, handed the ukulele back to Margie, and started back to his seat. Margie took the ukulele without protest and began to introduce the next number. Jerry rushed back, grabbed the ukulele and began to complain. "How come you give up so easy, eh?" he said.

Immediately Jerry plunged into "Stars and Stripes Forever." His nimble fingers flew up and down the frets as music filled the room. Jerry was truly professional on the uke. He played the bridge in a series of sliding chords and then attacked the melody again using a four-finger strum that made the little instrument ring like a banjo. When he finished, everyone clapped and shouted.

"Play 'Crazy G,' " somebody called out and Jerry was off again. He played number after number; the kids never seemed to get enough of his playing. Perspiration was shining on his forehead when Margie finally put her hand on his shoulder and announced, "Jerry's last number will be Malaguena." Margie left the hall. Jerry watched her go and said, "I guess she no like Malaguena." He started out very slowly. Each note was clear, and its tone, perfect. The crowd was hushed as the music began to build. The notes came faster and faster, and the volume expanded as if from some hidden source. Jerry's right hand was a blur, and his left, a frenzy of precise movements. As he finished, the little hall erupted with applause. Margie came walking up to the front of the room, dressed in the hula costume she had changed into during Jerry's last number. Jerry offered the ukulele to her, but she gave it back to him. Evelyn Akagi came forward without being asked and stood by Jerry. They sang, and Margie danced the hauntingly beautiful "Kalua."

This is the night of love, the shining hour of Kalua.

Her song is in the air, her lips are waiting there;
Who will be Kalua's only love?

Such a great party, Danny thought. Why did Margie have to spoil it by dancing "Kalua"? He had forgotten about Nori for the past two hours; now his mind filled with thoughts of her. To Danny, Nori was Kalua. Since he had seen her perform that dance, he could never hear the music without remembering how beautiful she looked. She had worn an all-white costume. The top was of white satin decorated with sequins that sparkled when the spotlight played on them. Below her tiny waist, the skirt was made of a band of matching white satin from which hung hundreds of silken strands that shimmered as she moved and parted to reveal her slender brown legs. Her hands were like little birds gracefully tracing patterns in the air around her. Now they were spread far apart, now at her lips, now together over her heart. Nori looked so grown up that night, and Danny had felt like a child sitting there in the dark, watching her dance.

Who will her lover be; who will her lover be?
Before the night is old, my arms will hold Kalua.

Margie dances very well, but not as well as Nori, Danny thought. Nori dances like Jerry plays the uke, effortlessly and flawlessly. Why did Margie have to dance "Kalua"? Why not "Sophisticated Hula" or "Beyond the Reef" or maybe a comic hula like "The Cockeyed Mayor of Kaunakakai?" The dance ended with Margie in the classic finishing hula position, her head bowed low, her hands together in front.

All the branch members helped put away the chairs and tables. With so many hands working, it didn't take long. Margie cleaned up the elder's kitchen and left hekka and rice for them to warm up the next day. Danny helped for a while, then he slipped away. He took an unusual route home to avoid running into any of his friends. The party was fun, but he didn't feel like talking anymore. When he got home, the lights were out, but the shifting shadows on the walls of the living room told him that his father was still watching television. The sound of distant gunfire reached his ears. Probably a Western, Danny thought. Pop really loves those Westerns, especially if there's a lot of shooting. Danny quietly slipped off his shoes and laid them on the porch. He went back out into the darkened street, closing the gate carefully behind him. He felt a little ashamed about avoiding his father, but he wanted to be alone.

Danny began to jog, his bare feet making a slapping sound on the rough asphalt road. He never wore shoes except to school or church. His feet were calloused and hard. He often played basketball on the asphalt court near his home in bare feet, pivoting, driving for the basket, stopping, changing direction, all in bare feet. When he went to Manele beach with his friends he would sometimes leave the winding road and make a bee line through the brush toward the white sand and kiawe trees that rimmed their swimming area. Sometimes he would cut his feet or pick up a thorn, but the salt water would wash the wound clean and he was never much the worse for his adventure.

After a few minutes of running, Danny found himself on a dirt road in the middle of a pineapple field near the edge of town. On the hillside above Lanai City, was the little enclave where the plantation officials had their homes. They were attractive brick houses and some had fireplaces. Lanai City was high by island standards and sometimes the nights could be chilly. In sharp contrast stood the rows of identical plantation houses down below where the workers and their families lived.

On nights like this when the low-lying clouds nestled in around the Norfolk Island pine trees that dotted the city, Lanai City looked like an Alpine village that had somehow been misplaced in tropical Hawaii. Three houses stood in a row at the top of a little rise. Nori's was on the far right and Danny could see a light burning in her bedroom window. He felt a lonely tug at his heart.

Chapter
6

Teru Yamada's fishing boat rocked lazily on the gentle swells that passed under it. A blue sky stretched unbroken in every direction, and the warm morning sun was becoming hotter and hotter. It would have been uncomfortably warm for the two men on board had it not been for the trade winds that fanned the deck of the little boat. The nets were out and, they hoped, were filling with fish. There was nothing to do but wait.

Hiromi Satō was wearing only a pair of tan shorts. He slept soundly on a small folding chaise lounge that had been draped with a huge beach towel. The gentle movements of the boat did not seem to disturb him at all. His body showed signs of the thickening that comes with middle age, and a few grey strands highlighted his black hair, but otherwise, Hiromi Satō was much the same man physically that he had been ten years before. In sleep, his handsome face looked peaceful enough, but a closer look revealed lines of tension and disapproval. This was not a man who smiled a lot. The natural folds of his face tended downward and made him seem stern and severe. On those occasions when he did smile, there was a remarkable transformation; he became the picture of good humor and contentment. People who spent a lot of time with him would do almost anything to deserve and prolong that smile.

Teru had the floor boards up and was tinkering with the old motor that had driven his boat for all the thirteen years he had owned it and probably several years before that. Teru was always making adjustments, cleaning, lubricating, and generally fussing with the motor. He had a small, but very complete, tool box on board and a supply of critical spare parts. If a problem occurred at sea, Teru felt confident that he could fix whatever had gone wrong, or at least cobble something together to get him back to the harbor. However, the little motor was very reliable and rarely gave Teru a valid excuse for using his tools, so he tinkered. Satisfied, at least for the present, with the adjustments he had made, Teru replaced the floor boards and sat back to rest.

He looked at Hiromi asleep on the chaise lounge and mused. He work five, sometime six day week, maybe twelve, fourteen hour each day. Just like da father, dis one—work, work, all time work. By 'n' by he die too quick, just like da father. Sometime go fishing wid' Teru for relax, but he no relax. 'Try fish over here, try fish over dere,' he tell Teru. 'Today we catch da most fish ever.' Teru like take easy, eh? Catch fish, no catch fish, all same to Teru. Da fishing da t'ing. He thought about that last statement and smiled. "Nice to catch fish, though," he said out loud. He laughed his soft, wheezy laugh and closed his eyes to the bright sky.

Teru had known Hiromi since his birth. He had been a close friend of Matsuo, Hiromi's father, when they both lived in Wahiawa on Oahu and worked for Dole Pineapple there. Hiromi looked very much like Matsuo did that day when he received the promotion that called for his move to Lanai. Matsuo had insisted on bringing Teru with him.

"Lanai is a sleepy little island, and there will be plenty of time for fishing," Matsuo had said with conviction.

But there was no time for him to fish. The Lanai Plantation had eaten Matsuo alive just as it was now eating Hiromi. When Teru had saved enough money to buy this fishing boat and "owe nobody," he quit the plantation. His little house at the harbor was paid for, and his thirty-five years with the company would bring him a small pension. He thought he could get by.

"Don't quit, stay on," Hiromi's father had said. "Some day I'm going to be a big potato in this company. They'll take me back to Honolulu, to the main office, and I'll take you with me."

But Teru didn't want to go. He could make it on his pension and the small profit he would make from fishing. In the end, Matsuo's striving had brought him disappointment and an early grave. Teru was still fishing, as always.

Hiromi yawned, stretched, and slowly sat up, blinking into the bright sunlight. "Is it time to start hauling in the nets?" he asked.

Teru shook his head. "Wait litty bit. Get plenty room in net for more fish. Try take easy, eh? Teru no pay you nothing for help him fish; for why you like busy busy, eh?" Hiromi smiled and lay back rubbing his eyes. After a few moments, Teru spoke again. "What you t'ink of da basketball team Lanai High get dis year?"

"They look good," Hiromi said, sitting up again. "Coach Manning's done a great job. That Danny Tolentino's the key—he's the floor general who sets up the plays and makes things work."

"Any kind people say dat Danny play like you, when you was young fella."

"Some people say that," Hiromi said. "Was I that good, Teru?"

"Same like Danny, some quick, some smart, some good shooter. If Nori was a boy, play like da father, Lanai High get two floor general on da team. Den for sure, dey win da Maui District championship, eh?"

"It would have been fun to have a boy. I think I'd be a better father for a son. I'd know how to handle him, what makes him tick. Nori's a wonderful daughter, but I worry about her a lot."

"What you worry, Nori? She some akamai wahine, plenty smart girl dat one." Teru tapped his temple with his finger. "By 'n' by, she marry some good basketball player; raise any kind boys. Maybe so, you get one whole team, play for grandpa. You be da coach, eh?" Teru chuckled at the thought.

Hiromi smiled, then became serious again. "I've got to get her off this island, so she can find somebody worthwhile to marry. There's an opening at the main office in Honolulu, and I'm going to try for it. Nori could live at home and attend the University of Hawaii."

"Maybe so, she like get away from da father, live wid another girl, live wid plenty girls in a big house at da school. You watch dat girl too plenty close, eh, Hiromi? For why you worry, all time worry. What you t'ink she gonna do, eh?"

"Look, Teru, you end up marrying the people you spend time with, right? I don't want her to marry some plantation worker and get stuck on this rock forever. It would be pretty easy for her to fall for somebody like Danny Tolentino, and then where would she be?"

"Danny Tolentino, pretty fine fella. He can marry Teru daughter anytime."

"That's easy for you to say; you don't have a daughter," Hiromi said grimly.

"You no like Danny?"

"Danny's all right."

"You no like Filipino, dat's it, eh?"

"The Filipinos are all right too, but I don't want one for a son-in-law, no." Hiromi said firmly.

"I know dis boy, Danny," Teru said. "I know Benito, his father, long time. Where you gonna find better people, Hiromi? Not on dis island, fo' sure. In Honolulu? I don't t'ink so. People is people, Hiromi. Get good Japanese, get bad Japanese. Get good Filipino, get bad Filipino. You plenty smart fella, Hiromi. How come you no find dis out already?" Then without waiting for an answer, Teru started pulling in the nets.

"That's very good," Mitsy said. She was watching Nori sketch a flower arrangement that they had made from the garden for her to use as a model. "I like this one of Annie too." Mitsy had a pile of pencil sketches in her lap that she was leafing through. "How did you get her to pose for it?"

"She brought me a picture, and I sketched it from that," Nori said. "Do you really like it? I don't think I'm very good at portraits."

"I like it very much. Would you do one of me sometime? I'd pose personally to get a picture like that."

"I'd be embarrassed to have you sit as long as it would take," Nori said. "It takes me forever. Sometimes I have to start over several times before I get the proportions right. Bring me a picture, and I'll do my best, though."

"I'm surprised that you find time to sketch, as busy as you are," Mitsy said.

"I have a lot of time on Sunday. Daddy almost always goes fishing with Teru on Sunday."

"Your mother was a wonderful artist, Nori. Her paintings of the ocean were as good as any I've ever seen. The walls of this house used to be covered with her paintings. Now they gather dust up in your attic. Have you ever tried working with oils or pastels."

"I think it might bother Daddy if I started painting. It would remind him of mother."

"He's got to get over being like that, Nori. I wish he'd take out all her paintings that he's packed away and hang them up again. It's been eight years—a man shouldn't mourn forever. I have a wonderful seascape that she did for me. I keep it in my bedroom because I know it bothers Hiromi to see it, but I'd love to hang it over the couch in the living room. That's where it belongs. If you want to paint, you should paint. Maybe I'll give you some oils for your birthday to get you started."

"What if Daddy got upset?" Nori said.

"Nori, you can't live your whole life trying to avoid things that upset your father. You just can't."

Chapter

7

When Danny got to church that Sunday morning, everyone was talking about the party the night before. The Elders were raving about the hekka they had warmed up for a late evening snack, and Margie was glowing from all the compliments. Danny taught his Sunday School lesson to a group of kids from seven to ten years old. They were a playful class, but when he started telling them about David and Goliath they became quiet and listened.

"Think of it," Danny said. "Goliath was nine feet seven inches tall!"

"Come on," David Tagavilla said. "Nobody dat tall."

"The Bible says, 'six cubits and a span,' and that figures out to nine feet seven," Danny insisted.

"Wow! Some kind basketball player he make, eh?" David's eyes were wide with wonder. "His head almost as tall as da basketball hoop. Too bad dat Goliath guy no go school Lanai High, eh?"

At sacrament meeting, the congregation was made up of one or two of the older sisters, an occasional older brother, and the young people. The last local branch president had died several years before. His widow was one of the ladies who attended regularly. She served as Relief Society president, and the senior missionary was called to be the branch president; all other offices in the branch were held by the youth themselves.

The elders were the stabilizing force in the branch. Sometimes they were outstanding; sometimes they were mediocre; always they were there. The Latter-day Saint kids loved the elders, and almost every one of them had a scrapbook filled with pictures of them. Usually the pictures had a note written on the back and were signed.

"To Kimo, who made Eagle Scout while I was on Lanai. I will never forget the night I pinned that badge on your uniform. Someday I hope you will be a missionary too. Remember the time you lost my watch at the beach. You were so worried. . . . "

"To Gladys, the girl who always smiles. Aloha, Elder Wilding."

"To Marie, always the first one at the church on Primary day. You will be such a beautiful girl when you grow up. Who will protect you from the boys when I am not here? Aloha nui loa, Elder Brimhall."

"Aloha pume hana, Elder Johnson."

"Aloha, Aloha, Aloha, Elder Erickson."

All the members had a supply of pictures of the many elders. They were printed in a photo mill of some kind and were of indifferent quality, but they were precious to the youngsters in the branch, who also kept an oral record of all the missionaries who had served on Lanai.

They used the elders as reference points to establish the time and order of remembered events. "I remember dat time; dat was Elder Nichols's time. You know, da one who could talk like Donald Duck. Was his companion da short guy wid da red hair?"

"No. Dat was two elders before. Remember? Before Elder Nichols was da elder wid da bald head. Before him was Elder McNeil, da football player. His junior was da red-headed one."

In any discussion about past elders, Elder Ihunui's name was sure to come up. He had baptized Kyoshi, who was Bernard's older brother, Danny, Bernard, and Margie, among others. He had been there when the branch president died suddenly of a stroke, leaving the branch without local adult leadership. The mission president had come from Honolulu to conduct the funeral, and before he left, he made Mike Parkinson the branch president, telling him not to expect a transfer for several months. A year later a transfer came through, and Elder Ihunui, as Elder Parkinson had come to be known, called the mission president and asked to be left on Lanai.

The nonmembers in town had always been able to recognize the elders, who wore suits and straw hats, but few of them bothered to learn their names, as the young men were transferred in and out so frequently. However, once they'd heard about "da elder wid da big nose," they couldn't forget his name. "Hi, Elder Ihunui," they would call, then turn and comment in Japanese or Filipino to their companions about the "funny kind elder name" and the big nose that inspired it.

When Elder Mike Parkinson left Lanai at the end of his mission, the whole branch and many of the townsfolk were at the airport to see him off. He was covered with leis up to his eyes, and his arms were full of presents. As the DC-3 took off, Elder Ihunui could see the boys in his Scout troop standing at the end of the runway, waving. It was a sight he would never forget, and it almost broke his heart.

Danny got up on Monday morning and looked out his bedroom window. Clouds still obscured the heights of Lanaihale and hung low over the city. He had been awakened several times in the night by the rain pelting down on the metal roofing overhead. A cock crowed off in the distance, and it was answered by one of Benito's roosters from the chicken coop behind their house.

By the time Danny left for school, the sun had broken through. Its fervent rays were bleaching the dull grey out of the clouds and scattering them into harmless puffs of misty vapor. The Norfolk Island Pine trees had been washed clean of Lanai's red dust by the drenching downpour, and their needles shimmered in the bright sunlight. Reddish mud puddles lined the roads and filled all the little concavities in the blacktop.

Danny saw Nori and some of her friends up ahead of him. They had taken off their shoes, to avoid staining them, and were walking barefoot. Even walking barefoot through the puddles, Nori looked elegant. She was carrying her shoes just like the other girls, laughing like them, calling to friends as they did, but she was different somehow, like a princess joining in a game with her subjects. She asked for no special privileges but seemed to deserve them.

By the time Danny reached the school, Nori was standing by the window in their classroom waiting for him and smiling. As he entered the room, she came over to talk to him.

"I talked to Jerry this morning, and he said the party was wonderful!" she said excitedly. "He said there was a fellow there that played the best ukulele in the islands—I assume that was Jerry."

Danny laughed. "That's our Jerry, always modest and shy. He was terrific though; I never heard him play better." Nori changed the subject and began to talk about plans for the pep assembly to be held on the next Friday before the team left for Lahaina. While she talked, Danny searched her face for clues of a changed relationship between them. He saw nothing but the little details and mannerisms that so endeared her to him. Her eyes were large by Japanese standards, and almond-shaped. Their dark brown color contrasted with the light tan skin of her face. Her features were finely cut and delicate, except her mouth, which tended to be more generous and full. She had a habit of pressing her lips together in a little half-smile and nodding her head when she was amused or wanted to show her approval of something. She did it as she finished giving Danny a rundown of the program planned for the assembly. "... that will be in the morning. The team will have lunch together, then after your meeting with Coach Manning, we'll all line up and cheer as you run past us to the bus."

"Sounds good to me," he said. The teacher called the class to order and began his instruction. Danny looked over at Nori during the class. She felt his gaze and turned and smiled. "It was nothing, the other night, nothing at all," he said to himself. "Why am I so stupid? She had to entertain her aunt—that's all." Danny felt a warm glow of relief pass through him.

After class Danny walked with Nori to her next class. "What if we lose to Lahainaluna on Friday, Nori? What if it's another Wailuku?" Lanai played Wailuku in the season opener and had been soundly thumped.

"It won't be," she answered. "You're a different team than you were when you played Wailuku. I think you're going to do just great! My cousin Tomo is bragging that they're going to beat us—he's so proud about them being in second place—but after the game you played last Thursday, I know we can win. If we do, Wailuku had better watch out."

Wailuku had already won the first half of the Maui District competition, but the second half gave every team a second chance. If Lanai could win the second half, they would force a playoff with Wailuku for the championship. If Wailuku won or tied for first place in the second half, the championship was theirs.

Nori pressed her lips together in the little mannerism that Danny loved, and then smiled sheepishly. "Do I sound like Coach Manning giving one of his famous halftime speeches?"

Danny smiled back. "I think you're lots better, but I'm not thinking about Wailuku yet. I'm just thinking about Lahainaluna and keeping our winning streak going. If we can win Friday night, that's four in a row. If we win that game, who knows? Maybe we can take the second half and force a playoff."

"Well, here's my class," Nori said. "I'll see you later."

Danny headed for the library. He had study hall this hour. As he sat in front of his books, trying to study, his mind filled with thoughts of basketball. Losing the first game of the season so badly in Wailuku had been embarrassing, but when they lost the week after in Kahului, the team was really down. Rudy Garcia had suggested that they just concede the District Championship to Wailuku and go spearfishing. Bernard had become furious at such talk and had backed him into the lockers, threatening to break his arm if he ever heard him say anything like that again. More from surprise than fear, Rudy backed down and said he was only joking. Then the team had looked at the two of them: Bernard, the aggressor, with hands at the ready, squaring off against Rudy, who towered over him and outweighed him by forty or fifty pounds. They began to laugh, and soon Rudy and Bernard joined in. Everyone seemed to relax, but there was no more talk of defeat. If anyone made a negative comment after that, someone was sure to say, "Hey, you no hear Bernard? By 'n' by he broke yo' arm!"

After losing the first two games, the team had turned around and won the last three by substantial margins. The big test was coming in the game against Lahainaluna High School on Friday night. Lahainaluna had been beaten only once, by Wailuku, in a close game. The other teams were a mixed bag of wins and losses, and none of them seemed likely to be a factor in the district competition.

The men of Lanai were avid sports fans, and three wins in a row were enough to get them excited about Lanai's team. A group of the men had gotten together and arranged for some fishing boats to take them across the Maui Channel to Lahaina. They invited the team to ride along. The principal, Mr. Watanabe, had accepted the invitation to save the round-trip airfares, and Coach Manning had reluctantly agreed. The mood of the basketball fans, so dismal at the beginning of the season, had changed dramatically, and he didn't want to do anything to stifle their enthusiasm.

Danny felt a heavy hand on his shoulder. "Waddascoops, brah; what's happening? Worried about da big game?" Danny looked up into Podogi's smiling face.

"Sure, aren't you? It kind of puts the pressure on to have everybody going over in the boats, doesn't it?"

"Pressure sometime good," Podogi answered. "Make us work mo' hard, eh?"

"If you can take the rebounds away from that big Hawaiian center, I think we've got a good chance," Danny said.

Podogi smiled and gestured with his hand, holding three fingers close to his palm, extending the thumb and little finger and waggling the hand and forearm. "Hang loose, brah, No worry, eh? Dat big Hawaiian Blalah eat too much poi; he come slow and sleepy. I cockaroach da ball away from him, no problem. He make like dis"—Podogi pretended to be holding a ball in front of him—"I make like dat"—he went through the motions of pulling the ball out of his opponent's hands. "I pass to you." He pretended to throw the ball to Danny.

In a reflex movement Danny put up his hands and found himself holding the imaginary ball. He looked around and saw that all the other students in the library were grinning. He became embarrassed and began to put his hands down.

"What-sa-matter you, you no gonna shoot." Podogi sounded disgusted. He reached out and took the "ball" back from Danny, dribbled twice, and mimed a hook shot from the top of the key. Following the "ball" with his eyes, he suddenly ducked his head and said, "Swoosh! Two points for Lanai High!" The other students clapped. Danny turned red as Miss Chen, the librarian, rushed into the room.

"What's going on, Keaka?" she asked, calling Podogi by his Hawaiian name.

"I jus' make two points for Lanai High—hard shot too," Podogi answered, looking very serious. The students began to laugh out loud.

Miss Chen looked confused. "In the future, I would appreciate it if you would confine your basketball playing to the gymnasium, Keaka." She opened the door and gestured toward the hall.

"No huhu, Miss Chen; I no like make you mad wid me, eh?" he said, and left the room trying to look repentant.

"Return to your studies," Miss Chen said to the room full of students.

Things quieted down. Danny stared at one of his books but was unable to concentrate. "That Podogi," he thought. "He's one crazy guy, but if we win on Friday, he'll have a lot to do with it. I hope his hook shot is working as well in the Lahainaluna gym as it was here in the library."

Chapter
8

On the Thursday night before the game, practice was short, and Danny got home early. He and Benito ate together and talked about the game. "You no worry, Danny," his father said, his voice full of confidence. "You too much good team. I bet ten dollar you win; I no worry too."

"I hope you don't lose your money, Pop. We'll try our best, but they're a big team and really good."

"I remember before time when I go cock fight." Benito's eyes shone as he told the story. "I look roosters; I say, 'What-sa-matter you guys, dis no fight, dis chicken murder.' One rooster big, strong." Benito raised his fists and flexed his biceps. "Da other rooster too much small, litty bitty bird." He held his hand down by the floor. "Everybody bet on da big one; me too. It chicken murder all right, you bet. All same dat little rooster push da big one round an' round. He like kill him, but he no can catch on his short legs. Dey stop fight. Dat big rooster in da pot dat night, I t'ink so; his boss so huhu his face come all red." Benito was laughing his high pitched hee-hee and gasping for breath in between words.

Danny laughed too. Something about Benito's good humor was irresistible. It was unpredictable too. Danny could never

69

tell what situation or turn of a phrase might spark his active sense of the ridiculous. Once he was tickled, laughter rolled out of him unrestrained, like sugar from a torn sack, until he was played out. Few could keep from joining him when he was like that, even if they didn't really know what they were laughing at.

"Mo' better you go sleep early," Benito said finally when he had regained control. "You get some big game for play tomorrow night. You no can play good if you no sleep, eh?"

When Danny woke the next morning his father had already left for the harbor to load the pineapple barges that took the fruit to Honolulu for processing. As Danny walked to school, he was greeted with words of encouragement from the Lanai High students, who were very much up for the big game with Lahaina.

"Give 'em, Danny!" Danny turned around to see nine-year-old David Tagavilla hitting the air with a raised fist. Danny smiled and waved. David was like a little brother to him. He was a handsome Filipino boy who reminded Danny of pictures he had seen of himself at that age.

"Le's go, Danny!" another voice called as Danny passed a group of sophomore girls headed for school. As he passed, the others picked up the chant. "Le's go, le's go, le's go!" Danny couldn't help smiling.

There was a large banner over the door at Akagi's Dry Goods. "Lahainaluna — no chance." It was Evelyn's work; her father owned the store. Evelyn was the same age as Danny, and he had known her since they were children. She was pure Japanese, but her skin was very fair, lighter than most of the missionaries. The elders called her an Oriental haole.

The front of the school was a patchwork of posters and

banners. One poster said, "Lanai Ono, Lahainaluna Pilau." Under the word "Lanai" was a picture of a girl with a pleasant smile on her face. Under "Lahainaluna" was a girl holding her nose. Another poster showed two roosters dressed in basketball uniforms. The game was represented as a cock fight. The Lahaina bird was very large and beefy, but he was lying on his back, out cold, with an X over each eye. Perched on top of him was the little Lanai bird, with large steel spurs strapped to his legs. The Lahaina bird's spurs were broken and bent. Danny recalled his father's story of the previous night and chuckled.

At each class that morning the teacher made some comments about the upcoming game and offered words of praise and encouragement to the team members who were in the class. Danny modestly accepted the kind words and smiled at the class. After the lecture started, he found it impossible to concentrate on the subject being taught. His notes consisted of diagrammed plays and the names of the players on the Lahaina team they would be facing that evening. Lahaina's great advantage was in the size of their center and forwards. Lahaina was the ancient capital of the islands, and Hawaiian blood was strong in the community. Hawaiians could be tall and powerful. Alfred Makanui, Lahaina's center and captain of the team, looked like the statue of King Kamehameha in Honolulu. He was well over six feet tall and built like a linebacker. The two starting forwards were not as big as Alfred, but they were considerably larger than the Lanai team members. Speed and quickness would win the game for Lanai, if they won, and it seemed like a very big "if" at this point.

At the pep assembly Nori introduced skits from each class depicting total victory for Lanai over the Lahainaluna team. The costumes left much to be desired, but everybody got the idea.

By the time the cheerleaders took over, the whole school was pumped up and ready to cheer. After the cheers, Evelyn Akagi sang the school song; then the cheerleaders led the crowd in singing it again.

Finally it was time for lunch. The team all sat together on game days. Coach Manning thought it helped them concentrate, and he came to the school to eat with them. Today he had scheduled a team meeting right after lunch since they would not be together again until game time. The team was going to Lahaina by boat, and he was going to fly over later. Coach Manning sat directly across from Danny at the table and picked at his food.

Dr. Charles Vincent Manning, Dr. "Chuck" to the people of the island who were his patients and friends, had been hired by the plantation to be in charge of the small hospital that served the people of Lanai. Dr. "Chuck" was just over six feet tall and had a slender, muscular body, a handsome face, and thick, curly, sandy-colored hair that he wore short. Coach Manning had been a pilot during World War II, and he still looked like a military man. He had flown off a carrier in the South Pacific and had described to the team his experience of landing on a carrier in the middle of a storm.

"When you make your approach," he said, "the heaving deck looks like a postage stamp in a bathtub that's being filled with water. Your only chance is to listen to the voice in your ear that's telling you what to do and to watch the man with the flags on the deck. They can see exactly what's happening. If you're coming in too high, they wave you over, if other adjustments need to be made, they let you know. If you try to fly by the seat of your pants in a situation like that, you'll either end up in the sea or smashed up against the barrier at the end of the deck."

He compared this to a basketball game. "In the heat of battle, against a tough team, sometimes you make the same mistakes over and over again. That's why you have a coach. When you're in a game and things are going wrong, call a time-out. Usually I can see what's happening. When I tell you the corrections to make, make them! When I tell you to do something, do it! When you're in control of the game, you don't need a coach; follow your instincts, go with your guts. But when you're in trouble, look to me, listen to me, and do what I say!"

Coach Manning had an uncanny knack for figuring out what was going wrong during a game. He would call a time-out and begin barking commands like a top sergeant. "Podogi, your man is overguarding your right side; take that left-handed hook shot you've been practicing every night. What are you saving it for, college ball? Danny, your man is expecting you to pull up and shoot the jumper and you haven't disappointed him all night. Give him a head fake and drive right down the middle of the key. It's wide open!" When they followed his instructions, they started racking up points.

If the other team liked to run and it was working for them, he would have his team slow the play down. If the opponents were getting more than a few points ahead, he would go into a full-court press, even early in the first quarter to wear them down and confuse them. "You probably think this will hurt your rhythm too, but it won't. The difference is that you're in charge! You decide when the play is going to be slow! You decide when to run and gun. They don't know what to expect; you do, because you're calling the shots." He ran the team like a conductor leads a symphony orchestra. Often they found that they didn't even need a time-out. They'd glance over at the bench, and he'd give them a look, a shake of the head, a gesture, and they knew what to do.

Coach Manning's strategy could be simply stated: "Out-hustle them every minute of the game, and be a balanced team. We want no standouts, no big guns, no stars. The man with the hot hand gets the ball, but it might be a different man each game. Everybody is a threat! Anybody can score and score big on a given night. If we really worked at it, we could make a hero out of any one of you, and the newspapers would love it. They'd tout you as a sure thing for the Maui District all-star team. But what do we do if you're cold on the night when we're playing for the district championship? Show the other team your newspaper clippings? We're not big, and we don't have a lot of depth on this team. We're quick and we're in good shape, but if we're not balanced, we're nothing."

The Lanai team had five good men. Jerry Tano and Danny were the guards, Darrell Fujimoto and Raul "Rudy" Garcia were the forwards, Podogi was the center. If they were all in top form, they had the potential to give any team in the league a run for their money, but the bench provided very little backup. If Darrell lost his confidence, or Rudy lost his head, or Podogi got creamed, they were in trouble. Danny was the glue that held the team together, and Jerry was his right arm.

Coach Manning had explained it in a private meeting with the five at the beginning of the season. "If Lanai High has a successful season this year, it will be because you five guys have found a way to play most of every game and play it as a team. No one of you can carry this team, but the loss of any one of you can destroy our chances for winning."

Danny caught Coach Manning staring at him. "What's the matter, coach, have I got gravy on my chin?" he asked, smiling.

"No. I was just thinking," Coach Manning answered.

"What about?" Danny asked.

"A game I played in college. It was so much like this game against Lahaina. They were big and physical; we were fast and canny. A lot hung on that game." He stared down at his plate. "I was the team spark plug like you are. I wanted to play forward, but I always ended up as point guard, calling the plays, taking the outside shots. Do you like your position, Danny?"

"I'm no good anywhere else," Danny replied. "I'd like to be a seven-foot center, but it's probably too late for that. Did you win that game you're thinking about?"

"No. We lost. It was very close, but we lost. That's what I'm thinking about now, why we lost and how to see that you don't. Excuse me, Danny, I have to talk to the principal for a minute." He got up and walked over to Mr. Watanabe, who was barely five feet tall. At six foot two, Coach Manning towered over the tiny Watanabe.

Danny knew Coach Manning's history as a player: three years all-conference guard in the Big Ten, played in the NCAA semifinals in two of those three years, accepted in medical school at the end of his junior year. He missed his senior year in basketball to study medicine and passed up any chance of playing basketball professionally. Did he regret his decision? Nothing he ever said would indicate that he did, but he loved the game, that was obvious, and missed being close to it. When the town council asked him to coach the high school basketball team, they apologized for the small salary they could pay him. He laughed and confessed he would be glad to pay them for the privilege. So, Dr. Chuck had become Coach Manning, and after three years of hard work and disappointment, Lanai High finally had a basketball team with possibilities.

In the team meeting Coach Manning carefully reviewed the strategy they would be using in the game at Lahainaluna.

He ended with some words of caution: "I really don't like the idea of your coming to the game in the fishing boats. Concentration is so important in getting up for a game like this; but we need the support of the town, and this seems to mean a lot to them. Spend some time thinking about what we've discussed because we won't have much time after you get to Lahaina." As the team left the locker room, he called out, "Make sure nobody falls overboard."

As the team members left the gym, they were met by a cheering crowd of students, who led them outside to the jeeps and pickups that would take them to the harbor, where the fishing boats were waiting for the trip to Lahaina.

Chapter

9

The road to the harbor was through the pineapple fields. The locals call the fruit "pine." "You like I bring you home fresh pine?" Danny's father would ask. "We get sugar pine on da road to harbor." Pineapple plants bore several crops of fruit before having to be replanted. The first two or three crops were large-sized fruit and were picked commercially. Pineapples that matured after that were small but very sweet. The local people preferred these and called them "sugar pine."

When seen from the air, the pineapple fields formed beautiful geometric shapes from the terracing and contour planting used to combat soil erosion. From the jeep, they didn't look quite so beautiful, and the constant cultivating and harvesting kept the air filled with red dust.

Will I ever shake the red dust of Lanai? Danny wondered. They passed a harvesting machine with a conveyor stretching far out to one side. Behind the conveyors plodded the pickers, fifteen or twenty of them, men and women working side by side, plucking the large pineapples from the plants and dropping them on to the moving belts. Dust swirled over, under, and all around them. Danny was glad that his father was a member of the harbor loading crew and not out in the fields.

A little farther on, a machine was laying down strips of heavy asphalt mulching paper and covering the edges with the red dirt. Swarming over the black strips were the planters, who jabbed holes in the paper with sharpened sticks and planted cuttings from the piles that had been dropped between the rows. The paper kept both the weeds down and the moisture in the ground while the cuttings were taking hold. I'll be doing that this summer, Danny thought. That is, if I'm one of the lucky ones who get a job. He was not looking forward to it. Working in the fields was hot, dusty, mind-numbing labor. You came home with red dust in your hair and in your ears. It even sifted through your outer clothes into your underwear, through the cloth masks and around the goggles you wore until it caked at the corners of your eyes and mouth.

The road began to curve and wind down toward the harbor. Kaumalapau Harbor was beautiful, compact, and deep. Danny had been spearfishing there many times.

"Hey, Danny," called Jerry. "You remember da big blue uhu you poked at da harbor last summer? Some big, dat one!" Danny smiled. He had a reputation as a spearfisherman that rivaled his fame as a basketball player.

"After we win the championship, we poke fish every day after school, eh?" He gave Jerry the thumbs up and smiled warmly. He turned to Bernard who was sitting next to him. "Bernard, have you ever noticed how the fish live in levels?"

"What do you mean, levels?" he asked.

"You know, up near the surface, are the manini and the black mamo and the humu humu nuku nuku apua'a, the little fish. A little farther down, the fish are bigger, and way down deep are the red and blue uhu. It's like they live in levels most of the time, in their own league, so to speak. They eat each other's little ones and stay away from the big fish down deep."

"I think I know what you mean," said Bernard. "I guess I never thought about it like that."

"Well, in these last three games, I feel like we've been fishing near the surface, poking the manini and the black mamo. They're not easy, but they're possible." Danny spoke more softly — he didn't want any of the others to hear him. "Tonight, we're going deep; we're after a big blue uhu. It can be done; I've done it, but it's different."

"I know what you mean," said Bernard. "I'm nervous too, not like you must be, because there's almost no chance I'll get to play, but I feel the difference like you say. It's like diving deep and hanging on to a piece of coral and waiting for an uhu to come by. You feel the pressure in your ears and your lungs, and you look up and see how far it is to the surface shining up there above you. You can stay a little longer, but you don't know how long. It's spooky all right."

"Don't get the idea that I think we're licked already," Danny said. "I'm going to give it everything I have. I just hate this uncertain feeling, that's all."

"I've got a very strong feeling that we're going to get that big blue uhu tonight!" Bernard said as he punched Danny gently in the ribs. "Now forget it and let's enjoy the boat ride."

They stopped next to the dock. Three small fishing boats were tied up there waiting for them. Teru Yamada called to Danny, "Hey, Tolentino come ride my boat. Bring some more guys, eh?" Danny headed for the boat, followed by Bernard, Podogi, Jerry Tano, and a couple of the younger boys on the team.

"Benito like I take you wid me, Danny. I told him come too, but he too busy busy load da barge. Try look, eh?" Teru gestured toward a barge being loaded further on down the dock. Benito was waving his hat. Danny waved back as Teru pushed off and headed his boat out to sea.

The southwestern coast of Lanai is spectacular from the sea. Towering cliffs, some higher than a thousand feet, rise right out of the ocean. The surf explodes into the shelf of rocks at their base, sprays of froth and foam arching into the air and smashing into the stony walls. The boats were a safe distance from the breakers, but Danny wondered what would happen if a boat had engine trouble in these waters, especially if it were alone.

As they passed the highest of the cliffs, Bernard gestured to a point on the shore. "That's Kaunolu Village, where King Kamehameha the Great used to spend his summers. The fishing was good there; still is. He'd bring all his cronies along for company and just fish and loaf the summer away." They rounded the southern tip of Lanai and headed east toward Maui.

"Dere Manele Beach," Podogi said excitedly, pointing toward a beautiful bay rimmed with white sand. "I never see da beach from da ocean side. Some pretty, eh. Around da point is some good place for poke fish. And dere da rock where we take easy in da sun, eh, Bernard? Now Black Sand Beach coming up."

"Hiromi like poke fish by dat rock too," Teru said. "I tell him, catch fish in net mo' easy, but he like poke fish mo' better. He say, 'It give da fish chance to get away.' "

"Dat Mr. Satō some good poke fish," Jerry said. "I see da bag of fish he poke one Saturday. Some big dat bag!"

The wind was picking up, and clouds were accumulating rapidly. "Are we going to have a storm?" Danny asked Teru.

"Maybe so, we get bad wind." he answered gravely. The waves were getting a little choppy. "You no can tell nothing 'bout dis water," he said, gesturing toward the Maui Channel. "Maybe so, we forget go Maui and try poke fish instead," He pointed at the tiny island to the south of them, Kahoolawe, which served as a target for bombing practice for the military. "Plenty fish, Kahoolawe."

Danny had heard stories of men who had driven boats to Kahoolawe during the night and spearfished at first light for a couple of hours, assuming that bombing practice, if scheduled, would not be that early in the morning. Supposedly the fish were not as wary in such an isolated place and could be taken in great numbers in a very short time. Danny smiled at Teru and lapsed into Pidgin. "Dat be good fun, Teru, but tonight we get some big fish for poke, Lahaina-side. Try be careful, eh? If dis boat sink and we have to swim Lahaina, we come too much tired for da game." Teru grinned, showing his ragged teeth, and turned his attention to the channel ahead.

As the clouds became darker, the light began to fail and the size of the waves grew larger. The slap of the boat against the swells was sharp and caused the hull to vibrate. The boys helped Teru stretch the canvas top back from the cabin and secure it to the sides of the boat. They hit a wave a little off center, and sea water splashed across the back half of the boat, drenching them all. The waves were white capped. They felt as if they were riding through a heavy surf. As the sky grew darker and the water rougher, the tiny boats yawed and pitched and became harder to control.

"Have you seen it this bad before?" Danny asked Teru. He nodded but said nothing. His eyes were on the front of the boat and the oncoming swells.

When they were in the troughs, Danny could see nothing but water around them. The other boats disappeared completely. When they rose to the top of a swell, he could see the dark mass that was Maui off in the distance and sometimes a part of a boat. He saw the propeller of the boat in front of them come completely out of the water and heard the whine of it revving up. He heard the same sound under their boat a moment later. The waves were crashing across three-quarters of the boat each time they took a swell head on. Nobody was seasick—they were too frightened. Danny knew he had a tendency to motion sickness, but he felt nothing in his stomach now but a tight knot of fear. The height of the waves seemed to increase. Water sloshed back and forth in the bottom of the boat, and they were all soaked to the skin. Luckily, Coach Manning had taken their uniforms, equipment, and overnight bags with him on the plane. At least they would have dry clothes to put on after the game.

I'm glad Nori isn't here, Danny thought, then he wondered almost out loud, "Why am I thinking about her now?" He knew why. If Teru made an error of judgment, if he allowed the boat to yaw too much and get turned sideways in one of those troughs, the next wave would capsize them. They all had on life jackets and were strong swimmers, so they would probably stay afloat and be picked up after the storm. But Nori, delicate little Nori, what chance would she have in a sea like this? Well, she wasn't here. She was safe and dry back in Lanai City, probably getting ready to listen to the game on the radio. Suddenly Danny didn't feel afraid anymore. He looked around at the ashen faces of his companions and began to laugh.

"What-sa-matter you, Podogi?" he shouted. "You no like this one boat ride? All same like Catholic carnival Ferris wheel: You go up, you go down, you go any kind way, no problem." Podogi had worked at the Catholic Carnival that year, selling tickets to all the little kids and telling them not to be afraid.

Podogi smiled back. "Some bumpy dis ride, I like get off, okay? Stop 'em, eh?"

"Get off anytime, but no can stop," said Danny. "We get plenty big game Lahainaluna. No more time for Podogi rest stop."

Bernard began to enter into the fun and make wisecracks in heavy Pidgin. Jerry Tano began a soliloquy in Filipino Pidgin. He spoke in a high squeaky voice and punctuated his sentences with psuedo-Filipino exclamations. "Beforetime I come a Lanai, I live in Pilipine Islands. Sollybollybalong! I no can find job, I no can make money for spend on girl. I no can have girl! Holy smokes! Girl like man wid plenty money for buy her any kind stuffs; I no mo' nothing, eh?"

They were all laughing now, and when an especially large wave came along, everyone but Teru raised his arms when the boat crested it and started down the other side, like riders on a roller coaster.

Jerry finished his bit by explaining that he had chosen to live in Hawaii because "Hawaii, no more snakes." Then he seemed to be talking to himself. "Lanai, no more snakes, but Lanai have too plenty pineapple. I t'ink so, mo' better have not so plenty pineapple, have a few snakes." Bernard was laughing so hard he was gasping for breath.

As suddenly as the storm had come, it passed, and the waves began to flatten into gentle swells. As the sky cleared, they could see the lights of Lahaina twinkling in the distance. They were the only lights visible on the whole northwest coast of Maui. Teru turned to Danny and smiled.

"How you like swim Maui Channel?"

"Not me!" he answered emphatically.

"Satō swim 'em," he said in a tone of voice that showed great respect. He was talking about Nori's father, Hiromi. Everybody on Lanai knew the story. As a nineteen-year-old boy, Hiromi Satō swam all the way from Keomuku on the east coast of Lanai to Lahaina, Maui. It was a remarkable feat even in a smooth ocean. A newspaper reporter had interviewed him after his landing in Lahaina, and Hiromi had said, "I read somewhere about a big, fat Hawaiian queen swimming over to Lanai to check on her unfaithful husband. I figured a young, strong Japanese boy shouldn't have any trouble making the same swim."

Hiromi Satō was brassy like that. His position as operations manager of the plantation put him in charge of all the people who crawled around in the dusty fields, planting, hoeing, and harvesting the ripening "pine" that flowed out from that little island to the kitchens and dining rooms of the world. He pretended to handle things in a democratic way with recommendations and suggestions, occasionally even calling for a vote of the workers, but it all came down to the same thing: what Hiromi Satō said was law. If someone crossed him, he didn't discharge the man, he merely made his life so miserable that he finally knuckled under or quit.

Mr. Satō was careful to break no union rules. It was not like the old days when an overseer in charge of field labor could do anything he wanted to the workers. To physically abuse a worker now would have brought on a strike like the one several years before that went on for months and left thousands of acres of pineapple rotting in the fields. Any official's head would roll if he started a strike, even Hiromi's. Hiromi was much too clever to let that happen. If a truck driver talked back to him, Hiromi would simply reassign him as a picker and let him wallow in the dust and get nauseated from watching the conveyor belt go by. He was soon pleading for his old job back, and sometimes Hiromi would give it to him.

After that, he became one of Hiromi's stooges. Those who had been so disciplined knew that Hiromi held both the carrot and the stick and that he would not hesitate to use either to accomplish his ends.

"How long have you known Hiromi?" Danny asked Teru.

"I know him since he small little boy," Teru answered. "He like my own son, dat Hiromi." There was obvious pride in his voice. "He work for Teru on dis boat sometime; work too much hard, no take nothing for working."

Danny said nothing, but his mind was full of questions. "How could a ruthless, swaggering bully like Hiromi Satō keep a friend like Teru, and how could he produce a daughter like Nori? It just didn't make any sense."

Teru reversed the motor and increased the power to slow down the boat as they came into the dock. Voices called out in the darkness, and hands caught and fastened the ropes Danny and the others threw from the boat. The rise and fall of the boat in relation to the stationary dock made Danny aware of the motion of the sea. He felt a twinge of nausea. "That's great," he chuckled softly to himself. "I live through a monster storm in the channel and get seasick on the wharf."

Chapter
10

A bus was waiting at the dock in Lahaina to take them to the high school. Lahaina was such a sleepy little town, it was hard to believe that it had been the ancient capital of the Hawaiian Islands under King Kamehameha I. Between 1820 and 1870, Lahaina had been one of the busiest ports in the Pacific because of the whaling industry that flourished then. As many as five hundred ships would visit the harbor in a single year. The Lahainaluna School was built on the cooler slopes to the east above the city and had a rich historical tradition. Originally a teacher's college, it was the oldest American school west of the Rockies. Now it was a high school, but it was a high school with a lot of pride. They would not roll over and play dead for a bunch of pineapple pickers from Lanai.

The carefree banter of the boat ride gave way to quiet reflection during the bus ride to the high school. Everyone was lost in his own thoughts. Danny's mind buzzed with questions. Will Darrell's corner shot be working tonight? Will Rudy keep his head? Can Jerry do the job on defense he's done the last three games? Can Podogi stop Alfred Makanui? Can I stop Tomo Satō? Wouldn't you know I'd be guarding Hiromi Satō's nephew?

The bus arrived, and the boys saw Coach Manning waiting for them. He jumped into the bus as soon as the door opened. "C'mon, you guys, the game starts in fifteen minutes. What kept you?" Jerry Tano started to tell him about the storm in Filipino Pidgin, but the coach cut him off. "Get dressed as fast as you can and get warmed up. This is the big one!"

They dressed quickly and in silence. Danny was praying silently, "Let us do our best. Let us play the best we ever have!" Then they were out on the floor shooting lay-ups. Danny loved the feel of the ball in his hands and the spring in his legs when he leaped up toward the basket and laid the ball softly against the backboard. Later, shooting from about twenty feet out, he dropped four shots in a row. Podogi was shooting hook shots to the left and then to the right. Bernard was practicing foul shots and, as usual, making one after another.

The buzzer sounded, and suddenly the game was under way. Podogi got the tip, and flipped it to Danny. Danny hit Jerry as he streaked down the court. Jerry made the lay-up and was fouled. All at once it was Lanai three, Lahaina nothing, and the crowd was howling for revenge.

Coach Manning called for a full-court press, and Danny stole the ball on the inbounds pass and dropped in a short jumper. A Lahaina guard tried to throw the ball to Makanui at midcourt, but it glanced off his fingertips out of bounds. Lanai's ball again. Danny faked a drive down the center and passed off to Darrell Fujimoto in the corner. He took the shot and sank it. Less than forty seconds into the game, the score was Lanai seven, Lahaina still nothing. Lahaina called a time-out. Whatever the Lahaina coach told the team seemed to work; they came back and made five unanswered baskets, and Lanai was down by three points.

The score seesawed back and forth all during the first half.

As long as Lanai pressed, they were able to stay ahead. As soon as they went back to a zone defense, their opponents would find a way to get the ball to Makanui, and Lahaina would start scoring again.

"Stay wid da press, coach," Podogi pleaded during one time-out. "We no tired; we run dese guys into da ground."

"Maybe you could," Coach Manning answered. "But you and Danny each have two fouls on you, and we're only in the middle of the second quarter. If you two foul out, who keeps Satō and Makanui from scoring at will? No, we'll press when we have to, but I want all five of you starters in there if this game goes down to the wire."

Lahaina was ahead by three points with ten seconds to go in the first half, but Rudy Garcia broke away for a lay-up and was fouled. The lay-up was good, and the foul shot tied the game.

Coach Manning gave the team guarded praise during half-time. They were playing well, taking only good shots and hur-rying back on defense. If they could keep the pressure on Lahaina and avoid getting into foul trouble until the middle of the fourth quarter, they would put on a full-court press and pull ahead at the end of the game. That was his strategy.

"This is their home court, and the pressure is on those referees," said Coach Manning. "Every time they make a call against Lahaina, those stands explode. I think the referees are fair, especially Chang. He's probably the best referee in the district, but he lives right here in Lahaina and works for the telephone company. He has to deal with these people every day. Will he make the tough call? I think so, but we have to play it very clean. If we make stupid fouls, he'll catch them, and he should."

"Makanui get mean temper," Podogi said. "He foul out in

third quarter wid Wailuku. How about we double-team 'em; by 'n' by he get huhu and make any kind dumb fouls. Dey get no mo' chance widout him."

"Okay, we'll try it," the coach answered. "Rudy, you and Jerry switch positions on defense. Jerry, that will put you down under the basket where you can help Podogi guard Makanui. Talk to him constantly, steal the the ball, then tease him about it. All right, let's go get 'em!"

The second half was like a replay of the first. Lanai took an early lead, only to go cold and get behind. The double-teaming was working well with Makanui, but then Lahaina's forwards started to score. Jerry was keeping up a barrage of Filipino Pidgin in Makanui's ear. "No go left, Makanui, you everytime miss you go left. All same you no can go right, son-of-a-gun boy, you some plenty pilikia, big trouble, you go right; I everytime steal da ball. No huhu now, brah; I try give you helping hand, eh?" Makanui was trying to remain cool, but the talk was getting to him.

There was never more than a four-point spread between the two teams during the whole second half until the last three minutes. Danny was all over Satō, stealing the ball, blocking his shots, making life miserable for him. Satō had only twelve points going into the last three minutes, and Danny had made twenty-three. Lahaina took a time-out with three minutes to go. Lanai was four points ahead and in a full-court press, but they had to be careful. Both Danny and Podogi were playing with four fouls. When Lahaina came back from the time-out, another tall Hawaiian was playing the post, and Makanui had gone to forward. Before Lanai could adjust, Makanui had scored two field goals to tie the game. They bottled him up again, and Satō began scoring. Danny did not dare guard Satō too closely for fear of committing his fifth foul. Lanai was matching them basket for basket, but could not get the lead back. With eight seconds to go in the game, Satō put Lahaina ahead with a twenty-five foot shot. Lanai took a time-out.

"Everybody is going to expect Danny to take the final shot," Coach Manning said. "Podogi, you take the ball out, fake the throw to Danny, and then hit Jerry on the far side. It's our best chance; they'll have two men on Danny for sure."

It worked! The whole Lahaina team was concentrating on Danny. Jerry got the cross-court inbounds pass and drove for the basket. Suddenly, Makanui's self-control left him—that Filipino Pidgin-spouting nuisance was headed for the basket half a step ahead of him. Jerry started his lay-up. In desperation, Makanui lunged at Jerry, smashing him to the floor. Jerry's head hit with a thump, and he lay absolutely still. The crowd went silent as the ball rolled free from Jerry's grasp. Chang's whistle pierced the air, just as the buzzer sounded ending the game. He indicated a two-shot foul, and the Lahaina coach ran out on the floor, yelling in protest. Chang's hands came together in the shape of a T—the technical foul would give Lanai three shots.

Coach Manning had run to Jerry's side as soon as the foul was committed. Jerry was sitting up now, still obviously dazed, holding the coach's blood-stained handkerchief to his eye. Danny and Podogi helped him to the bench as Chang signaled the two coaches to meet him in the middle of the floor.

"Look, coach," Chang said. "I say that boy was in the act of shooting; that's a two-shot foul. You came right out on the floor and called me a name I don't take from anyone; that calls for a technical. Coach Manning, you're a doctor. Is that boy capable of shooting his own foul shots?"

"I don't think so. It will take at least six stitches to close that cut over his eye, and it's already starting to swell."

"Choose a replacement for him then and shoot the three foul shots."

Coach Manning squatted down in front of the bench, and the team surrounded him. He was looking at Danny. "They're going to let us choose another man to shoot for Jerry," he said. "Now, Danny, when you shoot these fouls, take lots of time — " He stopped. Danny was shaking his head. "What is it?" he asked.

"Let Bernard shoot the fouls, coach. Nobody shoots foul shots like Bernard."

"But he's not even warmed up, and the pressure will be unbelievable."

"Let Bernard do it, coach," Danny insisted. Coach Manning looked around at the faces that surrounded him. Every head was nodding except Bernard's.

When Bernard went to the foul line, the Lahaina crowd hooted. Compared to the other players, he looked like a child. The arm holes of his uniform hung clear to his waist. Coach Manning almost called for another time-out so he could change his mind.

As soon as he reached the foul line, Bernard seemed to relax. This was home to Bernard Ōta, and he felt strangely at ease. He went immediately into his routine, planting both feet at the line, holding the ball in front of him. He bounced the ball twice, then brought it up to eye level where he sighted over it. He talked to the ball. "You know the way, old friend, up and in." He flexed his right wrist, released, and lofted the ball up in the air. The shot dropped through without touching the rim. The crowd fell silent. The silence seemed to unnerve Bernard slightly. He put a little too much backspin on the second shot, and the ball balanced on the rim for what seemed like minutes before falling in.

Suddenly the crowd realized that this little Japanese boy was for real. As he began his routine for the third time, the crowd behind the basket began screaming, jumping up and down and waving their hands, hats, and pom poms in an effort to distract him. As he brought the ball up to his face, Bernard felt a quiet assurance. In his mind he was back on the asphalt court across from Danny's house, shooting his hundred foul shots for the night. He could hear the roosters crowing and the dogs barking in the distance. He was all alone, shooting his last shot for the night, and he was feeling just fine. He smiled slightly, cocked his wrist, and let fly. The net made a little hula movement as the ball settled into it.

The Lanai fans in the stands rushed out on to the floor and surrounded the team, slapping them on the back and calling them the future Maui District champions. Among those who congratulated them on the win was a half-drunk Hiromi Satō, who apparently had flown over to see the game. "I won five hundred dollars on you boys tonight," he said, as he pressed two twenty-dollar bills into Danny's hand. "See that they have a victory celebration." Then he left the floor and put his arm around a younger version of himself, who Danny assumed was Tomo Satō's father. Hiromi was saying, "Okay, little brother, pay up." Some of the fishermen joined them at the door, and Danny knew they would all be celebrating far into the night.

The Lanai team was sleeping over in Lahaina, and Danny had been assigned to the home of a Filipino member of the Lahaina team who hadn't seen action that night. He stood beside Danny now and introduced himself. "Good game, Danny," he said. "My name Tony Guerrero. You stay my house tonight. You like go dance?" A band was setting up on one side of the gym.

Danny felt a small hand slide into his. When he turned

around, he saw Nori, smiling radiantly up at him. "Are you staying for the dance, Danny?" she asked shyly.

"I guess I am," Danny answered with a smile. Danny turned to Tony, who was still standing near him. "Okay with you, Tony?" Tony nodded and left to join the other members of his team. "Nori, I never expected to see you here. Are you staying with your Aunty Mitsy?"

Nori nodded. "Daddy decided at the last minute to come to the game. I coaxed him to let me come too. We're going back tomorrow afternoon on the two o'clock flight. Danny, I was so proud of you tonight; you played a wonderful game." She was still holding his hand.

"I'm glad you came, Nori," Danny said. "It makes everything better. I'll go shower and be back in a few minutes."

Nori squeezed his hand one last time, and then walked away. After a few steps, she turned around again. "I'll be waiting," she called back.

Danny looked over at Bernard, who was still at the foul line surrounded by the other substitutes from the Lanai team. They were thrilled that the bench had provided the winning points, and they were making a big fuss of Bernard. Then all at once, Podogi broke away from his well-wishers, grabbed Bernard by the waist, put him up on his shoulders, and headed for the locker room. Danny and the rest of team followed.

Coach Manning had taken Jerry into the locker room immediately after the game and was already sewing up his eyebrow when the team rushed in. After they were all showered and dressed, they sat in front of him waiting for the postgame critique. They knew that his note pad would be bulging with criticisms and suggestions; it always was. Coach Manning walked back and forth in front of them as he always did, gathering his thoughts and leafing through his notebook. When he looked up finally, he was smiling and shaking his head. He dropped the notebook into his dufflebag. "If I went back over this game tonight, I'd probably have a heart attack," he said. He gestured toward the door to the gym. "Go have fun at the dance."

They walked out of the locker room and on to the floor. The dance was already underway, but at their appearance the band stopped playing and a voice came over the loudspeaker system. It was Tomo Satō speaking into the microphone. "The guys on the Lanai team are our guests tonight," he said. "The next dance will be girl's choice." A group of Lahaina girls started moving toward them. For the second time that evening, Danny felt Nori's hand slip into his from behind. She had been waiting at the locker-room door. "I choose you, Danny," she said and led him to the dance floor.

All night long they danced together, and no one bothered them except for the occasional "Nice game, Danny," or "Not too close, you two," teasing. Danny was confused. Why would Nori show him so much attention tonight, be so loving and approachable after turning him down for a date less than a week ago? He decided not to think about it. Tonight she was happy and smiling, and her soft brown eyes said everything to him that he had ever wanted to hear her say.

Chapter
11

When Tomo Satō dropped Nori off in front of their Aunt
Mitsy's house after the dance, there was still a light burning in
the kitchen. "Aunt Mitsy?" Nori whispered softly. "What are
you doing still up? It's nearly twelve-thirty."

"I used to wait up for my girls when they were in high
school. We'd talk about the evening and all the fun they'd had.
I thought maybe you and I could do that. I miss those talks
now that they're all married and gone."

"Did you see the game?"

"Wouldn't have missed it for anything. I used to cheer for
Hiromi when he played in high school. He was very good."

"Was he as good as Danny?" Nori asked.

"It's hard to say—it was years ago. But I was pretty proud
of my little brother, I remember that part well enough. You
like Danny Tolentino, don't you?"

"He's the most wonderful boy in the world, Aunt Mitsy,"
Nori said. "Tonight watching him play so well, dancing with
him after the game, I felt something more than friendship. I
think I love Danny, Aunt Mitsy."

"Of course you do," said Mitsy simply.

"You really believe it?" Nori asked, a little taken aback.

"I absolutely believe it," Mitsy said with conviction. "I can see it in your eyes, and I'm happy for you."

"But I'm not even quite eighteen, Aunt Mitsy. Do you think I could know for sure?"

"If you're asking if I think you've found the man you're going to spend your life with, I have no idea. You're right — it is too early for that kind of decision, but it's not too early to fall in love. It's never too early. I was in love in the fifth grade with a boy who never knew it and doesn't to this day."

"But you're talking about puppy love, kiddy stuff." Nori was a little offended by the comparison of a fifth-grade infatuation with what she felt for Danny.

"It was love as real as the love you feel for Danny or that I feel for my husband now," Mitsy said. "It was younger, simpler, less complicated love, but it was not something entirely different. It was love. I still love that boy, and I haven't seen him since his family moved to Honolulu two years later." Mitsy became pensive. When she spoke again, her voice was husky and full of feeling. "Nori, love is not something that happens to you once in a lifetime. It is something you learn, something that grows inside you and is nurtured by every loving feeling you ever have."

"I never thought about it like that," Nori said. "You talk about love like it's a talent or a gift, something you study and work on and try to improve. Can you learn to love like you learn to play the piano?"

Mitsy laughed. "Let's not take all the magic out of it. If it was that simple, you could just take a good correspondence course and learn everything you need to know about love." She became more serious. "One thing I do know: you don't become a loving person by turning your back on sincere feelings of love."

"But what can I do?" Nori said. "You know how Daddy feels about Filipinos. If Danny came to the house to take me out on a date, Daddy would be furious. I'm afraid to think what he might do."

"It's a tough problem, Nori. Have you thought of talking to your father about it?"

"I don't dare, Aunt Mitsy. I'm afraid of what it might do to Daddy and how he might react. He'd feel betrayed, like I'd turned against him. He's such a lonely man, and I'm all he has. Everyone says I look like Mother, that I move like she did, that my voice is like hers. If he lost me, it would be like losing her again. I don't think he could take it."

"It's late, Nori. Let's sleep on this and talk again in the morning. I've got an idea. Why don't you stay over until Sunday, and we'll have lots of time to talk. I'll tell your father I need some help painting the kitchen. I really do want you to do some painting for me. Let me show you something." Mitsy led Nori to a back bedroom and opened the door. A blank canvas was mounted on an easel, and there were tubes of paint on the table next to it.

"Aunt Mitsy!" Nori almost shouted, then realizing how late it was, she clapped her hand over her mouth. "I hope I didn't wake Uncle Kenji. Is this for me?" She was whispering now, and Mitsy started to laugh.

"Kenji sleeps like the dead; you don't have to whisper. No, this isn't for you; it's for me. See this picture of Kenji and me? It's my favorite picture of the two of us, and I want you to make a portrait from it in oils. Will you do it?"

"Tomorrow? Oh, Aunt Mitsy, it takes me ages to do a sketch like the one I showed you of Annie. I don't know if I can even do a painting."

Mitsy laughed. "I don't expect you to do it in a day. You

can start tomorrow, and then I'll bring the canvas and paints with me when I come over to visit. Take as long as you want to with the portrait; I'm in no hurry."

"It would be fun to try painting, but what if Daddy sees me and it bothers him?"

"He'll just have to get over it," Mitsy said with a shrug, "but I'm hoping to keep it a secret from Hiromi and Kenji both. Our wedding anniversary is in July. If it's finished in time, I'm going to give it to Kenji as a present, and we'll hang it on the wall. When Hiromi notices it and asks who did it, I'll say, 'Nori painted it for me; you ought to get her to do one of you.' What can he say? He's never forbidden you to paint, has he? I think he'll be a little shocked at first, but then he'll be pleased and proud like any father would be of a talented daughter. What do you think?"

Nori put her arms around Mitsy and hugged her. "I think you're the most wonderful aunt in the whole world."

Chapter
12

At the dock the next morning, Danny, Podogi, and Bernard saw Teru Yamada smiling and waving them onto the deck of his boat. He had already tidied up the mess from last night's storm, and everything was clean and dry.

Knowing that Teru was at the helm had been a great comfort to them on the stormy trip over. He knew the channel waters better than anyone on Lanai. He fished in all weather, even when the other boats swung at anchor in Kaumalapau Harbor. Teru loved the sea in all its moods. He was like Manele Beach or the harbor — part of the island itself. He usually fished alone as captain and crew. He lived alone too, near the harbor in a tiny shack surrounded by half a dozen coconut palms, some of the few that grew on the island. Teru had great respect for sea creatures. He harvested the fish that he sold to make his living, but he never wasted life. If small sharks or other undesirable fish became entangled in his nets, he released them.

The fishing boats moved slowly into the channel. The fishermen, who were still nursing hangovers from the postgame celebration, were in no great hurry. The sea was glassy, with soft, rolling swells that rocked the boats gently. Danny couldn't believe that this quiet stretch of ocean had been raging and boiling the night before. On a day like this, maybe I could swim the channel, Danny thought. Then he shook his head. It's a long, long way. I have to give you credit, Hiromi Satō; that was quite a swim you made.

Podogi was tired—he hadn't been able to sleep much because he'd been so wound up from the win. So he slipped into the cabin for a nap. Danny and Bernard went to sit out on the bow, looking over the water at the islands in the distance. Molokai, to the north, looked substantial from where they were. Lanai looked very small, and Kahoolawe smaller still. Over his left shoulder Danny could see the clouds that shrouded the heights of Haleakala, a gigantic extinct volcano that made up two-thirds of the island of Maui. This was the way to see the islands, from the sea. When you were standing in the middle of a pineapple field, even Lanai seemed like a continent. When you were out in the ocean, you could see the shorelines and limitations of the islands and imagine them as tips of a mighty mountain range nearly buried by the sea.

"You really saved us last night," Danny said to Bernard.

"Oh, you could have made the foul shots," Bernard replied.

"Maybe, but with you we were absolutely sure."

"It was the greatest moment of my life," Bernard said quietly. He looked at Danny with shining eyes.

"It must have been a thrill," Danny responded, "to have everything left up to you and then to come through like you did. You were smiling when you made that last one."

"No, I mean in the huddle before," Bernard said. "All my friends nodding their heads and choosing me."

For a few moments they looked out across the channel at Lanai drawing nearer. "I really love it," Bernard said at last. "I love that little island. I'll go away to college, but I'm coming back to stay. You remember when I went to visit my brother

Kyoshi in Honolulu last fall? Honolulu is big and bright and exciting, and I had a wonderful time, but bigger is not always better. My folks lived in Wahiawa, on Oahu, for years before we came to Lanai, but I don't think they ever want to go back there to live."

"What's Wahiawa like?" Danny asked. "Do you remember it at all?"

"A city surrounded by pineapple fields, just like Lanai City, only bigger. I was only four or five years old when we left to come here, so I don't remember much about the place."

"What made your folks leave and come here to live?"

"World War II," Bernard said. "It changed everything."

"Where were you when the Japanese planes attacked Pearl Harbor?" Danny asked.

"We were in Pearl City, right by the harbor! I really don't remember much about it, just the noise and excitement. But I've heard my father tell about it so many times, it seems like my own memory. We were staying overnight at my uncle's house on that first Saturday in December 1941, and we were still there when the attack came on Sunday, December 7th. When we heard the sound of planes flying over, my father and uncle took Kyoshi and drove up into the hills to watch what they thought were military maneuvers.

"They hadn't been watching long when some planes flew right over them. They were flying so low, my father could see the red sun emblems on the wing tips and knew they were Japanese. They could see the bombs hanging from the bellies of the Mitsubishi Zeros and could even make out the pilots in their cockpits. The whole Pacific Fleet was in the harbor that day, just sitting like a bunch of ducks on a pond. It was a real mess. My father and my uncle were nissei — second-generation Japanese — born right here in Hawaii. They were Americans, and a foreign country was bombing their helpless ships, killing their navy boys. They were as shocked and angry as any American would be."

"It must have been tough being Japanese that Sunday night," said Danny.

"It was a bad time," Bernard said. "I've heard my parents talk about those days. 'Dirty Japs,' that's what we were, not Japanese or just Japs; only 'dirty Japs' would do. There were Japanese men already in the military there on Oahu, training, learning how to fire weapons, just like their buddies. Suddenly they were not to be trusted — they couldn't work around weapons of any kind. Americans of Japanese ancestry who wanted to join the army or navy were turned down cold. Hawaii was under martial law, and all Japanese were under suspicion, guilty until proven innocent. In the mainland, they moved all the Japanese away from the coastal areas and put them in relocation camps further inland. A lot of them lost their homes and businesses. In a way we were lucky — they didn't move us out of our homes, but I guess it was pretty grim."

"Wouldn't they let the AJAs do anything to help?" Danny asked.

"Not at first. Later on they decided to form a small AJA combat unit. It was to be just a token thing; they didn't expect many Japanese to enlist. I think they were a little surprised when ten thousand men volunteered. The 442nd Regimental Combat Team grew out of that early experiment, and they saw a lot of action in Italy. My uncle was in the 442nd and got wounded twice. By the end of the war, the 442nd was the most decorated unit in American military history. My father tried to join, but he was thirty-three years old and had a family. They told him to stay home and raise pineapple. That's when we moved to Lanai."

"Was it better on Lanai?" Danny asked.

"Just getting away from 'the scene of the crime' was an improvement. To speak Japanese in public, there on Oahu where it all happened, seemed unpatriotic in those days. My mother could hardly speak any English, so she was afraid to talk at all. After we moved here and people got to know us, they accepted us. That's one of the nice things about living on a little island. You know everyone, and it's very hard to hate somebody you know unless they really deserve it."

"It's funny," Danny said sadly. "They call Hawaii the melting pot of the Pacific, and it's supposed to be filled with happy, carefree people of different cultures living in love and harmony. I wish it were like that, but I'm afraid it isn't. I think I understand how your folks felt during the war. It's a terrible thing to know that somebody hates you just because of your race or background. It doesn't make any sense at all."

"It's easier to hate groups of people." Bernard said. "Hating individuals is more difficult, especially if you know them well." Then smiling broadly, he added, "Take you, for instance. After somebody gets to know you, even you are hard to hate." He punched Danny in the shoulder and laughed. "Anyway, I'm staying on Lanai forever. I'm famous! Twenty years from now people will still be pointing to me and whispering, 'That's Bernard Ōta, the guy who beat Lahainaluna, shooting free throws.' How long do you suppose it would take me to get famous in Honolulu?"

"Hey! What's that?" Danny almost shouted.

"What's what?"

"That sound! I've never heard anything like it. Don't you hear it?"

"Yeah!"

"Teru, what is that sound?" Bernard asked.

"Dat big kohola, humpback whale," Teru answered without looking up. "He like sing on such nice day."

They felt the sound vibrate the boat itself. The other boys looked nervously over the side. They could see a dark shadow under the boat.

"No pilikia, no problem. All humpback plenty good friend Teru. Dey sing any kind songs dis time year. Maybe so dis one got girl friend, like him sing. Maybe so girl friend over by Molokai. Dis humpback sing loud song for make her hear."

"Can they hear that far away?" asked Danny.

"Ocean some big, kohola not so many. I t'ink maybe so dey sing, talk to another kohola far away, by Molokai, by Oahu, maybe even by Kauai." There was some commotion from the boys at the back of the boat. The singing stopped.

"It's moving! It's moving!" somebody shouted. All of a sudden, the sea exploded about fifty yards from the boat. The gigantic humpback breached, hurling its fifty-ton body almost entirely out of the water, twisting in the air and landing on its back with a resounding splash. The backwash from the splash rocked the boat. Teru had cut the motor and was standing back with the boys, watching the display.

"I've never seen anything like that," said Danny excitedly, looking over at Teru.

Teru put his finger to his lips and pointed in the direction of a smooth patch of water that had appeared on the surface. "Humpback footprint," he said.

"What make da water look like dat," asked Podogi, who had jumped up from the cabin when the boat rocked.

"I t'ink so, kohola move his tail down deep, make water come smooth," answered Teru. He continued to point at the "footprints." Another appeared, then another—they were coming closer to the boat. The footprints stopped, the surface of the water was undisturbed. Then gently, slowly, the snout of the huge humpback parted the water right next to the boat. It rose higher and higher until an eye the size of a cantaloupe stared at them. The boys pressed themselves against the opposite side of the boat. Teru reached out and touched the whale's snout. Teru laughed. "Him spyhop. Him like see da team win big game wid Lahainaluna last night. No scared, eh? Dis kohola, Teru friend. Every year he go way, every year he come back."

"What are those things attached to his head and flippers?" Bernard asked.

"Dey barnacles." Teru answered. "Some big, and plenty, eh?"

"Some of those must be three inches across," Bernard said. "Do they hurt him?"

"You get barnacle too," Teru laughed, taking off his hat and scratching his head.

"You mean dandruff?" Danny asked, laughing too.

Teru nodded. "Same like barnacle to kohola."

"How did you get to know so much about whales, Teru?" Danny asked.

"When small boy, I live Lahaina. Old Hawaiian man sit every day under da big banyan tree in Lahaina Town, talk story about whale. Everybody say, 'Teru, stay way from old man. Old man pupule, all crazy in da head.' Teru like talk story wid old man. Old man all time laugh, tell any kind story. Old man, Teru friend."

"Was he a whaler?" Danny asked.

"From small boy he go hunt for whale. Plenty boat like catch whale for get oil, make plenty money. Old man go on boat, catch whale. He see any kind whale cut up, look inside. Sometime dey catch palaoa, sperm whale. Dey cut hole in head, reach inside wid bucket for oil; plenty oil dey get." He held up four gnarled fingers. "Sometime four ton oil, one palaoa."

Bernard gasped, "Four tons of oil in the head of one whale? They must be huge!"

"Blue whale da biggest," Teru said. "Old man say blue whale so big, his heart no can fit in small fishing boat like dis. Small man can crawl inside da big tube come out from heart."

"What happened to the old man, Teru?" Danny asked.

"One day Teru come for talk story, old man no come. All day I sit under da banyan tree, next day too. Maybe so old man die, eh?" A sadness filled Teru's eyes briefly, then they flashed. "He jump!" he shouted and pointed behind them. The great whale breached again, then again and again. The boys began counting "four, five, six, seven" times the mighty whale broke the surface and soared briefly above the surface of the ocean. Seven times it twisted like an acrobat and crashed into the sea with a thunderous slap.

"One humpback, I count thirty-eight times he jump," said Teru, still looking in the direction of the whale. The other fishing boats were watching too. The fishermen started their motors and moved off in the direction of Lanai, waving at Teru. He stood a while longer looking out at the sea as if expecting the whale to return.

"Teru, you said that whale was your friend, that you see him every year. How can you tell it's him?" Danny asked. "Don't they all look the same?"

"All your poppa chickens look same to me," said Teru with a smile. He started the motor and headed for home.

Chapter

13

At Kaumalapau Harbor the team was greeted by a cheering crowd of students. They had decorated the pineapple barges in the harbor with banners and slogans celebrating Lanai's victory. One read: "Bernard for President!" Another, "Three for Three—The Luck of the Irish!"

The team and their fans drove home in a convoy along the highway toward the city, honking horns and cheering and waving at the men and women working in the pineapple fields. The workers stopped and waved and yelled back. By now everyone on Lanai knew about the game. When they reached town, they all stopped at the saimin shop for the free soft ice cream cones that Sammy Lee gave them after every game. It was a tradition, and many people showed up to talk to the team then.

Danny and the team were amazed by the size of the crowd waiting there. This was their fourth win in a row, and the citizens of Lanai were getting excited. The branch members were out in force with arms full of paper leis. They decorated all the team members, but loaded Danny and Bernard clear up to their ears. If the team had lost, the players would have gotten all the advice and heard all the complaints at once. Now, though, the shop was buzzing with questions and play-by-play details. After that, everybody started talking about the next game.

Hiromi and some of the other plantation officials were there, and they all shook hands with the team and praised them highly. When Hiromi got to Danny, he smiled warmly and asked, "Did you have a big blow-out in Lahaina last night?"

"We decided to save the money and have a party after the season is over," Danny answered.

"Good idea! You keep winning, and I'll see that you have enough money to have a party for the whole school." Hiromi was expansive as he talked about the team's play the previous night. "All you have to do is beat Wailuku next week and you're on your way." He was all charm and compliments as he shook Danny's hand again and left.

"It's amazing!" Danny thought. "I feel like his best friend. When he turns on the hoomalimali and butters you up like that, you feel like running him for governor." Danny looked for Nori but didn't see her. "What if she was embarrassed about dancing with me all last night. What if—" He stopped himself short. Maybe she was coming in on the late evening flight, or staying over with her cousins for another day. Last night had been wonderful, and he wasn't going to spoil it with what ifs.

"Did you hear about the new elders?" Bernard was standing at his side, watching the crowd melt away and head for home.

"I knew Elder Larsen was leaving, but are they transferring both of them? They never transfer both elders at the same time."

"They did this time. Margie was just telling me. Elder Larsen is going home on the Lurline on Monday, and Elder Frost's asthma has been getting worse, so they want to get him to some place hot and dry."

"I hope they saved enough leis to give the elders a good send-off and greet the new ones. Maybe we'll have to use these again." Danny touched the leis around his neck.

"They're already here; they came in yesterday afternoon. And you'll never believe this, Danny—the senior companion is Elder Ihunui's little brother."

Danny couldn't believe it. "Elder Ihunui has a brother here in Hawaii?"

"That's what Margie said. She's making dinner for them tonight at her house. The branch is getting together later at the church for a welcome party. Can you come?"

"Pop will be waiting dinner for me," Danny answered. "But maybe I can make it later. What time is the party?"

"About seven. I'll see you there." Bernard left.

As Danny walked home, he thought about Elder Ihunui. They had talked alone the day before he left for home. The other elder was in the chapel teaching Primary, and Ihunui was in the apartment packing his bags.

"I guess you must be pretty glad to be going home, eh?" Danny asked.

"In a way I am. I've missed my family, but in another way I feel lonelier than I ever have."

"But you'll be home in less than a week. Why do you feel lonely now?"

"Not lonely for my folks, lonely for you folks." Elder Ihunui was smiling, but it was a sad smile. "You're right, I'll be seeing my family in a week, but when will I ever see you and the other kids again? If I save up my money and come back in seven or eight years, most of you will be gone. The ones who are here won't remember me. There will have been dozens of elders here in between. I'll be forgotten. That's what bothers me so much, I guess, being forgotten." He was quiet for a moment, then looked up. "You won't forget me will you, Danny?"

Danny walked up the front steps of his house. "I didn't forget him," he said, half aloud. Danny opened the door and smelled the aroma of frying fish. His father was busy at the stove when Danny walked into the kitchen.

"I'm home!" Danny said as he stepped up behind his father and looked over his shoulder. "Looks like Teru had a big catch."

"Too good catch and some fresh too. Dey still living one hour ago, flip and flop all da way home, boy. Some good game, Danny, everybody in Lanai come real happy, you bet. Maybe so, you beat Wailuku next week. Maybe so, by 'n' by, you come Maui District champs; I t'ink so."

"Maybe so, maybe so," Danny said, smiling. The Maui District championship seemed a long way off. Wailuku had won the first half of the season. Even if Lanai won the second half, they would still face a play-off game with Wailuku.

"Bernard some good shoot foul shot. Too much small that one, but everytime practice, practice; come too much good shooter," Benito went through the motions of shooting foul shots one after another.

Danny loved his father's cooking, and tonight's meal was no exception. After dinner, he helped clean up, and they talked about basketball, and cock fighting, and loading pineapple at the harbor.

"We have some new elders on the island, Pop," Danny said. "One of them is a brother of Elder Ihunui."

"Ihunui, too much good elder," said Benito. "Some funny, two brother both come Lanai. Dis one get big nose too?"

"I haven't seen him yet," said Danny. "There's a party at the church later, I thought I might go."

"Go, Danny," said Benito. "I some tired work harbor. I like go sleep."

Danny went into his room and took a photo album down from his closet shelf. He sat down on the bed and laid the book across his lap. The album opened to where some recent pictures still waited to be mounted. Danny turned backward page after page and watched himself and his friends grow younger and younger. There was one of Podogi, Bernard, and Danny with fresh crew cuts. It had only been taken a couple of years before, but Danny was surprised how young they looked. Mixed in with the snapshots were formal photographs of elders who had served on Lanai. Some of them were obviously reprints of their high school yearbook pictures. One elder was in a white dinner jacket. Then Danny came to a place in the album where there were lots of colored snapshots. This was the Ihunui Era.

Elder Ihunui was a photography nut, and under his influence Kyoshi Ōta became one too. Both of them had flooded the branch with pictures. At first the kids had been camera shy — they would turn their heads or cover their faces when approached. Those who posed willingly, though, began to get copies of the pictures. Danny and Bernard loved having their pictures taken, so they ended up with lots of pictures to keep.

Danny laughed at a picture of Bernard sitting cross legged on the beach at Manele looking very solemn. Danny was behind him smiling but cross-eyed, his chin resting on Bernard's head. Above Danny was Podogi with his thumbs in his ears and his fingers extended. Above him was Margie with her tongue sticking out. Elder Ihunui was at the top of their totem pole with a pineapple balanced on his head. Another picture, taken that same day, was a silhouette of Danny, Bernard, and Podogi looking at the sunset with their arms draped across each other's shoulders. They had been inseparable even then. It was that night around the campfire that Elder Ihunui had told them all about his brother Wes, who died on the battleship, Arizona, when the Japanese bombed Pearl Harbor.

There were more pictures of various Scouting activities during the Ihunui Era. He had been an avid Scouter and revived the branch Boy Scout troop by recruiting some of the non-member town kids. One of these was Kyoshi Ōta, who became his first convert on Lanai. Danny and Bernard had followed the same pattern. They joined the Scout troop first, then the Church. There was a picture of Margie, all in white, being baptized by Elder Ihunui in the protected children's pool at Manele Beach. "Elder Ihunui is in a lot of these pictures," Danny thought. "Maybe that was his way of trying not to be forgotten." Danny remembered the time when he asked Elder Ihunui what he had thought when he first found out he had been assigned to Lanai. "I was sick," he admitted. "The other missionaries teased me about being 'banished to Lanai.' Everybody wanted to go to Kauai, Maui, or the Big Island, but assignments to Lanai and Molokai were dreaded. I wanted to go to Pearl City. I'd been stationed at Pearl Harbor when I was in the Navy and had lots of friends there."

"How do you feel now?" Danny had asked.

"I think I'm the luckiest elder in the islands. The feeling in the mission is changing too. My junior companions are spreading the word about Lanai, the branch, the Scout troop, and all you kids. Everybody wants to spend some time here now."

Danny wondered if the new Elder Parkinson would be like his brother. He couldn't wait to find out.

Chapter

14

The party had been going on for about half an hour when Danny arrived, and everyone was cheering for the survivors of a group ping-pong game. The game had started with all the players surrounding the table, one person at each end holding a paddle. One of them would serve, then set the paddle down for the next person in line. Each one in turn hit the ball, then moved around the table. If somebody failed to return the ball, he or she had to drop out. As the players became fewer, the pace of the game became more frantic. By the time Danny arrived, the game was down to six people, two of them the new elders. They were all good players, and the game went on and on, getting faster and faster.

There was no mistaking Elder Ihunui's little brother. He had the Parkinson family nose all right. The other elder was heavy set and had a baby face. Perspiration trickled down his forehead as he ran from one end of the table to the other to pick up the paddle and hit the ball. Now they were down to four players: the two elders, Bernard, and Podogi. Podogi gave Bernard a wink, and they both made mistakes in quick succession, leaving the elders alone at the table. Elder Ihunui's brother served the ball, dropped his paddle, and raced for the other end. The heavy elder had to return the serve, run to the other end, pick up the paddle, and return his own shot. He made a noble effort, but halfway round the table he stumbled, fell forward on his ample stomach, and slid to a stop right at Danny's feet. Danny helped him up and shook his hand warmly.

"I'm Danny Tolentino," he said.

"Elder Goebel," the panting elder answered.

"The missionaries call him 'Elder Gobble,' " put in Elder Parkinson. "You should see him eat."

"We call him 'Elder Global,' " said Bernard. "One of the kids called him that by mistake, but we think it fits." Elder Goebel smiled good-naturedly. He seemed to enjoy the teasing as much as anyone. "I assume," he said with a great deal of dignity, "that you refer to my almost total familiarity with every aspect of this world upon which we live." Everyone laughed.

Danny turned to Elder Parkinson and shook his hand. "I can tell who you are," he said. "The hair is lighter, but otherwise you're Elder Ihunui, six years ago."

"Actually my name is Chris Parkinson, but so many people have called me Elder Ihunui that I'm beginning to feel comfortable with it."

"Maybe we call him Elder Ihunui Opio," said Podogi. "Dat's Hawaiian for 'Elder Bignose, Junior.' "

"Nah! Too long name," said David Tagavilla. "Call him Elder Opi; mo' easy for say, sound good too!"

So Elder Chris Parkinson became Elder Opi. If his parents had visited the island, they would have been terribly disappointed to find out that, though they had sent two missionary sons to serve on Lanai, few people knew the name Parkinson.

Elder Opi was bombarded with questions about his big brother, Ihunui:

"Is he married?"

"How many kids he get?"

"His wife plenty good-lookin', eh?"

"He still play ukulele?"

"Why he no come back for visit?"

Elder Ihunui would be relieved to hear that he had definitely not been forgotten. By the end of the evening Elders Opi and Global felt completely at home. They'd had a lei greeting at the airport, a home-cooked meal at Margie's, and now they had been christened; they were part of the Lanai Branch family.

That night after the party, as the elders lay in their bunks, talking, Elder Opi said, "They're just like Mike described them, 'the sweetest, most lovable kids in the whole world.'" Then he smiled and asked, "How do you like your new name?"

Elder Global laughed his high-pitched childlike giggle. "Am I really stuck with that?"

"I'd say that you are. I like mine. I like being thought of as Elder Ihunui, junior. Mike's a great brother. I hope you can meet him sometime."

"I bet he was excited about your mission call, wasn't he?"

"He was ecstatic! He came over to the house and talked to me until two in the morning. He loved the islands so much and especially this one. I remember one thing he said that you'd be interested in."

"What's that?"

"Chris," he said, "there are three kinds of elders in the mission field: the Goof-offs, the Squares, and the Boys. The Goof-offs are there for all the wrong reasons. They don't want to be missionaries, they want to be returned missionaries. They're just marking time, doing as little as possible themselves, and getting in the way of others who really want to work. The

Squares are spiritual to the point of nausea; sanctimonious is what they are. They make a decision about which necktie to wear a matter of fasting and prayer. They're like the old Pharisees—appearance is everything. They're almost as worthless as the Goof-offs. Then there are the Boys. When the Boys work, they really work; when the Boys play, they have more fun than anybody. It's not against the principles of the gospel to have fun. If you go on a mission for two years and don't have any fun, you will not have been as effective as you could have been. Now that's the gospel according to Mike Parkinson."

"I've always wanted to be one of the boys." Elder Global grinned. "Maybe this is my chance."

Elder Opi and Elder Global worked hard and had fun in the best tradition of the "Boys"; Elder Ihunui would have been proud of them. They had the records of the previous elders, and they took up tracting where the others had left off. They knocked on doors and launched into their presentation, just as they had done in Honolulu: "We're ministers of the gospel, calling through the neighborhood today, leaving a thought and a prayer in the homes." Often the women gave them blank stares and shook their heads. Many of the housewives spoke very little English. The Filipino bachelors smiled and said, "I no can sabe dis one talk-talk."

They began to understand why the previous elders had moved so quickly through the city. They changed their approach. Now when a woman came to the door, Elder Opi would point to himself and say, "Elder Opi," and Elder Global would nod and say, "Elder Global." The women, who often had heard how they got their names, would smile and relax. The elders pretended to be thirsty and were always invited in to have a drink of juice or water. Once inside the houses, they often found that the women understood more than they had let on, and sometimes they were able to give a lesson. Using the same technique, they got into the Filipino bachelors' homes. They learned a few words of Tagalog, the major dialect of the Philippines, to communicate better with them.

The thirsty-door approach was especially hard on Elder Global, who insisted on frequent rest breaks to return to their apartment. "I don't mind giving my heart and soul to the work, but do I have to sacrifice my kidneys too?"

The adults on the island thought of the LDS church as sort of a children's church since most of the active members were young people. They would listen to a lesson or two, but they rarely became serious investigators. The elders had their best success with the young people. They still felt that visiting the homes was valuable — that way they became acquainted with the parents and put to rest any fears they might have had about the haole elders their children spent so much time with.

On one wall of the elders' apartment was a height chart of all the missionaries who had served on the island since Elder Ihunui. He had begun it by standing against the wall and having his companion mark his six feet two inches on the wall behind him. He then signed his name neatly next to the horizontal mark. As his companions came and went, each of them left their height mark and signature. Other elders had followed suit, and there were now quite a few marks and signatures, most of them in about a twelve-inch band. There was one name that stood by itself, far above the others. Elder Hartvigsen was over six feet seven inches tall, a towering Scandinavian with a thatch of colorless blond hair. The children had named him "Elder Everest." Soon after Elders Opi and Global arrived, they added their names and heights to the list. Elder Opi was almost exactly the same height as his brother, and their names appeared side by side. A few days later some of the younger boys were visiting the elders, and one of them looked up at the chart and gasped.

"Look," he cried. "Somebody higher den Elder Everest!" They hurried over to read the name. There on the wall, up near the ceiling, was a horizontal mark and a signature. It read: Elder Global and Chair.

Elder Global liked to brag about his culinary talents, and his size seemed to bear testimony of his skills in the kitchen. When pressed to confirm his companion's boasting, Elder Opi would say, "He cooks like nobody else in the world" and let them draw their own conclusions. A few of the younger members came over early one morning and found them in the middle of their morning meal. They thought the elder's breakfast was, if not appetizing, at least colorful. Elder Global loved to use food coloring, and that morning they were having blue scrambled eggs.

The story spread throughout the town, and when the Elders were doing their weekly shopping at the grocery store that week, they noticed two little Japanese ladies looking at them with obvious interest. As they passed, one of them looked up at Elder Global and smiled broadly. "Blue scramble egg?" she asked with unbelief. "Every Tuesday," he said with great dignity. "Every Tuesday." Elder Opi nodded his confirmation. They moved on down the aisle without further comment. The two ladies held their hands over their mouths, trying unsuccessfully to stifle their giggles.

Chapter
15

It was a happy time for Danny, the happiest he could remember. He was still glowing from the night in Lahaina when everything seemed to come together for him. Nori was warm and friendly. He looked forward to being with her in class, in the school's executive council meetings, and at school activities. A group of their friends had begun going to the movies together on Saturday nights or meeting at somebody's house to watch their favorite television show, "The Hit Parade," with Snooky Lanson and Giselle McKenzie. They went together as a group, but Danny and Nori always ended up sitting together. Sometimes when they were talking, they would almost feel as if they were alone. She would look at him as she had done that night in Lahaina, and he would forget that anyone else was in the room.

After their big win in Lahaina, the Lanai team seemed to jell better than they ever had. It was as if they could read each other's minds. As Danny ran the plays, he felt as though the other team members were an extension of himself: just as he knew the exact position of his arms and legs at any time, so he seemed to know the location and movements of his teammates as they ran down the floor on a fast break. Their greatest asset was their team play. Any individual recognition they received was secondary. Podogi alternated with Makanui from Lahaina as the top rebounder in the district, and Danny was crowding Liu, the rangy Chinese-Hawaiian who played center on the Wailuku team, in individual scoring. No one on the team talked much of individual statistics, though; they just wanted to keep on winning.

The first game of the season's second half was a critical one. Wailuku came over to play Lanai on their home court. After a perfect record for the first half of the season, they were riding high. Nothing Lanai had showed them in Wailuku gave them any reason to be concerned. They felt that the Lanai win in Lahaina had been a fluke. Wailuku certainly would not let Lanai High get close enough to win on foul shots after the buzzer.

It was a gambler's field day. The Wailuku fans were flushed with confidence and gave attractive odds, and Hiromi and his friends sensed an upset in the making. They covered the Wailuku bets and came to the game ready to collect.

The game itself was almost an anticlimax. Lanai took an early lead and held it throughout the game. The team could do virtually no wrong. The contest was a complete reversal of the first-half opener in Wailuku. Danny had made thirty-two points when the coach replaced him in the middle of the fourth quarter. The bench played the last three minutes, and Wailuku made up part of the deficit, which made the game seem closer than it really was.

After the last buzzer, the crowd engulfed the team and carried them to the locker room. A jubilant and slightly drunk Hiromi Sato pressed a fifty-dollar bill into Danny's hand. "For the party," he said. Bernard marched triumphantly around the locker room. "I'm sweating," he shouted. "I actually played enough to sweat!"

The betting crowd was at the bowling alley collecting their money, but almost everyone else seemed to be at the saimin shop when the team arrived. Sammy Lee was doing a good business after the game. He was beaming as he handed out the soft ice cream cones to the team. Nori and the gang were there, and she found a chance to talk to Danny.

"I knew you would win tonight," she said with a happy smile. "It was like Lahaina, only better."

"I think we were kind of lucky," Danny said. "They were so sure they were going to roll over us. I think they kept expecting us to fold, and then couldn't adjust until it was too late."

"You could have beaten anybody tonight," Nori said. "I didn't see you make one mistake."

Jerry was giving a play-by-play account of the game in Filipino Pidgin, and everyone else was watching him and laughing. Danny looked into Nori's eyes and thought he saw something more than excitement and admiration. He put his hand over hers, and she made no effort to move it.

The next few weeks were a happy blur for Danny. Monday through Thursday the team practiced hard and long to maintain the knife-edge preparedness necessary to extend their string of victories. Coach Manning drove them relentlessly through the drills, scrimmages, and special situations that might come up. When they stopped for rests, he had his notebook out reviewing the strengths and weaknesses of the team they would play the upcoming Friday night. They beat Kahului, Kihei, and Paia, stretching their winning streak to eight games. The postgame sessions at Sammy Lee's were turning into celebrations that everyone took for granted.

"Don't get cocky," Coach Manning warned one night after an especially good practice. "Remember what overconfidence did to Wailuku? They fell apart that night we played them, and the same thing could happen to us. They've won every game since then by big margins, and they destroyed Lahaina. We may be leading the league this half, but one loss and we're tied with Wailuku. We can't force a playoff with a tie; we have to win. If we get past Hana, that still leaves Lahainaluna." He smiled and looked over at Bernard "And we can't count on Bernard to save us this time." Everybody laughed.

Podogi put a headlock on his tiny friend. "What-sa-matter you, Bernard? You no gonna help us wid Lahainaluna dis time? By 'n' by, I step your neck, you lazy guy!"

Coach Manning waited until the boys stopped laughing and continued, "Even if we're lucky enough to win the second half, we still have to play Wailuku for the championship. We can't afford to let up for a minute."

The times when he was alone with Nori on Saturday nights were precious to Danny. Some nights they would sit on the back steps of the house they were visiting while their friends watched television. The group pretty much stayed together, but there was time for quiet talk in twos and threes. One night, while everyone else was watching television in Margie's front room, they sat alone in the kitchen.

"What's the matter, Nori?" Danny asked. "You seem a little quiet tonight."

"Today is my mother's birthday. She would have been thirty-nine years old. Have I ever shown you her picture?" She opened the locket hanging around her neck and held it out to Danny.

"I've seen you wear that locket before, but I didn't know it had a picture of your mother in it," Danny said softly. He looked at the tiny black-and-white photograph. She was beautiful, and she looked so much like Nori that he must have looked surprised. "When was this taken?" he asked.

"On her birthday. She was eighteen."

"She looks just like you with an old-fashioned haircut.

"I guess we do look a lot alike."

"Has your father ever thought about getting married again?"

"If he has, he's never said anything to me about it. They were very happy, Danny. We were a happy family. I wish you could have known my father then. He smiled a lot in those days and didn't work such long hours. He liked to be at home with us. My mother was an artist and loved to go down and paint at the beach. We'd go down to Manele almost every Sunday. Daddy would spearfish, Mother would paint, and I'd play in the tide pools and gather shells on the beach. They had such great plans. Mother was pregnant, and the doctor said he thought it was a boy. They were going to name him Matsuo, after my grandfather. She was in her ninth month when it happened; she hadn't been able to carry a child that long since I was born."

"What went wrong," Danny asked.

The doctor called it toxemia and put her to bed. We woke up one morning, and she was gone. My father had slept beside her all night and hadn't realized that anything was wrong. It was a blood clot. She just died. A person shouldn't die like that, Danny, just breathe out and never breathe in again. She looked as if she were still alive, as if she were just resting. Her hair wasn't even mussed up." Nori began to cry softly and Danny put his arm around her and waited.

"The night after Mother died, everybody came to the house and stayed for hours and hours. It's a Buddhist custom to visit the home when somebody dies. The people come and sit up all night with the family. We were so full of pain, we didn't feel like seeing anyone, but the people came and stayed and stayed. Of course it was only good manners for us to provide food for them. Fortunately, some of our neighbors helped me. My father just sat and stared off into space. People came by and tried to talk to him, but he just nodded and said nothing. I spent the whole night carrying trays of food around the house. I've never been so tired. Maybe it was good for me to be busy, there was less time to think."

"Hey, Danny, Nori, you're missing a great show," one of the guys called from the living room. Two of the Nori's friends came into the kitchen, took some soft drinks from the refrigerator, and returned to the television, chattering excitedly.

Nori continued: "My father chartered a DC-3 and brought family from the other islands here to Lanai for the funeral. He flew in a photographer from Maui to take the formal pictures. You've seen them in Buddhist homes—everybody crowded around the casket looking grim."

"I've seen them," Danny said. "But I never could understand why they would want pictures to remember such a sad occasion."

"I don't understand it either, but we have one, a big one, hanging on the wall next to our Buddhist shrine, and there I am, standing by my father, trying not to cry. Well, then, we flew to Maui and had the cremation ceremony, and finally everybody went home, and we were alone. Daddy had been strong through it all, never showing his emotions, just solemn and quiet. That first night when we were alone, he held me in his arms and cried like a child. I thought I'd cried my eyes dry, but when I saw him sobbing like that, I cried too. We just sat there for the longest time. Finally, he wiped my eyes and his and said, 'It's over Nori, it's over.' He gave all her clothes away. He has a beautiful picture of her that he keeps in a drawer; I have the locket. There's a cedar chest in the attic that has some of her things in it, but Daddy keeps it locked. He took all her paintings off the walls after she died; they're up there too. We don't talk about her at all, Danny. We never have since that night."

Chapter

16

The senior prom was coming up — the social event of the year at Lanai High. The girls wore formals, and the boys had tuxedos flown in from Honolulu. A band would come from Honolulu too, and their contract would require them to play as long as anybody wanted to dance. Usually that wasn't much past midnight, but with this senior class it was hard to be sure how long they might have to play. One of the teachers said that high school classes were like the waves at Manele Beach on a calm day. Most of them were uniform in height and intensity, but every now and then a big one would come out of nowhere and drive you into the sand if you weren't watching. Danny's senior class was like one of those big waves. They were talented, inventive, and they had initiative and determination. The senior prom would reflect their creative flair, and everyone wanted to be part of it.

As student-body president and a member of the senior class, Danny would be expected to be at the dance. He wanted to go, and he wanted to take Nori, but he could not get himself to ask her. Everything had been so wonderful since that night in Lahaina. They were closer than they had ever been. He knew she admired and respected him, and he hoped she felt even more. The way she had opened up to him the previous Saturday night had seemed like a declaration of trust and regard, maybe even love. But if I ask her, and she turns me down again, what then? he thought. Do I just say, 'Oh, that's okay, Nori, I understand' and act like nothing has happened? If I ask someone else, what would she think? Would she understand, or would she be hurt and disappointed? The more Danny agonized over the decision, the clearer it seemed that he had no choice; he had to risk asking her.

That afternoon after the executive council had met, Danny and Nori were alone reviewing some plans for the next council meeting. Nori was sitting at the table, and he was standing at her side with his hand resting lightly on her shoulder. Nori was talking about an idea for a student activity that they wanted to present to the council the following week.

Danny interupted her. "Nori," he said. She looked up, and when their eyes met, he felt his cheeks flush. A message of affection passed between them as real as if it had been put into words. "Will you go to the senior prom with me?" he asked. He hesitated, then added, "We'd double with Podogi and Margie." Danny felt a slight shiver pass through her body and saw her eyes change; they became furtive and she looked away.

"Can I tell you for sure tomorrow, Danny?" she asked. She picked up her books and started to stand up. For a moment Danny considered holding her in her chair and asking her what was wrong. He wished he could take the words back. He wished he hadn't asked her. But he had asked and now she was in a hurry to leave. He let her go.

Danny rushed down the hall. He was late for basketball practice.

"Hey, Danny," Jerry shouted as he entered the gym. "Mo'

better you wiki wiki, change quick. Coach Manning be plenty huhu you come practice late."

Danny might just as well have missed basketball practice altogether. His usual crisp execution of the plays was flawed. His passes were behind the men or too fast and hard for them to reach. His shots were short, with nothing behind them, no strength, no confidence, no follow-through.

"What's the matter, Danny? Are you sick?" Coach Manning finally asked.

"I think I've got the flu," Danny lied. "I feel kind of sick to my stomach." That was true enough. He had a knot in his stomach that felt the size of the basketball in his hands.

"Why don't you take a shower and go home and get some rest," Coach said. "We can't have you laid up this Friday night when we play Hana. That little team has been improving lately."

"I think it's just a one-day thing, Coach," said Danny, throwing the ball to Jerry. "I'll be okay by tomorrow." He headed for the showers.

Danny didn't go straight home. His father would have wondered why he was home so early. He didn't want to talk about his feelings tonight. He just needed to think. He walked into Sammy Lee's shop and ordered a bowl of saimin.

"Okay if I sit back in the banquet hall?" Danny asked. Sammy nodded. There was small room in the back with a table that accommodated ten people. The area was only as big as a small bedroom, but Sammy called it the banquet hall. There was a pass-through window at counter level from the kitchen to the room. A similar counter served the main shop. Sammy, standing in the kitchen, could see everyone in both rooms, but the thin wall and door that separated the banquet hall from the main shop afforded Danny at least visual privacy. Sammy Lee seemed to sense that Danny was not in the mood to talk.

He served the saimin and busied himself in the kitchen. Danny wasn't hungry. He stirred the bowl and took a couple of spoonfuls, then sat quietly.

Danny heard two men talking outside, then the door of the shop opened as they entered.

"Hey, Sammy, how about some service?" a voice called. It was Hiromi Satō's. Danny couldn't tell who the other voice belonged to. Both men had been drinking; he could tell that much. Satō was speaking.

"Do you know how a Filipino makes sausage?" he asked as the opening line of his anecdote. Sammy's eyes darted back to where Danny sat. He hurried out front with two bowls of saimin and set them before the two men. He tried to speak, but Hiromi held up his hand and continued, "He ties up a dog out in the sun and feeds him nothing for several days. He gives him all the water he wants, but no food. Then when the dog is really hungry, he mixes up some spicy meat and rice and gives him all he'll eat." Hiromi started laughing and couldn't finish the story. He finally regained control and blurted out the punch line. "Then he kills the dog and ties the intestines into neat little sections and calls them 'Pilipino sausages.'" Both men convulsed with laughter.

"You like somet'ing for drink?" Sammy asked, hoping to distract them. They paid no attention to him.

"What do they do with the rest of the dog?" the other man asked facetiously.

"They don't bury it!" Hiromi said, and the laughter began again.

"Have you ever been to a Filipino luau?" Hiromi asked. "You won't find any dogs hanging around."

"Watch out for those laulaus!" his friend gasped, and they

both laughed hysterically. When they finally wound down and started eating, Sammy went back to the kitchen.

"That daughter of yours is a real beauty; do you have a good Japanese boy picked out for her?" Satō's friend asked between sips of saimin.

"She's got a mind of her own, that girl," he answered. "I think she'll be picking her own husband. She's going to the University of Hawaii next year. She'll have plenty to choose from there. I have set some limits though. I told her I would like her to find a Japanese boy if she can, hopefully a rich one." Satō chuckled and went on. "If she can't find a Japanese, I'll take a Chinese, Hawaiian, even a haole, but no Filipinos! I don't want any Filipinos in the family—those guys just crawled down out of the trees last week!" They paid for the saimin and left.

Danny was stunned. He expected the Filipino jokes from Satō, especially when he had been drinking, but that last statement showed that Hiromi Satō had no respect for the Filipino people at all. He considered them subhumans, barely more than animals. Filipinos were off limits as boyfriends for Nori; that was clear. No wonder she shivered when he asked her to go to the prom. Her father would never stand for a Filipino boy coming by the house to pick her up for the dance. Danny paid Sammy and assured him that his untouched saimin had been very good. He just wasn't very hungry.

"Sorry, Danny," Sammy said. Danny nodded. He knew Sammy wasn't talking about the soup.

It was still too early to go home. Danny walked up toward the little golf course that stood on the hillside above the town. No one was playing so he just walked around the holes in rotation. The plantation owned the golf course, and there was no charge to play. Danny wished he had some balls and clubs.

He felt like hitting something. He wouldn't care which direction the ball went.

Why did she say she would tell me tomorrow? Danny thought. I know what the answer will be. She'll have guests coming in from Maui, or she'll have to go to Maui, or she'll have a sick goldfish to sit up with or something. Why doesn't she just say, "Danny, you're a nice friend, but I just can't go out with you." Why can't she be honest with me?

Why can't she be honest with her father? Why doesn't she say, "Look Dad, I'm almost eighteen years old and I've never been on a date. Want to know why? Because the only boy I care anything about is a Filipino, and you hate them. Well, Danny has asked me to the prom, and I'm going to say yes. If you don't like it, I'm sorry, but I'm going to the senior prom with Danny."

It didn't even sound like Nori. She couldn't talk like that to her father; she couldn't talk like that to anyone. That's why tomorrow, he felt sure, she would come up with some excuse to explain why she couldn't go to the prom at all.

"What am I supposed to do, Nori?" Danny said out loud. The sound of his own voice startled him. He looked around to see if anyone could have heard him.

He began to walk toward the road to Keomuku. As he walked, he spoke softly, under his breath. "What kind of a man are you, Hiromi Satō?"

As the road began to turn up the hill, he quickened his pace. Nori, I can't let you do this to me. I can't pretend to believe your excuses, and I can't pretend that it doesn't matter to me when you tell me a lie. If you'd tell me the truth, I'd accept it for now, or I'd offer to go with you to talk to your father. We'd work something out. But you'll lie to me again tomorrow; I know you will. You'll come up with another weak excuse, and I'll know that it's always going to be like this.

For a long time Danny strode along the road in silence, his thoughts muddled and confused. When he spoke out loud again, there was resolve in his voice. "I'm going to forget you, Nori, and go on with my life." He went on speaking in his mind. Want to know how I'm going to do it? I'm going to get so angry that I can't feel anything. That's how we Filipinos solve our problems; we get angry and take a knife and cut out whatever threatens us. I love you Nori Satō, and I think you love me, but I'm not going to wither up and die.

Danny began to run. It always made him feel better. The road to Keomuku was uphill for the first few miles or so, and soon he was sweating profusely. He kept running, feeling the muscles in his legs crying out for rest. Let them suffer, he thought. The knot in his stomach was beginning to unwind, the lump in his throat was dissolving. He could breath again. As he climbed higher and higher, he felt the strings that bound him to Nori grow tense and then snap one by one. He felt free.

Chapter

17

When Danny went to school the next day, he was changed. His mind was clear, and his confidence was back. He wouldn't be over Nori completely for some time, he knew that, but he had made a start. They had their first class together, and he went all the way through it without looking at her once. When she stopped him to talk after class, he tried to appear casual.

"Danny," she said hesitantly, then looked away. "I'm sorry, but I guess I won't be able to go to the prom with you. My father has a company meeting and dinner in Honolulu on Saturday, and he insists that I go with him." She looked up to find Danny smiling down at her. It wasn't a happy smile. It was an ironic, knowing one, so different from Danny's usual smile.

"That's okay, Nori," he said. "Maybe some other time." His eyes were hard, and she saw it. He stood there, looking directly at her, saying nothing, making no move to go. She finally looked away again.

"I guess we'd better get to class," she said at last.

"I guess we'd better," he said, and left. As he turned the corner, he caught a glimpse of Nori still standing where he had left her.

That same day Danny asked a Filipino sophomore to go

to the prom with him, and she accepted immediately. Her name was Juanita Presa, and she was a beautiful girl with dark eyes that glistened when she smiled. Nita was so excited that she kept asking, "Danny, are you sure?" It was a heady experience for him, and he thought, Imagine someone that gorgeous being that excited about me. She's not ashamed to be seen with me in public.

Nita was new to Lanai; her family had just moved from Maui, where her older sister had been Miss Maui Aloha during Aloha week the previous year. The glamour of that title imparted a special promise to Nita, which she exploited to the fullest. She already had a date for the prom, but she couldn't pass up the opportunity to go with Danny Tolentino, the student-body president and captain of the basketball team. She'd figure out a way to break the bad news to the boy who had asked her.

At basketball practice, Danny was his old self. His timing was perfect, his passes flawless. After he had made five straight baskets during the scrimmage, the coach said, "Nice going, Danny. If a night off from practice can turn you around like that, maybe we should send you home and just see you at the game on Friday night."

"I was feeling lousy last night, Coach Manning," Danny said. "I think everything's okay now. In fact, I feel better than I have for years!"

"Pilipino sophomore girl make Danny feel too much good, I t'ink," said Jerry, smiling. The word was out already.

What do I care? Danny thought. His first thought had been about what Nori would think when she heard that he was going to the dance with Nita. Let her think what she likes. Does she expect me to just wait around to catch any spare minutes she might toss me. I'm through with that stuff. I'm through with

Nori! Danny smiled at Jerry and laughed with a mirth he did not really feel.

"Dance with the girls on Saturday night if you still have the strength after the Hana game on Friday," Coach Manning broke in. "Until then I want your undivided attention. Now run that fast break again and try not to dribble on your feet."

The practice went well. The Lanai team was in top form. Danny was playing as if it were a game, not a practice session. He pushed the team hard, never letting up. Finally the coach sent them to the showers early. He was obviously pleased.

The last two games of the regular season would be played in the Lanai High gym. On the Thursday night before the Hana game, they had a very light workout. Coach Manning knew that they were at the peak of their game and didn't want them to go flat. Mostly they talked strategy.

"Don't imagine that this Hana team is a pushover," he said. "We beat them easily in the first half of the season, but they've improved a lot. They're fast, very fast and pesky. They reach in and steal the ball. They talk to you, and they get you talking back. They're clever, and they can run all night. Kahului beat them in the first game of the second half, but they beat Kihei and Paia. I think Lahaina was very lucky to win their game against Hana last Friday."

"Don't worry, coach," Danny said. "We're not going to get cocky like Wailuku did in the first half of the season. We're winning because we work harder."

"And when it comes to talking, nobody can beat Jerry," Bernard offered. "He's our secret weapon."

"Jerry's mout' no secret to nobody," said Darrell. Everybody broke up. Darrell rarely made a comment, but when he did, he was right on target.

The Lanai team was up for Hana, and so were the townspeople. When the game started, there was hardly room in the
gym for the players to play. The Hana team was exactly as
Coach Manning had said—fast and pesky, and they did everything he had warned the team about, but it was to no avail.
Lanai was an inspired team. Podogi's hook shot was working
both to the left and to the right. Darrell was deadly from the
corner, and if he missed, Rudy was there with the tip-in. The
Hana team was relatively short, so Podogi and Rudy ruled the
backboards. Danny was phenomenal, driving down the middle
for lay-ups, potting the short jumpers, stealing the ball on
defense, leading the fast break; he was playing the best game
of his life.

In Danny's mind this was not a game of Lanai High against
Hana, it was a Filipino boy showing Hiromi Satō what he could
do. Danny was running the team, that was obvious. He was
leading all scorers; he was stealing the ball and blocking shots.
The Lanai High team was an extension of Danny Tolentino,
and they were winning big!

Lanai was twenty-three points ahead at the half. Danny had
made exactly that many himself—it was the most he had ever
scored in one half of play. Coach Manning didn't say much
during halftime except to warn them about overconfidence.
Danny hardly heard that. As the team went out on the floor to
warm up for the second half, Danny looked up at the place
where Nori and her friends usually sat and caught her looking
at him. She smiled; Danny looked away, pretending he hadn't
seen her. As they did their lay-ups, Nita called out from the
stands, and Danny acknowledged her with a nod. Her friends
saw the nod and began to talk to her excitedly. Danny flushed
slightly.

The Hana team had gone to the dressing room stunned,

but they came back fighting. They got the Lanai lead down to fifteen points midway in the third quarter; after that it was all Lanai High. The whole crowd stood and applauded when Danny came out of the game with a record high forty-two points. It was a school record and also a district record. Danny looked up at the cheering crowd and saw Nita and her group jumping up and down chanting, "Danny, Danny, Danny!" He resisted an urge to look over at Nori.

They beat Hana by eighteen points, even with the bench playing the last three minutes. When the buzzer sounded to end the game, the students descended on the team, and Danny found himself in the arms of an ecstatic Nita who had worked her way over to the bench during the last few minutes of the game. This is how a high school hero is supposed to be treated, he thought, feeling the color rise into his cheeks. Why do I feel like I'm doing something wrong? He returned Nita's embrace and told her he would meet her at the saimin shop after his shower.

Hiromi grabbed Danny by the shoulder as he headed for the locker room. "Nice game, Tolentino," he said. "Beat Lahaina next week, and we get a chance at Wailuku for the championship." Danny could smell the alcohol on Hiromi's breath. Hiromi had some money in his hand. As he extended it, Danny grabbed Bernard and pulled him between them. "Bernard's the treasurer for the team," he said without smiling. "Give it to him. He's a fine, honest Japanese boy; he'll take good care of it." Bernard, a little confused, took the money and thanked Hiromi. Danny left them talking together and headed for the locker room. He shook his head. "I insulted you, Hiromi Satō, but you were too drunk to notice."

An excited throng of students was waiting at the saimin shop when the team arrived. Sammy Lee is one smart Chinese,

Danny thought. He gives the team a few dollars worth of free ice cream, then sells ice cream and saimin to half the school. The students crowded around the players, and the congratulations started all over again. Nori was there with two of her girl friends. They came up together and started talking to Danny. Just then he heard a voice call his name from the front of the shop. "Danny, I'm saving you a seat." It was Nita.

"I've got to go," he said. "Have fun in Honolulu!" As he turned and walked toward Nita, Danny thought, "What a perfect night—we destroyed Hana, I broke the individual scoring record, I snubbed Hiromi Satō, Nori got what she deserved, and that beautiful Filipino girl over there is crazy about me. So why do I feel so lousy?"

Chapter

18

Danny stood on Nita's porch, feeling stiff and uncomfortable in his rented clothes. He looked at his reflection in the glass in the front door and shook his head. The white dinner jacket was clean and well-pressed, and his tie was straight. He looked down at the front of his clothes. The ruby studs in his shirt sparkled, and his highly polished black shoes gleamed. The press in his pants was so sharp it seemed hazardous. That was the problem—he felt too perfect. He would have been more comfortable in a T-shirt, jeans, and bare feet.

Nita answered the door, and suddenly he felt underdressed. She was wearing a dark red silk formal with thin straps over her bare shoulders. The fabric followed every contour of her body. She stood for a long moment, framed in the doorway, smiling and saying nothing. Danny felt very young and unsophisticated. He looked down to make sure he was not dressed in the T-shirt and jeans he had been thinking about a couple of minutes earlier.

"How do you like my dress, Danny?" she asked. "My sister let me borrow it when I told her I was going with you. I'm sure no one else will be wearing one like it; this was made just for her by a Honolulu designer."

"You look wonderful!" Danny croaked. He cleared his throat and went on. "I love the dress."

"You look very handsome in that jacket, but it needs something, come inside." Danny followed her in, feeling more uncomfortable by the minute. She produced a red carnation and pinned it on his lapel.

Her closeness and the smell of her perfume were unsettling. Just then, Danny remembered the box in his hand. "I have a flower for you too," he said, haltingly, and held out the box containing a white orchid.

"What a beautiful orchid! Will you pin it on for me?" Danny looked around for a mother or sister to help him, but he and Nita were alone in the living room.

"I'm afraid I'm not very good at this," he stammered.

"Pin it on like this," Nita said, holding the flower up to her dress. He made a couple of false starts, but Nita made no move to help him. She just stood still and smiled. Danny realized that he would have to slide his fingers under the top of her dress to guide the pin. The warmth of her skin sent a shiver through his body. Somehow he managed to pin the corsage on the dress. Nita turned and looked in the mirror. "That's perfect," she said. "I bet you've done this lots of times."

Where's the family? he thought. Doesn't her father or mother want to tell me to get her in early or something? He could hear the low murmur of conversation in the kitchen. Apparently her parents had been warned to stay out of the living room while he was there. Why am I so nervous? I'm the senior; Nita's the sophomore going to her first prom. Would I be like this if I was going with Nori? Why am I thinking about Nori? Danny felt anger welling up inside him. He was back in the executive council room, pleading with Nori to go to the prom with him, seeing her gather up her books and rush out of the room, only to listen to her weak excuse the next morning. Anger drove out his feelings of apprehension and self-consciousness. He smiled at Nita and opened the door. "Hope you don't mind riding in Podogi's jeep, Nita; Pop's Cadillac convertible is in the shop having a new top put on it." Nita laughed. Danny took her hand and led her down the stairs.

"Hey, Nita." Margie called as they came through the gate. "Your dress is gorgeous!" Podogi was speechless for once as he helped them into the back seat.

"Drive carefully," Danny said. "We don't want any Lanai dust on these two pretty girls."

The senior class had gone all out on the decorations for the prom. The entrance to the gym had been made to look like the inside of an airplane. Freshmen girls dressed as stewardesses showed them to their seats, served them drinks, and gave them safety instructions. Each chair was fitted out with a safety belt that had to be secured before takeoff. The pilot turned on a recording of an airplane taking off, and they were on their way. Then they "deplaned" through a door that opened into the darkened gym. The high ceiling had been lowered with blue crepe paper, and foil stars hung just below it. In the center of the room, a large silver ball covered with bits of mirror reflected the beams of intersecting spotlights. The ball turned slowly and little patches of light played on the walls, the ceiling, and the dancing students.

The band played and sang all the familiar songs from the hit parade plus some of the Glenn Miller-style big-band favorites. Nita was a wonderful dancer. She anticipated Danny's every move and made him appear much more graceful than he felt. If there was a lull in their conversation, Nita was quick to fill it with a pleasant comment or a question about something that Danny was interested in and knew something about.

"Wasn't that recording of the airplane terrific? It sounded as though we were really taking off . . . Whose idea was the ball with the mirrors? It turns this old gym into a wonderland . . . Would you teach me how to spearfish? I'm a good swimmer, but I've never used a snorkle . . . How do you stand the pressure in your ears when you dive down deep? . . . What's the biggest fish you have ever speared? . . . Have you decided what to study in college? . . . What part of the Phillipines did your parents come from? . . ."

Whenever Danny started talking, she would look right into his eyes and seem to hang on every word. When he ran out of things to say, she would ask another question.

Nita was getting admiring glances from other guys in the room, but she seemed not to notice. All her attention was centered on Danny. After several fast numbers, the band slowed things down.

Nita snuggled in close, and Danny became aware of the silky texture of her gown and the softness that it covered. Several times he offered to trade dances with other couples. Her answer was always the same: "If you want to, but I'd rather dance with you, Danny." They traded with Margie and Podogi a couple of times; otherwise, they danced the whole evening with each other.

To be as exclusive as they were made a significant statement in friendly Lanai High. Danny knew that they would be thought of as "steadies" by the other students. He wondered what Nori would think when she heard about it. He was immediately angry at the thought and pulled Nita even closer to him. She took the opportunity to press her cheek against his. Let Nori think what she likes, he shouted in his mind. She's having a wonderful time in Honolulu with her father, and I'm having a wonderful time here with Nita!

Later that night, he thanked Nita for a lovely evening. As he turned to leave, she called him back. "Thanks for taking me to the dance, Danny," she said, holding her face very close to his. Then in a move that seemed totally natural, as though it had been expected, she stood on tiptoe, lifted her arms and placed them around his neck, leaned against him, and kissed him softly on the mouth. A little off balance, Danny put his hands to her waist to steady himself. Nita moved closer and kissed him again. An image of Nori watching them flashed briefly through his mind, anger welled up inside him, and he pulled Nita closer still. This time he initiated a kiss that left her breathless. When they finally parted, Nita let herself into the house and stood smiling at him as he left.

Nori looked out the window of her beachfront room at the Moana Hotel on Waikiki. The moon was full, and its light reflected off the white sand of the beach below her and imparted a pearly glow to the breakers that rolled in from a turbulent sea. The surf was up, and the stiff breeze blowing in from the ocean had pushed the few clouds up against the Koolau Mountain Range, which brooded in the darkness high above Honolulu.

Nori opened the window, and the breeze blew the curtains back into the room. The wind was warm and moist and carried the tangy smell of the sea. She looked up the beach and saw the dark outline of Diamondhead silhouetted against the star-filled sky. Out there in the darkness beyond Diamondhead, beyond Molokai, the surf was probably up at Manele Beach too. On this night there would be no one to see it. All the Lanai High students would be at the senior prom or sitting at home wishing they were.

Nori glanced at her watch. It was nearly eleven o'clock,

time for her to go to sleep in Honolulu; but in the decorated, music-filled gymnasium at Lanai High, on this special night, all eyes would be bright, and nobody would be thinking of sleep. The thought of Danny and Nita dancing, as she and Danny had done in Lahaina, caused Nori more pain than she had anticipated.

It's funny, she thought. On a dance floor, you can be in each other's arms all evening, and nobody thinks anything about it. If you were to take up that same position in the park or in the hall at school, the whole island would be buzzing with gossip.

She thought of Nita, her shining black hair and flawless skin, dressed in a clinging gown that showed off every curve. Dancing would be a "contact sport" with Nita. She'd see to it that Danny became aware of every contour of her body before the evening was over, all in the name of dancing. "I can't believe I'm thinking thoughts like this," Nori said under her breath. "I'm acting like a jealous fiancée."

It's my fault that Danny's dancing with Nita tonight and not with me. Daddy invited me to come to Honolulu with him, but there was no real reason for me to be here. Several men came to the dinner by themselves; one brought his mother. Daddy could have brought Aunt Mitsy; she'd have loved it.

Danny asked me to the dance, and I turned him down; it's as simple as that. Oh, I came up with this trip as an excuse, but that's all it was, an excuse to avoid having to face Daddy, or risk going to the dance behind his back and worrying for fear he'd find out. Now I'm jealous of Nita for accepting a date with Danny and being excited and wanting him to hold her close on the dance floor. I can't blame Nita, I can't blame Danny; I can only blame myself.

I'm going to talk to Daddy tonight. I'll stay awake, and when he comes up from the meeting, I'll hear him. I'll knock on the door, and I'll talk to him. There'll be no Annie bursting in from the kitchen with dessert, or a phone call from the plantation, or a member of his bowling team coming by to pick him up, or one of his poker friends to disturb us, or even Aunt Mitsy. I'll tell him how I feel, and he'll have to listen. I've got to do it. If I go on like this, feeling as I do, pretending, always pretending, I'll resent him. I'll stop loving him, and we'll lose each other. He's always in a good mood after one of these meetings. He makes sure he's up for them, his brightest, best self. He even limits himself to two cocktails.

Nori remembered a conversation between her father and Aunt Mitsy one night at dinner:

"Sure, production records are important, but they're not the only thing. You've got to handle yourself right at those big dinner meetings in Honolulu too," he said.

"You mean they choose top management people based on their small talk at the table?" Mitsy asked.

"All the plantation managers have pretty good statistics, or they would have been fired long ago. When a big promotion comes available, the board brings everybody in and puts their feet to the fire. They ask tough questions. If they like your answers, they offer you the job.

"It's like basketball. You see an opening, you shoot, you score. If somebody fouls you, you make the foul shots, and at the end of the game, you win. I know the job I want, and when it opens up, I going after it."

The job he wanted was coming available, and he was making his move tonight. He was all confidence on the way over in the plane, and while they were shopping in the afternoon, they even rented a car and drove up into Manoa Valley to look for homes that might be for sale. He was counting on this promotion and the move to Honolulu that it would call for.

146

There was a new member of the board, a haole from the mainland, who had recently purchased a large block of Dole stock and had just moved to Honolulu to watch over his investment. Hiromi hadn't met him, but he wasn't nervous. If the man had invested lots of money in the company, he would be anxious that the best men possible were in charge of operations. Hiromi figured that included him.

For nearly an hour, Nori sat before the open window, looking out at the moonlit sea, rehearsing what she was going to say to her father. Finally, a little before twelve, she heard a door slam in the adjoining room. She walked over to the door that separated their adjoining rooms and leaned her back against it.

"Daddy, can I talk to you?" she practiced softly to herself.

"Tonight? It's nearly midnight. We'll talk in the morning. What are you doing up so late?" He'd probably say something like that and start to close the door.

"No, now; we have to talk now, tonight," she said in a frightened, breathy whisper. She shook her head and walked back to the window, her mind filling with doubt and fear. It won't work! I can't do it! she thought. She looked at her watch; it was five minutes after twelve. The band would be playing more slow numbers at the dance back on Lanai, hoping to calm the students down and get them ready to quit and go home. Danny and Nita would be holding each other very close, rocking gently to the music. Nori pictured the scene in her mind and felt her courage return. She walked to the door, knocked firmly, and heard her father's footsteps approaching.

Hiromi opened the door and spoke before she had a chance to say anything. "They're going to treat me just like they treated Pop," he said simply.

"What do you mean, Daddy?" Nori asked.

"This new guy, the haole from the mainland, he hates Japs."
Nori had never heard her father use the word *Jap* before.

"I don't understand," Nori said, bewildered.

"He asked me what I did during the war. He wanted to know why a healthy young guy like me wasn't in the 442nd in Italy instead of sitting out the war on Lanai. He never asked me about production figures. He didn't ask me about personnel management. He wanted to know where I was on December 7, 1941. He must have bought a lot of stock; he practically ran the whole meeting, asked all the questions, made all the suggestions, drew all the conclusions."

"Why didn't you tell him about your brothers who were in the service during the war?" Nori asked.

"He'd have said something like, 'Well, they set you a good example; why didn't you follow it?' "

Nori had never seen her father like this. He seemed beaten. He didn't even sound angry, just hopeless. "What are you going to do?" she asked.

"I'm going to go back to Lanai and run that plantation until they fire me," he said, without emotion. "You'd better go to bed, Nori; it's a little late. Sleep in if you want to; I think I will." As he stepped away from the door, Nori saw a bottle sitting on his bedside table. She knew it would be a long time before he actually went to sleep.

Chapter

19

When Danny passed the dry goods store on the way to school on Monday morning, he saw Nita standing out in front talking to Evelyn. Nita hurriedly excused herself and joined him as though it was an established routine for them to walk to school together. Danny felt a little uncomfortable, but Nita soon put him at ease. She said nothing about their date but concentrated excitedly on the upcoming game with Lahainaluna on Friday.

"Do you think we can beat them again?" she asked.

"I don't know, it was pretty close last time."

"But you're playing so much better now—look at what you did to Hana last Friday. Oh! You've just got to do it, Danny. That would force a play-off with Wailuku! We could be Maui District champions!" Her dark eyes snapped with excitement.

"Hold on! Don't you think we'd better concentrate on beating Lahainaluna?" Danny was laughing at Nita's enthusiasm and total confidence.

She took hold of his arm and hugged it. "You can do it— I know you can!" Out of the corner of his eye, Danny saw Nori standing at the window of their first-hour classroom. Impulsively he took Nita's hand and walked with her up the front steps of the school. The knowing looks exchanged by the students in front of the school left little doubt in Danny's mind that the rumor circulating about him and Nita had just been confirmed.

Though Danny did nothing to plan it, he spent a good deal of every day with Nita. She waited for him every morning at Akagi's store. She saved a place for him in the cafeteria at lunch. When he walked down the hall between classes, she seemed to appear at his side. She never asked him to meet her at a certain time, she was just there. If he was with friends, they went on without him, leaving him alone with her; and Nita's friends did the same. The time with her was always pleasant. Their conversations were interesting and animated—Nita saw to that. Nita kept the talk light, and she was careful not to discuss their relationship. But an unspoken contract was being drawn up, signed, and notarized. Danny was dumbfounded. He had been on one date with her, and he was already beginning to feel as though she was his fiancée.

When Nori saw Danny walking toward the school with Nita, she felt a tightness in her throat and an uncomfortable feeling in her stomach. Nita was walking slightly in front of Danny with her head turned to look back up into his eyes. She would talk excitedly for a moment, then listen intently to his response, nodding her head and smiling. Every few steps, she would reach out and touch him as if to get his attention. It seemed unnecessary; his eyes never left hers for a moment. Nita's tight black skirt and bright red sweater emphasized her appealing figure, and her long black hair, drawn back in a ponytail, bounced and swayed as she laughed and turned her head.

Jealousy and resentment welled up in Nori's heart, embarrassing and confusing her. I have no right to feel like I do, she thought. I brought this on myself. I can't blame Nita—of course she's crazy about Danny. And why wouldn't he feel the same way about her? Look at her — she's beautiful and exciting, and she loves being seen with him.

When Danny greeted her in the classroom, he was respectful and pleasant, but Nori could detect no warmth in his voice as he talked to her. He smiled, but it wasn't the affectionate smile she had known for so long.

Later, in executive council meeting, he joked with her, but his humor had an edge to it, not anything that the other members of the council would pick up, but a subtle irony that Nori could not help but notice.

All that week, Nori handled the situation gracefully — the rumors, the frequent sight of Nita and Danny together, the coolness in Danny's voice when he talked to her. She handled it, but the inner light that was always part of her dimmed. The school was buzzing with talk about Danny and Nita. Some of it was critical of Danny. Nori never took part in these discussions, nor in the ones that criticized Nita.

Once when she was talking on the phone with her cousin Tomo, Nori asked him how well he knew Nita Presa when she lived on Maui. What he said unsettled her: the Presa girls had a reputation for getting what they wanted, not caring who was hurt in the process.

Nori was not really prepared for how much losing Danny hurt her. She hadn't realized how much and in how many ways she depended on him. He had always been a known quantity in her life. But they had become very close during the weeks since the game and dance in Lahaina. Nori had felt the difference, enjoyed the closeness, but refused to recognize the emotional implications that went along with their changing relationship. In a way, she wanted to think of Danny as her friend, her best friend, like the brother she had never had.

Nori wanted things to stay the way they were, the way they had always been, but she was also surprised to discover that she wanted more.

Danny quickly tired of the needling he took from his friends and the members of the team, but how could he blame them? He and Nita were inseparable, or so it seemed. Danny felt manipulated by Nita, but the process was so pleasant, and the manipulator so charming that he couldn't bring himself to do anything about it. The students at Lanai High weren't used to the kind of exclusive togetherness that Danny and Nita seemed to be enjoying. The boys and girls spent time together, but usually in groups—there wasn't a lot of pairing off. He didn't want to hurt Nita; he really enjoyed her company, but he chafed at her subtle control, an approach that seemed to be considerate of him but that seemed to leave him little choice.

On the surface, Nori seemed to be unruffled by the situation. She acted as friendly as ever, as though nothing had changed. Sometimes Danny wondered if she had even noticed what was happening. Why is it so important to me that she notice? he asked himself. Why can't I just forget her or just have her for a friend like Margie or Evelyn? Such conversations with himself always left him with a knot in his stomach.

The turmoil didn't help his concentration during basketball practice either. "Have you got the flu again?" Coach Manning shouted at Danny after his third bad pass in a row. "Sharpen up! Those Lahainaluna guys will be pumped up for this game. With two losses this second half, they're out of the running. Their only chance for glory is to beat us tomorrow night and kill our chance for a play-off. They know Wailuku will win in Hana. This will be the game everyone is watching. This is the game that decides everything. Now run that fast break again and see if you can make it work!"

When the referee tossed the ball up to begin the game with Lahainaluna, Makanui surprised Podogi by grabbing the ball and flinging it far down court to Tomo Satō. Satō had broken past Danny in anticipation of the pass and made the easy lay-up. The coach was right, the Lahaina team was primed for this game with Lanai.

Lahaina put on a full-court press and made the simple task of getting the ball across midcourt an ordeal. Satō was all over Danny, reaching in for the ball, bumping him with his body when the referee wasn't looking, and baiting him verbally. "You gonna try to break the scoring record again tonight? This isn't Hana you're playing, Tolentino. You have to work for your points in this game." Everytime Danny pulled up to shoot, Satō's hand was in his face, and Satō's voice in his ear. "Shoot, Tolentino, think of the glory!"

Danny did shoot and scored. It relaxed him, and he began to function. He ignored Satō's banter and implemented Coach Manning's strategy. It started to work, and Lanai went ahead by six points by the end of the first period.

Lahaina came out charging in the second quarter and made eleven unanswered points. Satō continued to press Danny, but his pressing got him into foul trouble, and the coach had to take him out. Danny began to score again and had fourteen points by the end of the half. By going to a man-to-man defense and pulling out all the stops, Lanai was able to go into the locker room with a four-point lead. Coach Manning wasn't comfortable with it.

"You're probably thinking that we're four points better than we were in Lahaina at halftime, and we ought to be feeling good. Maybe we should, but I'm worried. There's something wrong out there. Danny, you're not yourself. That Satō boy is pushing you all over the place. If they hadn't pulled him out you'd be sitting here with six or eight points instead of fourteen and we'd be behind."

Balance saved them during the third quarter. Jerry began hitting jumpers from the top of the key. Then Darrell got the hot hand. Danny called plays to get the ball to the man who was hitting and watched for signals from Coach Manning. Slowly and steadily Lanai increased their lead.

Early in the fourth quarter Lahaina took a time-out. When they came back on the floor, they had that now-or-never look in their eyes. Makanui threw his body into Podogi as they went up for a rebound and knocked him sprawling on the floor. He got up limping and had to be taken out for a couple of minutes. Makanui then made three straight hook shots, manhandling the gawky sophomore who replaced Podogi. Coach Manning called a time-out.

"We've got an eight-point lead, and there's a little less than five minutes left to play. We can win it, but we've got to keep our first five on the floor. Danny, you and Podogi have three fouls on you. They'll be trying anything to get you to foul out. Keep cool. You have to play hard, or they'll beat us anyway, but don't commit any dumb fouls."

As Danny dribbled the ball down the floor, Satō looked right into his eyes, smiling. He started to talk to him in a low, confidential voice. "Well, Tolentino, I understand you have a new girlfriend." Danny passed the ball to Jerry. Satō continued to talk. "Nita Presa, eh? She's a pretty hot number. I'm surprised you have the energy left to play basketball." The ball came back to Danny. "Is she up in the stands watching you? Why don't you try one from here and really impress her?"

In spite of himself, Danny started asking questions in his mind. "How does he know about Nita? Did Nori tell him?" He looked at the grinning Satō and realized that his smile was very much like the smile of his uncle, Hiromi. In the instant that Danny let his mind wander, Tomo Satō batted the ball out of his hands and started down the floor. Furious with himself, Danny streaked after him in a desperate effort to recover the ball he had lost so foolishly. As Tomo went up for the lay-up, Danny lunged for the ball and felt his hand strike Satō's wrist. The ball bounced crazily on the rim and fell in. The referee's whistle pierced the air, and his raised hand ducked sharply indicating that the basket would count. Satō made the free-throw, and the Lanai lead was cut to five.

Coach Manning pulled Danny out and sat down beside him. "Danny, that's just what we can't have happen. Losing the ball was bad, but you had no chance to get away with that foul. Cool off for a minute." He turned away from Danny to watch the play on the floor. In less than a minute's time, Coach Manning turned back to Danny. "I've got to put you back in there. Satō's made two more baskets while you've been sitting here. Now, get that game under control!"

Tomo greeted Danny with a broad smile. "Kind of hot-headed aren't you, Tolentino? Does it make you mad when I talk to you about Nita?" Danny paid no attention. He gave Satō a head fake and drove past him down the key for a lay-up. Satō seemed not to mind. "Very nice! I hope Nita saw it." The next time down the floor, Satō whispered to him, "I could tell you things about those Presa girls you wouldn't believe, or maybe you would!" He raised his eyebrows in a suggestive way. Danny bounce-passed the ball to Podogi, who hooked one in. Lahaina was answering Lanai basket for basket, but Lanai had a five-point lead with two minutes to go.

Satō made a twenty-footer over Danny's head to cut Lanai's lead to three and stepped up his verbal barrage as Danny brought the ball down the floor. "I'm glad you and Nita got together, Tolentino, at least I don't have to watch you dancing with Nori anymore. You're not good enough for her. It's better that you 'Pilipinos' stay together." Danny saw Darrell all by himself in the corner and knew that he should throw the ball to him, but instead he drove for the basket, right past the grinning Tomo Satō. Satō feigned contact and threw himself to the floor. His academy award-winning performance fooled the referee, who cancelled the lay-up and sent Danny to the bench.

The stunned Lanai team sputtered, and Lahaina tied, then took the lead. By the end of the game, Podogi had fouled out too and was sitting dejectedly by Danny. The final score was eighty-two to seventy-four, in favor of Lahainaluna.

At the sound of the buzzer, the audience sat in stunned silence. A few of the Lahainaluna fans tried to be jubilant, but they soon became self-conscious, like people caught giggling at a funeral.

Danny's team, accustomed to being engulfed by cheering fans at the end of each game, moved awkwardly toward the locker room. Benito came out on the floor, as he always did, and shook Danny's hand. "Some tough luck this one," he said, shaking his head. "Some tough luck, you bet."

Not many students came out of the bleachers to talk to the players. It wasn't that they blamed the team; they just didn't know what to say. They filed quietly out into the darkened night in small, quiet groups. As Danny reached the door of the locker room, he saw Nori standing there, speaking to each player in turn. "Maybe she feels like it's her responsibility as student-body vice-president to cheer up the losers," Danny thought grimly.

"Don't feel bad, Danny," she said, looking up into his face. "You did your best." As their eyes met, Nori's filled with tears. "Oh, Danny, I'm so sorry."

Danny looked at her and smiled a very sad smile. Then he went on into the locker room.

Coach Manning didn't keep them long. He knew they had one more stop to make before they could go home — the saimin shop. He tried to help them shake off their depression, but his speech didn't seem to do much to lighten the mood.

The team all walked together to Sammy Lee's shop; nobody wanted to be the first one there.

"Maybe Sammy close up already," Rudy said. "We just go home, eh?"

"We're going to the saimin shop for soft ice cream, like always," Danny said in a tone that left no room for discussion. "If nobody's there, then we go home."

The lights were blazing at the saimin shop, and people were milling around outside.

"Maybe they like hang us," joked Podogi. Nobody laughed.

Suddenly someone in the crowd spotted them and pointed in their direction. Everybody formed up outside on either side of the doorway. As the team nervously walked between the two lines, somebody started a chant, "Give 'em! Give 'em! Give 'em!" The sound echoed across the park. From the streets nearby came the sound of running feet. The area in front of the shop began filling up with students, all smiling and taking up the chant: "Give 'em! Give 'em! Give 'em!" All at once they stopped.

Danny shouted out over the crowd, "Hey, what-sa-matter

you guys; you lolo? You all go crazy? We just lost the game, remember?"

From somewhere in the crowd came the answer: "What-sa-matter, you guys all stink-face, look so sad? Hana beat Wai-luku! Lanai, da second half-winner! We play Wailuku for da championship next week, here on Lanai!" Everyone cheered.

As the sound died down, Sammy Lee stuck his head out the door and shouted at the team, "Hey, you guys, I like go sleep sometime tonight. You like eat soft ice cream or wot?"

Chapter

20

It was true! The great Wailuku team had been upset. Hana, a scrappy little team with more courage than talent, had beaten Wailuku in triple overtime. Sammy Lee had turned on the game when he left the Lanai gym to open the saimin shop. He expected to hear a lopsided score in the Hana-Wailuku game and the announcement of Wailuku as the district champs. Instead, he heard the beginning of the first overtime. Wailuku seemed to have an infinite capacity for overconfidence. After Lanai destroyed Hana, Wailuku felt as if the regular season was over. They had only to go to Hana and collect the win.

When things didn't go as planned, the haughty Wailuku five began to pout and commit foolish fouls. They blamed the referees; they blamed each other. By the middle of the fourth quarter, Wailuku didn't have a starter left on the floor. The Hana team kept their cool, drew the fouls, and made their free throws. With Wailuku's starters on the bench, the game with Hana, which was supposed to have been a mere formality, turned into a dogfight. At the end of three overtime periods, the score was Hana 65, Wailuku 63.

The few students who had wandered into the saimin shop after the game found Sammy glued to the radio. During the time out between the first and second overtimes, they began making phone calls. All over Lanai City people were turning on their radios and resurrecting the excitement that had died during the fourth quarter of the Lanai game. The Wailuku-Hana game ended just as Danny and the team left the high school and headed for Sammy's. When the buzzer sounded in Hana, the Lanai students left their radios, spilled out into the streets, and headed directly for the saimin shop.

At the shop another surprise awaited them. The location of the championship game, which was determined by the flip of a coin, had been announced on the radio: the game would be played in Lanai. By the time the team reached the saimin shop, everybody knew but them.

During the next week, everyone on Lanai was eating, drinking, and sleeping basketball. People who knew nothing about basketball were talking about it. The little Japanese mama-sans clucked about it at Okimoto's grocery store while they shopped. The Filipino bachelors had the pin setters at the bowling alley write "Wailuku" on masking tape and attach it to the head pins. They got some terrible splits, but the head pins always went flying. The twenty best seats for the game were raffled off by the PTA, and they made nearly five hundred dollars for the library fund. The cheerleaders and songleaders worked out new routines. All three hula teachers on the island joined forces to plan the half-time entertainment. Dole Corporation bought new uniforms and sent them to Lanai for the team to wear in the championship game.

Every public building was decorated with slogans and banners. One read: "Waddascoops? Lanai, Da Champs For Real!" Another: "Wailuku, Mo' better you stay Maui!" All the rooms at the Lanai Inn were booked for Friday night, and the people of Lanai offered to open their homes to Maui people who wanted to come over for the game. A team member couldn't spend his money anywhere in town. If they made a small purchase at the bowling alley, the saimin shop, or Okimoto's, someone always seemed to step forward and say, "On me, eh?"

Usually, there was very little entertainment on Lanai. Any unusual amusement that became available got the people's enthusiastic support. The Catholic church had a carnival every year with rides brought in by barge. The merry-go-round was a tired-looking affair with horses badly in need of paint and no music. The ferris wheel was a stripped-down model that creaked and groaned under its load. It was the color of rust and had no decorations or bright lights. Both of them were full from the time they started until the very last turn at the end of the carnival. A magic show from one of the other islands could fill the Lanai High gym to the bursting point, and every kind of sporting event or school play drew large crowds.

Having the Maui District High School Basketball Championship Play-offs in Lanai City was the most exciting event anyone could remember taking place on the island. Everybody was caught up in the event. Classes were held as usual, but even the teachers had difficulty concentrating. After school every basketball hoop in the city was surrounded by kids pretending to play the big game.

" . . . a long pass down floor to Tolentino. He dribble, he shoot—two points for Lanai High!"

"Kanahele get da rebound. He try hook shot from da left. Nobody can stop. Lanai ahead by fifty points in da first quarter."

"Ōta at da line. . . . He make one free throw. . . . He make anotta free throw. . . . Lanai High win—one point!"

Danny was feeling the pressure. The losses early in the season to Wailuku and Kahului had been painful, but the expectations were not as high back then. If the team had just recovered and won more games than they lost, it would have been considered an acceptable performance by a gutsy team without any real shot at the championship. Winning nine games in a row had changed all that. They were expected to win. The agony of the loss to Lahaina on the previous Friday night had been swept away by the implications of Hana's victory over Wailuku: Lanai High School had a shot at the Maui District championship, and they would have it right here in Lanai City.

After basketball practice, Danny went over to the missionaries' apartment to talk. He and Elder Opi sat on the steps while Elder Global cooked dinner.

"I think I had forgotten what it was like to lose," Danny said.

"It's no fun," said Elder Opi. "I was the only senior on a team of sophomores and juniors. We lost seven games that season, so I had a lot of experience at losing. But I never developed a taste for it. It was what my coach called a 'building season.' He never planned on winning many games that season. He just experimented with different combinations and got ready for the next year. His plan must have worked—they took state two years later."

"He just threw away your senior year?"

"We didn't have what it takes, I guess. He took the opportunity to give the juniors and sophomores some experience. It paid off, like I said. He won it all a couple of years later. You can't quarrel with success. What I'm telling you is, losing basketball games doesn't kill you. I'm living proof."

"Maybe that's what Coach Manning has been doing," said Danny. "Our starting five has been playing together for three years. Even during our sophomore year he would put the five of us in at the same time and let us play for a few minutes. The seniors got a little upset sometimes; they figured we cost them some games. I think this season is pretty important to Coach Manning. Bernard says his father told him Dr. Chuck is leaving this summer. He's going to some big hospital in Boston to study a specialty. I'd like to win the championship for him; he's been a great coach and a good friend."

"Maybe losing the other night will help you do it," said Elder Opi. "Or maybe losing the championship will help you in some other way. If there's one thing I've learned in my short life, it's that you never know when to be happy."

"What do you mean?" Danny asked, a little confused. "You mean I should be happy about losing to Lahaina last Friday?"

"It might be the best thing that could have happened. If you'd won, you might have gotten cocky just like Wailuku did and blown the big one."

"But you said it might be good for us to lose the championship, too."

"What I said was, you never know when to be happy. You can't! You can't see far enough ahead to know how the present is going to affect the future. Take my brother, Mike, for instance. When Wes was killed in the attack on Pearl Harbor, Mike couldn't wait to get in the service and start fighting the Japanese. When he turned eighteen, it was happy time, right? He could join the navy and start getting revenge. Wrong. The war ended before he could get into action.

"Then he was stationed in Pearl Harbor and went to the Pearl City Branch. The branch president was a Japanese guy named Oshiro. Bad news, right? Now he has to work closely with the people he hates. Wrong. The Oshiros became like second parents to him, and he forgot all about hating the Japanese race. Later when he got his mission call to Hawaii, the reason was clear: The Lord was sending him back to Pearl Harbor where he had so many friends. Right?

"Wrong. The mission president sent him to Lanai where Mike was sure he would waste six months of his mission on an isolated little rock before he got back to Oahu where the real action was. He thought he'd hate it. He was wrong again — he loved it so much that he convinced the mission president to let him spend his whole mission here.

"See what I mean? You never know when to be happy or sad. So you might as well be happy. Now come on around behind the church and let me show you my favorite shot. It's a doozy! It even helped us win a couple of games during my senior year." Elder Opi turned to yell through the door, "Hey, elder, toss out the ball, okay?"

"Well, all right," came the reply. "But this repast will be ready in a few minutes." Elder Global appeared at the door, wearing an apron and holding a basketball.

A few seconds later, Danny was following Elder Opi around the house. The elder stood out in front of the basket about twenty feet, dribbling the ball. "Okay, I'm coming in for a lay-up, and you try to stop me without fouling." Danny took up a defensive stance. Elder Opi stayed in one spot, dribbling the ball slowly, alternating hands and shifting his weight first to the left, then to the right. All at once he broke for the basket. Danny cut him off and raised his hand to reject the ball. At the last moment, Elder Opi swung the ball down under Danny's arm and with a little two-handed flip banked it off the backboard and into the net.

"If you can get under his arm, you've got it made," he said. "If his arms stay high, you have your lay-up. If he tries to drop the arm to stop you, you're shooting two from the foul line. Here, you try it now, and I'll guard you."

Time after time Danny practiced the shot, first from one side of the basket and then the other. Elder Opi guarded him tenaciously in the conventional way, which made the shot difficult but possible. Sometimes Danny made the lay-up; sometimes he went to the line; almost always he got his two points. Elder Global had tapped on the window several times with a fork, gesturing with his finger toward his open mouth or rubbing his stomach to indicate that dinner was ready. Elder Opi nodded but kept practicing with Danny. Finally Elder Global came around to the back, still wearing his apron.

"I worship your basketball skills, elder," he said. "In fact, I have some burnt offerings I would like to lay before you if you can break away for a moment. Did you remember that we have a meeting with the Felipes this evening? You just have time for a very cold shower before we have to leave."

Elder Opi smacked his forehead with the palm of his hand. "I did forget!" he said with a grimace. "Guard Danny while I get ready."

Elder Global took a position between Danny and the basket. Danny was laughing at the figure the missionary cut with his white shirt and tie on and his apron fluttering at his knees. "Come on, come on! Don't judge my skill by my uniform. I guarantee you'll never score on me!"

Danny dribbled toward him slowly, waiting for his chance to drive for the basket. It never came. Totally ignoring the ball, Global rushed at Danny, pinned his arms to his sides with a tremendous bear hug, and carried him to the grass where he held him down and sat on his chest. "Do you admit I beat you one on one? I'm not leaving until you plead for mercy."

Danny's face was scarlet from laughing and from the weight on his chest. "I give! I give! No squash me, eh?"

Elder Global stood up and ceremoniously dusted off his hands. "I wonder if Wailuku would be interested in my services. I'd be willing to play for a nominal fee, and if they couldn't afford that, maybe they'd pay me an exorbitant price. Either one would do nicely, as long as it's a lot of money. I'd pay an honest tithing on it too, no matter how much they paid me. That's the kind of Mormon I am, 'virtuous, lovely, or of good report or praiseworthy.' . . . " He droned on and on, gesturing broadly. Danny left him with a wave of his hand and trotted off toward home.

On the night of the championship game, most of the team members were in the locker room dressed and ready an hour before game time. When Coach Manning came in, he sensed the tension in the room. He sat down on a bench in the middle of the team and began to talk.

"When I was in the South Pacific, flying for the navy, I got shot down on Bougainville in the Solomon Islands. I walked away from the wreck unharmed but scared nearly to death. The island was crawling with Japanese soldiers, and I was sure I would be discovered any minute. I lay in the undergrowth at the edge of a lagoon for three days, not daring to move. I knew there were fish in the lagoon, but I couldn't force myself to leave cover to catch one. I was just too scared.

"Finally, I was so hungry, I couldn't stand it any longer. I walked to the edge of the lagoon. There were fish everywhere, and the water was shallow. I guess I lost my head. Before I knew what I was doing, I had pulled the pin on a grenade and tossed it in. As I dived back into the brush, the whole lagoon sounded as if it had exploded. When I peeped out, there were dozens of fish floating on the surface. I waded in and began picking them up.

"Suddenly, I heard a fiendish laugh echoing over the water from the other side of the lagoon. I dashed out of the water and went head over heels into the jungle again. I have never

166

felt such terror before or since. I wrapped my arms across my chest to muffle the sound of my heart, which seemed to be beating loud enough to be heard across the bay.

"Then I heard this voice with a heavy Australian accent calling to me, 'Come on out, Yank; nobody's goin' to 'urt ya.'

"I came out sheepishly and found a scrawny, pint-sized Aussie smiling at me. He was what they call a coast watcher, and I learned later that he was only happy when there was a war on. He was half my size, but he was afraid of nothing. He had a bunch of Samoan jungle fighters with him, and they kept track of all the Japanese on the island. They radioed their positions to our forces in the area, and our planes bombed and strafed with deadly efficiency. When Japanese patrols went out in search of their tormentors, they were wiped out by the Aussie and his gentle giants. After a few days with them, my fear left me. I was with them for nearly a month before they could find a way to get me out. We were outnumbered a hundred to one, but I was calm as a Boy Scout at summer camp. I decided that fear was a state of mind that had little to do with the facts of a situation.

"Now, statistically we are outgunned by this Wailuku team. They're bigger and taller than we are, and they've demonstated the ability to score almost at will when they get a game going their way. Overconfidence has just cost them the championship and forced this play-off, so it's unlikely they'll be cocky tonight. Liu is one of the most talented high school players I've ever seen. On the right night he could put fifty points on the board all by himself.

"That's the bad news, and if we let ourselves, we could freeze up like I did on Bougainville and go out there and get stomped." He looked around the circle of faces that surrounded him. They looked tense and frightened and unsure of themselves.

"What da good news, coach?" croaked Podogi, whose throat had gone dry all of a sudden.

Coach Manning smiled and took a deep breath. "The good news is that we've already won!"

"We've what?" Bernard shouted.

"We've won!" said Coach Manning. "You're the best team Lanai High has ever produced. Against all odds, you've fought your way into a tie for the Maui District championship with the biggest school in the league. You've covered yourselves with glory. Whatever you do tonight is icing on the cake. I'm already satisfied. Now don't get me wrong! I'd love to win, and I think we can do it, but don't go out there and win it for me. I'm happy now.

"Win it because you're having so much fun making baskets that you just can't quit. Run them into the ground because you're in terrific shape and you love to run. Beat them because you're more relaxed and because you've played together so long that you can read each other's minds. Out-think them, take chances, do the unexpected, see if you can put a hundred points on the scoreboard. If they can make a hundred and one, give them the championship, they'll deserve it! The only way you can lose tonight is if you let all the pressure get to you and don't have any fun. Now relax! Take a nap, talk about girls, eat a candy bar; I'm going to go up and mingle with the crowd. I'll see you guys on the floor at game time."

Chapter
21

When the Lanai team walked out on the floor, the entire crowd jumped to their feet. They clapped and shouted as the team began doing lay-up drills. "What will they do when the game starts?" Danny said. "Maybe they think these baskets count."

"Dis crowd all crazy," Podogi said. "We listen to dem, we miss any kind shots."

"Not us, brah, us too cool, eh?" Jerry was smiling. "Hey, Podogi, da coach say Liu could make fifty points. How about we shut him down, eh? I talk plenty Pilipino Pidgin in his ear. By 'n' by he come lolo, all crazy, like Makanui in Lahaina."

Danny heard a chant starting. "Danny, Danny, Danny!" That would be Nita and her friends. Danny hadn't seen much of her in the past week. He told her he had to concentrate on the game. He saw Nori sitting with the executive council. Danny had skipped the council meeting for the first time since he became president. He asked Nori to take over for him, and she agreed to.

Nori had been quiet all week, and the distance between them seemed to be growing. When they did talk, it was strained and uncomfortable. Sometimes Danny would look over at her in class, when she wasn't aware of his glance. His eyes would trace the contours of her face. Then he would remember the good times when he lived to be with her and when he saw tenderness and affection in her eyes as she looked at him.

As Danny went in for a lay-up, a flashbulb flared nearby. A photographer from the *Honolulu Star Bulletin* was there covering the game. High up in the stands a Honolulu radio station was getting ready to broadcast the play-by-play. The local games were usually covered by small stations and transmitted to the Maui listening audience. This game was being broadcast to all the islands. Hawaii's sportswriters and broadcasters smelled a story in this "David and Goliath" contest that pitted tiny and obscure Lanai High against the vaunted Wailuku team.

Danny felt his mouth suddenly go dry, then remembering the coach's comments, he shook off the tension and began to talk and joke with Jerry. "Hey, Jerry, I no can wait for all da fun we gonna have in dis game."

Jerry looked at him strangely, then chuckled. "Me too, boy! Fun, fun, fun, dat's all we gonna have tonight." He rebounded a ball and threw it to Podogi. "Have some fun, Podogi. Try make a lef'-hand hook shot from da top of the key, eh?"

Podogi looked up nervously and saw Danny and Jerry laughing at his tense face. "Have fun, eh? Try look at dis!" He faked left, then moved right and released a high arching shot toward the basket. It swished. Soon everybody was talking about having fun.

They did have fun. The team clicked from the opening jump ball. Podogi's hook was working, and Darrell's shot from the corner was deadly accurate. Danny drove the key for lay-ups and dropped twenty-footers from out front. Rudy made tip shots, and Jerry was having his best offensive game in weeks. They were relaxed, confident, and at the top of their form. There was only one problem: so was Wailuku. Wailuku matched them basket for basket, fast break for fast break, foul shot for foul shot, and at the end of the third period Wailuku had a two-point lead.

Coach Manning squatted down in front of the bench, and the players circled around him. "We've got to do something different," he said. "Both teams have had a feeding frenzy at the basket during the first three quarters. Look at that score, seventy-one to sixty-nine. If we keep going like this, you could probably make your hundred points, but they'd probably end up with the hundred and one I talked about earlier. I've changed my mind." Coach Manning smiled and shook his head. "We're so close. Let's win this thing!" The team members murmured their approval.

"If we're going to win, we've got to change something. We're like a couple of tennis players slamming it out from the baseline; the harder one player hits the ball, the harder it comes back. It's like playing a baseball game, and the batters keep seeing nothing but fast balls right across the numbers. You can fatten up your batting averages, but you still might lose the game. We've got to do something to break their rhythm. There's a chance that it might break ours too, but like I've always said, it's easier to adjust when you're the one who's making the changes."

"Just tell us what to do," Danny said with conviction. "Tell us what to do and we'll do it!"

"All right, we've got the ball. When you go out there, I want you to play as if you're protecting a ten-point lead. Stall, hold the ball, use up the clock, don't take any shot but a sure thing. We've been running and gunning for three quarters now; it's bound to confuse them if we do a slowdown. Podogi, I want you to come out front with Danny. Jerry you go in and play the post. That way if somebody gets in trouble, they can just throw the ball high out toward Podogi, and he'll get it. Don't try anything but a layup. No jump shots, no set shots, no nothing. Work it around until somebody's under the basket alone. I'd be perfectly satisfied to win this game seventy-three to seventy-one. On defense it's a full-court press every minute from here on in. This is the last game of the year; you can rest during spring break."

They put their hands together with the coach's, barked "Let's go!" and returned to the floor.

Danny brought the ball down the court. The change at the post confused Wailuku—Liu followed Podogi out to his guard position, leaving the middle open, and Danny drove the lane for a lay-up. The score was tied for the tenth time in the game. The whole thing had taken only about ten seconds.

"Not much of a slowdown," Danny thought. "But it was a lay-up." He looked over at the coach, who was clapping enthusiastically.

Nishimura, Wailuku's point guard, was bringing the ball down the floor. Danny worried him, stabbed at the ball, rushed at him, then backed away. Nishimura tried to get the ball to Liu at the top of the key, but Podogi and Rudy had him sandwiched. Rudy's man broke for the basket, and Nishimura tried to hit him with the ball, but it was deflected off Podogi's elbow right into Jerry's outstretched hands. He pulled the ball in close and pivoted away from the Wailuku players, who streaked by him toward the other end of the floor to stop the fast break they fully expected.

As Jerry began his slow, deliberate dribble down the floor, his man made a rush at him, and Jerry passed the ball to Danny and ran up the floor to his post position. Podogi came out to the guard position, and the stall was on. They moved the ball back and forth around the perimeter, making no move toward the basket until the Wailuku men started to press them. Then Danny faked a drive down the middle. As they collapsed on him, he passed off to Podogi, who started the perimeter passing again. Forty-five seconds went by, a minute, a minute and a half. Darrell Fujimoto broke for the basket, and Podogi hit him with a two-handed overhead pass. Lanai High was in the lead.

Wailuku took a time-out and came up with some innovations of their own. They regained the lead and went into a zone defense. The coach nodded at Danny, and he made three outside shots in a row that forced them back into a man to man. With twenty seconds to go, Lanai had a two-point lead, and Wailuku had the ball. Nishimura got the ball to Liu, who headed for the basket a half a step ahead of Podogi. Knowing that Liu would not miss a close shot, Podogi fouled him and sent him to the line. There were seven seconds on the clock. Lanai took a time-out to let him worry about his free throws.

Coach Manning pretended to be calm as they huddled near the bench. "Are you having fun?" he asked. The surprise of the question broke the tension. "Now listen. If he misses either one of his foul shots, call another time-out. If he makes them both, take the ball out as soon as you can and get the ball to Danny. Danny, I don't want you to pass and I don't want you to shoot a hail Mary from midcourt. I want you to dribble the full length of the court and put the ball in the basket. They won't dare guard you too close for fear of fouling. You'll use up the clock and either win the game or get us into an overtime. I prefer the former."

"You prefer da wot?" Jerry asked involuntarily.

"Never mind," Coach Manning said. "Just make sure we get the rebound if there is one. Okay?"

Liu stepped to the line. His body was wet with perspiration. Concern was evident in his handsome young face, but he was an athlete, a good one; he refused to let the pressure get to him. He took his time, went through his routine, and then raised the ball to eye level. The first shot dropped through the hoop. The second one followed a moment later. The game was tied.

Everybody expected Lanai to call another time-out. They didn't. Jerry took the ball out and passed it to Danny before the Wailuku team realized what was happening. Darrell, Podogi, and Rudy streaked for the other end of the court as though they expected a long looping pass. Liu and the two Wailuku forwards rushed down the floor to cover them.

Danny dribbled down the left side of the court, then broke to the right. Nishimura, who was backpeddling right in front of him, smashed into Jerry on his blind side as Danny changed direction. Danny drove for the basket, but in his path stood the six-foot-four Liu. As Liu reached up to reject the ball, Danny suddenly remembered Elder Opi's shot. At the last possible second, he dropped the ball down under Liu's outstretched arm and flipped it up against the backboard with his two hands. As it dropped through the net, the buzzer sounded, ending the game.

Nothing they had experienced during their nine-game winning streak had prepared the team for what happened next. The little gym actually shuddered under the impact of the shouting, foot-stomping fans. Thirty or forty students swooped down on the players and raised them to their shoulders, not just the five starters but everybody in a uniform. Then the coach was lifted up, and the team manager, the cheerleaders, even Mr. Watanabe, the principal, were hoisted up on the shoulders of the jubilant students. The townspeople stood and applauded as the delegation began making a circuit of the gym.

The pep club appeared with their arms full of flower leis to drape around the necks of the victorious heroes.

The *Star Bulletin* photographer was beside himself trying to record the celebration. Spent flashbulbs spilled out of his pockets and littered the floor behind him as he rushed from shot to shot. The sports announcer was shouting into his microphone, trying to describe the scene to his radio audience.

Nita began a purposeful advance through the crowd surrounding Danny. He was in the middle of the swirling mass of celebrants, and she wanted desperately to be at his side where the glory of the evening could shine on her as well. With a determined smile, the wiry little Filipino beauty made steady progress toward her goal. To her left she spied the photographer forcing his way in for a close-up of the captain of the winning team. She redoubled her efforts, and the smile became a grimace as she forced her way forward.

Then Danny spotted his father standing nearby and waving, tears of happiness running down his cheeks. He jumped down from the shoulders of the students who were carrying him. The crowd parted to let him go. Danny gathered his father into his arms and hugged him with great affection. Then he turned to the crowd and, placing his left arm around Benito's thin shoulders, raised his right hand high in tribute to his father. The photographer broke loose from the crowd at just that moment and snapped a picture with his last available flashbulb. That was the picture heading the feature article on the front page of the *Honolulu Star Bulletin* sports section the next day.

Chapter
22

Bernard had a surprise for the team when they reached the locker room, but before making an announcement, he whispered it to Danny. Danny listened with alarm and then grabbed him by the throat and pretended to choke him. "What if we hadn't won?" he whispered hoarsely into Barnard's ear.

"You have to have a little faith," Bernard protested. "Columbus took a chance . . ."

Danny removed one hand from Bernard's throat and put it over his mouth. By then both were laughing gleefully.

When Hiromi Satō began giving Danny money after each game, Danny had assigned Bernard the job of team treasurer and turned the money over to him. The fund had grown to a substantial sum before the Lahaina catastrophy. Then after the play-off game was slated, Satō had let it be known that an additional fifty dollars would be forthcoming if Lanai was able to win the championship.

The optimistic Bernard had run some calculations and decided that the available funds would cover food and drink for as many students as could get permission from their parents to attend an all-night beach party at Manele. During the past week, with Margie Morita's help, he had planned a menu and shopping list and organized a calling committee to alert the students to the plan immediately following the game. Bernard's father had connections in the plantation motor pool that transported workers to and from the pineapple fields. Mr. Ōta had arranged for buses to take everyone to the beach if Lanai won. Mr. Okimoto had agreed to open his store after the game so the supplies could be purchased for the party.

All these plans were kept secret until game time, but soon after play began, the whispering started. During halftime, the whispers became excited chatter that swept through the crowd. By the beginning of the third quarter, only the boys on the playing floor and the coach were unaware of the plans for the big party. Bernard now filled them in. "Hey, you guys? You like go beach?"

"Go beach? Tonight? You lolo, Bernard," Jerry said. "Who like go beach nighttime?"

"About half Lanai High like go," said Bernard after pretending to do some quick calculations in his head.

Jerry pulled down his lower eyelid with his finger—the extreme gesture of disbelief. "Go beach, my eye, no joke me, Bernard; what you talk?"

"We gonna have big blowout, Manele Beach, for celebrate dis victory. Try listen, eh; no talk, talk, all da time!" Bernard said. Then he quickly explained everything.

By the time the team had showered and changed, Margie and some of her friends had done the shopping, loaded the food into Mr. Okimoto's pickup, and headed for the beach to get started on the food preparation. As Danny trotted toward his home, buses were cruising the streets of the city, picking up students. A small special bus called for the members of the team so they could ride down to the beach together. Danny was pleased to see Coach Manning on board when it stopped in front of his house.

"You didn't think I'd miss this party did you?" Coach Manning asked. "Remember me? I'm the one who likes to have fun! I won't stay the night; they need me at the hospital in the morning. But I wouldn't miss one of Margie Morita's feeds for anything. Besides, Jerry has promised to teach me how to play the ukulele."

Danny dropped into the empty seat next to Bernard and behind Podogi, who turned partway around so he could talk with them. Bernard beamed up at Danny, his face barely visible in the glow of the interior bus lights. Then the driver closed the door and plunged them into darkness. Jerry was in the back of the bus, playing the ukulele and singing the "Hawaiian War Chant."

"Is that Darrell singing with Jerry?" Danny asked. "I didn't even know he could sing."

"First time ever he sing I t'ink," Podogi said, laughing.

"Maybe he just learned tonight," Bernard added. "What's one more miracle among so many?"

"It was a miracle, wasn't it?" Danny said softly. "It could have gone the other way so easily. I could have dribbled on my foot or missed that screwy shot. I just learned it the other night from Elder Opi, and I never even thought of using it until then. I don't know what made me try it. Maybe it was an answer to my prayers. I prayed about this game, I really did."

Podogi nodded. "Me too. I pray like crazy. Maybe we get little bit help, eh?"

"I don't know," Bernard answered. "It felt like a miracle, but why should the Lord choose us to help? I'll bet those Wailuku boys were praying too. Liu's a good Catholic boy. Didn't you see him crossing himself before his free throws?

Nishimura's Mormon. He was probably praying for help too. I don't know how the Lord works it out; maybe he just watches the game and lets things happen naturally. But I'm like you; I pray like anything."

Jerry had started the group in the back of the bus singing, and Podogi, Bernard, and Danny joined in.

> Dis ol' man, he play two,
> he play nick-nack on my shoe.
> Wid a nick-nack, paddy-wack,
> give a dog a bone,
> dis ol' man went rolling home.

They continued until the rhymes became ridiculous and the song degenerated into noisy laughter.

"Hey, coach," Danny called out. "What happened to the Aussie coast watcher you told us about? Did he make it through the war?" Everybody became quiet to hear the answer.

"He did," Coach Manning said. "I saw him after the war at a ceremony on the island of Eniwetok in the Marshall Islands. They were giving out medals, and he got a ton of them. It was a pretty big deal, lots of high-ranking officers involved, but he seemed unimpressed. After the ceremony he came over to say good-bye. He was smiling that strange lopsided smile of his and talking in his high-pitched Aussie accent. 'Well Yank,' he said, 'it weren't much of a war, but it were better than no war at all,' and he walked away. I never saw him again."

The bus came to a stop in a grove of kiawe trees near the beach. The door opened, the lights came on, and everybody piled out.

The beach was alive with celebrating students. Two large fires were burning on the sand. Folding tables filled with plates of food were set up between them. Paper plates were piled high with carrot and celery sticks; others held sliced papayas and mangoes, quartered limes, whole bananas, and wedges of sugar pine. Suspended over beds of red hot charcoal were large woks filled with chicken and beef hekka, boiling and bubbling and giving off the sweet aroma of Maui onions and ginger. On other portable barbeques, steaming pots of rice simmered. Two large grills had been set up, and the smell of hamburgers, hot dogs, and teriyaki chicken mingled with the scent of the sea. Tubs of crushed ice bristled with soda pop bottles; others contained ice-covered cartons of ice cream.

"Okay!" Margie shouted. "The team's here; we can start eating."

The crowd of hungry teenagers engulfed the tables and began filling paper plates with food. They scattered into little groups eating, talking, and laughing all at the same time. Margie and her committee worked diligently to refill the serving dishes that the insatiable students quickly emptied. Nori and the executive council members, which included Danny, pitched in to help. Bernard and Podogi went directly to the tables to fill their own plates with food.

"It's nice not to be the student-body president sometimes," Bernard said loud enough for Danny to hear.

"You could starve to death in dat job," Podogi added with a chuckle.

Nori and Danny ended up working side by side. "It was a great game, Danny," she said softly. "That last basket you made was so exciting!"

As Danny looked at her and smiled, he suddenly felt weak and helpless. Their eyes met, and he felt his face flush. There was that look again, the look that said everything he had ever wanted to hear her say. He wanted to return that message, wanted it so much that he ached inside. But if he did, she would change again, those eyes would fill with uncertainty and dread.

What do you want from me, Nori? he thought. How long will it last? Tomorrow? What'll you do when I ask you for another date? You couldn't have me come to your house to pick you up. Your father would be furious. You just can't face him, can you? Better to think of another excuse. Just keep me near, close enough, but not too close. Then one day you can just get on an airplane and fly to Honolulu and forget all about me.

As before, anger came to his rescue. The pain lessened, and the feelings of weakness left.

"Danny!"

Danny turned just in time to catch Nita as she jumped into his arms. "Oh Danny, you're the most wonderful basketball player in the world! I tried to get through the crowd to tell you after the game, but there were so many people. Then I missed the bus. I made Daddy bring me down in his jeep. Have I missed anything?" She threw her arms around him again and hugged him.

Nita never left Danny's side all evening. By the time he was through helping the food committee, she had filled a plate for him and found a place for them to sit. He wanted to be with Bernard and Podogi, but her attentiveness made it difficult. They would join small groups for few minutes, but everyone seemed to think they wanted to be alone. It wasn't boring. Nita relived almost every play of the game with him. "When you took the ball away from Liu in the second quarter, just took it away, I couldn't stop screaming! And that long shot just before the half—oh, Danny, I don't think I'll be able to sleep for a week!" Her brown eyes twinkled in the firelight, and they never left Danny's face for an instant.

After they had taken the edge off their appetites, the more energetic of the group began looking for something fun to do. Some went swimming and body surfing in the gentle waves that washed the beach. From the shore came warning calls from those who were not swimming.

"You lolo guys. No swim so soon after eat, eh? By 'n' by you get cramp, sink to da bottom; nobody can find, eh?"

"You call dat eat? Only small little snack. After swim, we show you eat!"

Two of the younger high school teachers who were acting as chaperones had organized a touch football game in the surf. With about twenty boys on each team and only the light from the fires further up the beach for illumination, the game degenerated into a water fight.

On the dark sand where the light from the fires couldn't reach, guys were chasing sand crabs. Someone with a flashlight would hold it so that the beam marked a bright line on the beach surface. He'd slowly sweep the beam up and down the sloping sand until a crab was spotted. Mesmerized by the light, the crab would freeze. The guys, who had filled their hands with wet sand, would creep up silently on the unsuspecting crab till they were just outside the flashlight's beam. The leader would shout, "Now!" and the crab would be bombarded with the handfuls of wet sand. Then the guys would try to catch it before it could dig its way out. If they were successful in catching the crab, they would attempt to terrorize some of the girls with it. If the girls refused to be frightened, they just tossed it into the ocean and went back out into the dark to catch another one.

A large group had gathered around Jerry Tano, who was playing the ukulele while they sang.

... I wanna go back to my little grass shack
In Kealakekua, Hawaii ...

... Night and you and blue Hawaii ...

None of them would have sung alone in the daylight, but
there on the beach in the darkness, with only the flickering
camp fire to light their faces, they sang and sang.

... It isn't Waikiki or Kamehameha's pali,
Not the beach boys free ... "

Some began harmonizing and smiled at the results. As they
finished each song, Jerry went into a vamp to continue the
throbbing beat until someone called out the name of another
favorite: "Beyond the Reef," "Old Hawaii," "King Kamehameha." Jerry would adjust the rhythm, and if a key change was
in order, he went through a complicated progression of chords
that ended in the proper key. Under Jerry's skillful leadership,
they sang like professionals.

Finally, Jerry started playing "Crazy G," signaling that a
ukulele concert was beginning. The singers sat back, contented,
while he played old favorites and some new numbers they
hadn't heard. The music tempted the swimmers, the water
football teams, and the crab chasers away from their games,
and the whole group sat in a semicircle around Jerry. As he
finished "Malaguena," he called out, "Hula! Try move back litty
bit, make some room, eh?" The crowd moved back. Margie
and several other girls jumped up to dance, and Jerry launched
into the chords of "Huki Lau."

Oh, we're goin' to a huki lau,
a huki huki huki huki huki lau ...

The smiling girls pulled their hands one way and moved

their hips the other in a graceful action meant to simulate the pulling in of a giant huki lau net filled with fish. Spreading their arms wide, they brought them together over their hearts to signify that everybody loves a huki lau. Then they pretended to scoop the contents of delicious laulaus from their hands into their mouths. They threw imaginary nets out into the sea and, by placing one hand over the other and rotating their thumbs, imitated the action of fish swimming into those waiting nets. Finally they went back to tugging at the nets.

Everybody was singing and clapping. Then Coach Manning called out a request. "Nori, how about doing 'Kalua' as a last number? I've got to leave pretty soon."

Jerry started the introduction, and the crowd hushed. Nori stood up and began to move to the music. The fires had died down to a flickering glow that flared up occasionally whenever the sea breeze picked up. Nori was wearing white shorts and a light blue blouse. In the firelight she looked like a sea sprite swaying rhythmically in the air. Her feet seemed not to touch the sand. Jerry's clear voice carried over the sound of the lapping waves:

> This is the night of love,
> The shining hour of Kalua.
> Her song is in the air;
> Her lips are waiting there.
> Who will be Kalua's only love?

Nori's hands and arms caught the firelight and traced graceful patterns in the night air. Her face seemed to glow. Her lips formed the words of the song.

> Who will her lover be?
> Who will her lover be?

Before the night is old
My arms will hold Kalua.

Danny was hypnotized by the scene. He listened to every word and followed every movement with his eyes. When Nita tried to whisper to him, he pressed his finger to her lips without taking his eyes away from Nori. All his memories came flooding back. When will I be over you, Nori, he thought sadly. When?

"How about a standing ovation," Coach Manning called out. "For the dancing, the singing, the ukulele playing, the great food, and uh, oh yes, the basketball! I'll see you all tomorrow. You can let the sun wake you up, but I have to be at the hospital by six in the morning."

Everybody jumped up and clapped. The coach walked off into the trees with one of the teachers who was driving him to the city. The players left the crowd and followed them. They stood quietly by as Coach Manning jumped into the jeep. He looked up as if surprised to see them standing there. Finally Bernard spoke up. "We know you're leaving this summer, Coach Manning. We just wanted you to know, we'll never forget you, ever."

The darkness could not completely mask the tears in Coach Manning's eyes. He said nothing for a few moments. Then he cleared his throat and, in the best Aussie accent he could muster, said, "Well, it weren't much of a basketball season, but it were better than no basketball season at all." He clapped his driver on the back, and they drove away.

Chapter
23

At the urging of the chaperones, the students began to get ready to sleep. It was a simple process. Each student looked for a likely spot above the highest point that the tide could be expected to reach, wrapped up in the blanket he or she had brought, dropped down on the sand, and wriggled around until the sand conformed to the shape of the body. As the students split up into little groups and began going through this ritual, they looked like grunion burying eggs in the sand at high tide during a full moon in Southern California. The chaperones scattered themselves along the beach and tried to get some sleep, but they were kept awake by restrained laughter or the splash of young legs running in the shallow water of the receding waves.

Exhausted by the game and the party, Danny, Bernard, and Podogi finally gave up trying to get to sleep near the group and trudged down to the far end of the beach where the rhythmic dashing of the waves upon the rocks drowned out the sounds of those still at play. At least the noise of the surf was dependable. It had a hypnotic quality, and the three dropped off immediately.

Danny woke suddenly to the soft pressure of a hand over

his mouth and another squeezing his fingers. He opened his eyes — Nita! But Nori was bending over him with a solemn and determined look on her face. She removed her hand from his mouth, put her finger to her lips, and gestured for him to follow her. Then she moved off swiftly toward the rocks.

Danny stood up unsteadily and followed her, though he was still half asleep and wondered if he could be dreaming. The wind had freshened, and the waves crashed against the rocks, tossing a fine, salty, dewlike spray into the air. The roar of the surf covered the sound of their movements. The scattered clouds, wind-driven past the full moon, created a strobe effect as bright moon light alternated with darkness.

After a few moments, Nori turned and waited for him. Wide awake now, Danny hurried to catch up. When he reached her, he tried to speak, but she signaled for him to remain silent. Taking his hand, she led him at a brisk pace along the flat lava rocks toward the point. Expertly she picked her way among the scattered rocks and boulders. As a child she had spent almost every weekend playing on the beach and in the tidal pools that spread like a garland along this stretch of lava.

Danny followed, but as they walked he began to think, What's this all about? Why is she doing this? Why am I going along? Her hand felt soft and warm in his. He admired the graceful movements of her slender body and remembered her as she had looked when she was dancing a few hours earlier. Danny felt a swelling in his chest that made breathing difficult. No! Not again! Danny was sorry he had come. All the old wounds had reopened, and the salt spray seemed to sting in them.

Then they were around the point, cut off from the wind. As they walked away from the rocks, the sound of the pounding surf receded, and Danny could hear only the hiss of the waves hitting the beach and sliding swiftly over the fine sand. There in the shelter of the cove, Nori stopped.

The wind was dying down, and with the clouds swept away, Danny could see her clearly in the bright moonlight. "What do you want from me?" he asked her quietly. But sensing his weakness, he called upon his old friend anger and found the strength to be sarcastic. "Why you bring me here, eh? Your papa come plenty huhu wid you for go walking wid Pilipino boy. You no scared? Every time Pilipino fight." Danny walked toward Nori in a menacing way, talking very rapidly in a heavy Filipino accent. "Pilipino come plenty crazy, every time poke knife. Maybe so he like cut Japanee gorl in little pieces! Maybe so he like—"

"Danny, please stop; I want to tell you something."

"For why you no talk when we school? I every time in meeting wid you, in class wid you. I every time ask you for go any kind place wid me, but you no mo' time. You no time for me! For why you get so plenty time now? Maybe so, I no mo' time now! Maybe so, I like go sleeping nighttime. Mo' better you find nice Japanee boy who like talk, talk, in da nighttime, eh? Mo' better—"

Nori rushed up to Danny, put her arms around his neck, and kissed him full on the lips. At first, Danny made no move to take her in his arms. He just stood there with his hands hanging helplessly at his sides, feeling her soft lips on his and becoming aware of the tears running down her cheeks. He finally put his arms around her and felt her slump against him, dropping her face to his chest. For a long time she cried, her body shaking and her breath coming in gasps. After the sobbing finally stopped, Nori sat down on the sand, pulling Danny down to sit beside her. She took a deep breath and began to speak.

"Oh Danny, I love you. I've always loved you. These past

few weeks have been terrible for me. My father, oh you know my father." She began to cry again, then swallowed hard and continued. "He loves me, wants the best for me, but he's all mixed up. If he knew we were together alone like this, that you had held me in your arms and kissed me, I don't know what he'd do."

"Then why did you bring me here tonight?" Danny asked. "Don't you know how I feel about you? Was it to tell me to stay away? I was doing that already. I won't say I was over you. I'll never get over you, Nori, but at least I was angry at you, and that helped."

Nori took his hand between her two hands and held it tightly. "I told myself that we were just good friends, that we could always stay that way. After the dance in Lahaina, I knew that what I felt for you was more than friendship. The long talks we had on those Saturday nights before the prom were wonderful. I've missed them, Danny; I've missed them so much." Her voice caught, and her grip on Danny's hand tightened. "When you asked me to the prom, I panicked and came up with that weak excuse. When you got angry, I tried to get angry back, but I couldn't. You were hurt, and I had hurt you. I thought maybe it would be best for you to forget me, and maybe it is, but I couldn't stand it."

Tears were rolling down her cheeks again. "I don't know why I brought you here except, except . . . Oh, Danny, I couldn't live another minute having you look at me like you have for these past few weeks."

Danny reached out and took her in his arms. They talked on and on into the night, sharing feelings that they had never had the courage to share before. At last they decided that they had better go back to the group before they were missed. The clouds had moved in again, and darkness settled in among the rocks and stretched along the sand. They slowly made their way back to their blankets. By now everyone was asleep, but there was one pair of eyes that noticed their return. Those same eyes had seen Nori wake Danny and had not closed all the time they had been gone.

Chapter

24

Danny rejoined the group that got together at Evelyn Akagi's house on Saturday nights. Nori was there, as before. And, as before, Danny and Nori found time to be alone. They weren't alone as they had been that night at the cove, but they could talk with an openness and understanding they had never had before.

On Sunday afternoon, they hiked up to Mahana and looked out over its grassy slopes at Molokai to the north and Maui to the east. The day was crystal clear. The only clouds visible were off in the distance, hiding the crest of mighty Haleakala from their view. They sat on the grass-covered ground and talked about a future that they knew was mostly wishes and dreams.

"Up here I can forget for a little while that meeting alone like this is dangerous," Nori said. "My father is with Teru spearfishing right now. I know his habits so well." She glanced at her watch. "He'll still be diving by that big rock in the bay. He never quits before five o'clock, no matter how good the fishing is. He's always trying to break his record for the most fish taken in an afternoon in the bay."

"What does he do with the fish?" Danny asked.

"Oh, he doesn't waste them. He cleans them all and puts

them in a wet gunny sack. We keep a scale in the garage, and Daddy always weighs the sack, marks down the weight, then takes out enough fish for supper and gives the rest away."

"Who does he give them to?"

"Do you remember Susumu Kobayashi?"

"The man who caught his foot in the conveyor last year?"

"That's him. He loves fish. Daddy gives the fish to him. Susumu takes some and gives the rest to people he knows will like them. Some people who are having money problems really count on the fish Daddy gives them. He gives them other things too. We don't eat all those groceries I buy every week. Susumu's boys take the fish and food around on their bicycles."

"I've seen them do that. I thought they were doing it for the Buddhist church."

"That's what everybody else thinks too. Daddy doesn't want anyone to know about it. He says it's nobody's business. He warned Susumu that he wouldn't give him any more fish if he told."

"I don't understand your father, Nori. If he really cares about people, how can he do some of the things I've heard about, like sending old men back into the fields to work after many years in another job, just because they complained about something he told them to do? The men of this city are scared to death of Hiromi Satō. They obey him, but they hate him for the power he has over them."

"I don't understand it either, Danny. It's as if he's two different people. One is a kind, loving father who tries to help people. The other is a cruel and heartless person who crushes anyone who gets in his way. He rarely shows his bad side to me, but I know it's there. I just don't know what to do about it."

"What would he do if he found out about us?"

"I don't know. Maybe send me to Maui or Honolulu to finish high school."

"But we've only got a few months to go until graduation."

"I know, but he wouldn't be thinking clearly. He'd just decide what to do and do it, whether it made sense or not."

"Are you going to keep seeing me?" Danny asked.

"Yes, I am," she answered firmly. "I tried to choose him and forget you, and I almost lost you. I can't, I won't, do that again. If he finds out and sends me away, I'll have to go, but until then, I'll see you as much as I can."

Hiromi came to the surface, spouting like a humpback whale. He handed his spear gun to Teru and swam around behind the boat and climbed up the ladder.

Teru chuckled. "You get two fish dis time, one trip down. Too good, Hiromi. Some long time you stay, Teru count almost one whole minute. You no scared?"

"You just have to stay calm; that's the secret of long dives," Hiromi said confidently.

They sat quietly for a few moments while Teru removed the fish from the heavy string attached to the end of the spear. Hiromi took the time to get his breath back. Teru finally broke the silence. "What you gonna do about da big haole boss man, eh?"

Hiromi dried his face with a towel. "Well, I'm not going to let it destroy me like it did Pop. I've decided to produce so much pineapple that he'll forget I'm Japanese and how he feels about us. It's hard to hate somebody who is making you lots of money. That promotion is coming up this summer, and I'm going to have it if I have to work the people of Lanai to death."

"Some worker say you push too hard already. By 'n' by you get plenty trouble. If da worker strike, you no get dat promotion. Mo' better you take easy, eh? For why you like get promotion and go Honolulu? Push, push, busy, busy; you just like your fadda, Matsuo. Push, push, busy, busy kill my good friend Matsuo, by 'n' by kill you too, eh?"

"Look, Teru," Hiromi said gently. "I know you mean well. You're worried about me, and you don't need to be. I'm strong; I can take it." He smiled and cuffed Teru playfully. "Remember me? I swam the Maui Channel from Keomuku to Lahaina. You were in the boat by my side, saying, 'You can do it, Hiromi, keep going, don't give up.' I didn't give up then, and I'm not giving up now. I want that promotion. Nori's going to Honolulu to school, and I want to be there with her, to look after her. Also I want to beat the system and fight my way to a place in top management in this company. I want to do that for Pop. He earned it, and they took it away from him because he was Japanese and we were at war with them. Well, the war's over, and it's time they forgot about it."

"Forget is good," Teru said quietly. "Everybody be mo' better if dey can forget and start new, but sometime hard, eh? You remember dat Filipino who get your fadda promotion?"

"Balderas," Hiromi said bitterly.

"You no forget, eh?" Teru said. "Sometime I wonder if you t'ink all Filipino named Balderas."

Chapter
25

Nita was waiting in front of Akagi's Dry Goods, as usual, on Monday morning when Danny came by on his way to school. "You're late," she chided. "We'll have to hurry to make it to school on time."

Danny looked at his watch. It was late; no wonder he didn't see any other students walking by in the park. "I guess I overslept," he said awkwardly. He felt nervous and self-conscious being alone with Nita.

She chattered happily as they walked. "I heard about the big assembly on Thursday. I think it's wonderful that the plantation officials are coming in from Honolulu to honor the team. That was a great picture of you and your father in the *Star Bulletin*. I cut it out and put it in my scrapbook."

Danny became more and more uncomfortable as they got closer to the school. What if she meets me in the halls and in the cafeteria like she's been doing? he thought. Of course, she will—she has no reason to think anything has changed. Danny stopped and faced Nita. She seemed a little surprised but smiled up at him and waited for him to speak. "Nita, I owe you an apology," he said finally.

"Why?"

"I've been taking up all your time, and it's not fair. People are getting the idea that we're going steady or something. You're a beautiful girl, Nita. There are a lot of guys who would like to get to know you better who have been holding back because of me."

"I like spending time with you, Danny," Nita said. "I'm not interested in any other boys." She was looking directly into Danny's eyes, which was not helping him concentrate on what he was trying to do. Her face was a study in trust and affection. Danny felt awful.

"Nita, you should be having lots of different boyfriends. I shouldn't be tying up your time like I have been. In a little school like Lanai High, guys tend to stay away from a girl who seems to be spoken for."

Nita smiled and took Danny's hand. "You're so wonderful, Danny. You're worried about me, but you don't need to be. I'm not afraid of what other people think; let them think whatever they want to."

Danny extracted his hand from Nita's, took a deep breath, and began again. "I'm afraid I haven't been totally honest with you, Nita. I've given you every reason to feel that you're my special girl. It's my fault. I've misled you, Nita, and I'm sorry. I want us to be friends, but we can't be sweethearts."

Nita's expression changed in a moment. Her face flushed, and her brown eyes narrowed. The smile was gone, and her mouth formed a thin, hard line. "It's that Nori Satō, isn't it? She's been telling all the girls that she could have you back any time she wanted you. I guess she was right. I'm disappointed in you, Danny. I didn't think you'd be so easy to fool. Do you think she's really interested in you? Don't you know it's just because you won the championship and got your picture in the paper?"

Danny was surprised and disgusted. Any tender feelings he had for Nita evaporated as he heard her attacking Nori. He cut her off short. "Look, Nita, I'm sorry if I hurt you. It's all my fault: the prom, spending so much time together and everything. I made a mistake, and I apologize, but it can't be like it was with us; it just can't."

"You made a mistake all right, but not the one you think you made. You're living in some kind of a dream, Danny Tolentino, but don't expect me to be around when you wake up. You're on your own from now on!" She stalked away, leaving him standing alone feeling upset, but also relieved to have the confrontation over.

She handles her problems just like I do, Danny thought. She gets mad at them. It dulls the pain for a while, but what does it do to the person?

Danny expected some awkwardness when he ran into Nita at school. As it worked out, he rarely saw her. Her thorough knowledge of his schedule and habits had made arranging chance meetings possible several times each day at school. That same knowledge now made avoiding him easy, which she did.

Danny didn't spend a lot of time thinking about Nita after their talk on the way to school that day. Actually, there was very little room in his mind for anything but Nori; he thought about her constantly. She was always standing in the window of their first class each morning, waiting for him to arrive. She smiled and waved when she saw him, and he waved back, trying to appear nonchalant but feeling a warm flood of affection course through him. He arrived at school earlier now so they would have a chance to talk before class began. Their conversation was light and pleasant, but their eyes spoke of deep feelings and shared secrets. Danny almost forgot about Hiromi

Satō and the threat he was to them. They walked to their classes together and usually had an excuse to talk for a while after school. Danny had never enjoyed his student-body work with Nori more than the next few days as they prepared for the big assembly on Thursday.

The assembly was an big success. A public relations man from Dole had flown in with a reporter and photographer to handle the presentation of the jackets to the team members. Hiromi Satō and other local plantation officials were seated on the stage along with two members of Dole's board of directors from Honolulu. Many townspeople had come to watch the proceedings, and the fathers of the team members had been given half a day off to be in attendance. Since Danny was to be honored with the team, Nori conducted the assembly. Her beauty and poise greatly impressed the visiting officials, and they had the photographer include her in photographs they took of the team and the cheerleaders. They also took a picture of Danny and Nori together as president and vice-president of the student body.

The jackets were made of white nylon. On the back of each one was silk-screened "Lanai High School, Maui District Champs, 1954" in large green letters trimmed with gold. Each player's name was embroidered on the left front of his jacket, and a small golden pineapple emblem was sewn at the top of each sleeve. Each player was brought to center stage and helped into his new jacket; even Coach Manning got one. As each boy received his jacket, a shout went up from the audience.

"Way to go, Podogi!"

"Smile, Darrell!"

"Hey, Bernard, dey get your size jacket?"

When Jerry's turn came, they called, "Speech, speech!" The P.R. man from Dole, who was acting as master of ceremonies, went along and handed Jerry the microphone. "Sollybalaba-longdongding," Jerry exclaimed in psuedo-Filipino. "Dis one Pilipino boy no can tink good, eh?" He wiped imaginary perspiration from his brow. "Whew, holy smokes boy, some hot in here; almost I wish Wailuku win da game." The students roared. "Just make joke, eh?" Jerry said quickly and handed the microphone back.

When Coach Manning received his jacket, the entire audience rose and gave him a standing ovation. The M.C. offered him the microphone, but he pointed to the lump in his throat and shook his head. His eyes were filled with tears.

Nori closed the assembly with a tribute to the coach, the team, the students, and the people of Lanai. She asked the team to remain on stage for more pictures. Most of the students stayed to watch the photography session. As each flashbulb went off, the students cheered.

As Danny and Nori were walking to the cafeteria after the assembly, he noticed that she was pale and agitated. "What's wrong, Nori?" he asked. "Did the assembly make you nervous? You seemed so calm; I thought you were having a great time."

"It's not that," Nori said quietly. "It's something that happened afterwards. Danny, have you ever talked to Nita about me?"

"We talked on Monday morning. She was waiting for me at Akagi's like she has been the past few weeks. I apologized for leading her on and tried to part as friends. She started to say some things about you, but I wouldn't listen to them. When she left, she was pretty angry, but we haven't talked since then. What happened?"

"When I came down from the stage just now, I walked right by her. I said hello, and she didn't answer. She just looked at me. I've never had anyone look at me like that before, Danny. She just glared at me, and her eyes said, 'I hate you, Nori Satō!' "

Chapter
26

When Danny got home from school on Friday afternoon, he was surprised to see his father sitting in his chair in the living room watching television. Danny opened the door and stepped in. The shades were drawn, and shadows from the action on the screen flickered on the walls in the darkened room. Benito's face was lit by the screen.

"How come you're home so early, Pop?" Danny asked. Benito seemed not to hear him. He continued to stare vacantly into the TV.

"Pop?" he called a little louder. Still no answer. Danny walked over to the front of the television set, switched off the sound, and turned to face his father. "Are you all right, Pop? What's the matter?"

Benito finally looked up at him. His eyes seemed to have difficulty focusing. "Danny, you come home!" Benito seemed surprised to see his son.

"What's the matter, Pop? I've been talking to you. Didn't you hear me? Why are you home so early?"

"Oh Danny, Danny." Benito looked down into his lap and shook his head slowly from side to side. "For why you no listen, Danny? I every time tell you Japanee gorl no mo' good

for you. You no listen, Danny. Now we get too plenty trouble."
He shook his head sadly and muttered to himself in Filipino.
When he finally looked up, his eyes were filled with pain. "Satō
say, 'Take rest of day off, Benito; get plenty sleep. Nex' week
you go back pick pineapple in da field, dat what he say. Hard
for me go work in da field again, Danny! I no mo' young now!"

Satō had demoted Danny's father to a field worker. For
years he had helped with the loading of the barges at Kaumalapau Harbor. He was a respected man there, clever with
machinery and handy in making repairs. Even Satō couldn't
cut his pay, but he could make him pick pineapples in the red
dust of the fields until he got sick or quit. Benito had only two
or three years to go until retirement, but he would never
survive in the fields, and an early retirement would cut his
pension substantially.

"Forget Japanee gorl, Danny," the old man pleaded. "By
'n' by, maybe so Satō let me go back harbor."

Danny's hands formed into fists, and his fingernails bit into
his palms. What a coward Satō was, using his power over Benito
to punish Danny for daring to be interested in Nori. "Pilipino,
Pilipino poke knife!" He remembered the line from the hated
song. He could understand how a man might feel like reaching
for a knife to settle a score with someone like Satō, but the
Tolentinos didn't solve their problems with knives, not even
when the offender was a monster like Hiromi.

"Don't worry, Papa," Danny said softly. "I won't cause you
any more trouble." He went into his room, closed the door,
and cried bitter tears of frustration.

Nori rushed up the street toward her home. Aunt Mitsy
would be there cooking dinner. When Aunt Mitsy was visiting,
they were like a real family. Nori burst into the house, out of

breath. "Aunt Mitsy, I'm home! Sorry I'm late. What's for dinner?"

"I'm in the kitchen, Nori. Come in and help me."

As Nori entered the kitchen, the smell of chicken and long rice cooking on the stove filled the room. "You're making my favorite, I was hoping you would. Where's Annie?"

"Annie's mother is not feeling well. I told her to take the night off," Mitsy said. "Why don't you cut up some fresh vegetables for dinner?"

"What's the matter, Aunt Mitsy? You seem kind of quiet tonight."

Mitsy wiped her hands on her apron and looked out the window without speaking.

"Is something wrong? Is Daddy all right?"

"He's not hurt or anything, but I am worried about him, Nori. I'm afraid he's done something terrible. He's sent Benito Tolentino back to the fields."

The words struck Nori like a slap. "He did that to Mr. Tolentino? I don't understand."

"You've been spending a lot of time with Danny lately, haven't you?" Mitsy asked sadly.

Nori's face flushed and then went pale as she realized what had happened. "But why didn't he come to me?" she said, tears beginning to form in her eyes. "What has Mr. Tolentino got to do with us? Oh, I knew we were taking a chance of being caught, but I never thought he'd do anything to Danny's father."

"When he came home at lunchtime, I could tell he'd been drinking. It surprised me; he never drinks during working hours. He was so angry—I couldn't talk to him at all. He said something about you and Danny being alone down at the beach. He told me to tell you to stay home tonight, then he left and drove off toward the harbor in his jeep. What's this about you and Danny at the beach?"

"It was the night of the beach party—we went off to talk. It was my idea, not Danny's. I was losing him completely, and I just couldn't stand it."

"Why didn't you tell your father how you felt? Wouldn't it have been better that way?"

"I tried to talk to him when we went to Honolulu, but he was so down that night. I've never seen him like that. I was afraid he might fall apart before my eyes. He seemed to snap back after we got home, but I don't believe it. I think he's lost his confidence, Aunt Mitsy; I really do."

"He may have gone too far this time," Mitsy said. "I made some phone calls to find out what was going on. Everybody in town knows about it. Hiromi's been pushing the workers pretty hard, and I'm afraid he's made a lot of enemies. This business with Benito may be the last straw. Annie thinks there might be a strike. When he sobers up, he'll know it was a foolish thing to do, but he'll never admit it—he's too proud for that. There's been a change in him since the Honolulu meeting. He's always been a hard driver, but now he seems obsessed with production statistics. He works long hours and then pours over the reports every night trying to figure out a way to make them better."

Tears were running freely down Nori's cheeks, and she was trembling. "It's all my fault, Aunt Mitsy." She dropped down on a chair and buried her face in her hands. "What am I going to do?" she said, sobbing. "Oh, I've made such a mess of everything."

Mitsy moved closer and put her arm around Nori. "You were probably foolish to imagine you could keep your relationship with Danny a secret for long, but I can understand why you tried. Facing Hiromi when he's angry even scares me a little, and I practically raised him." Mitsy took a handkerchief out of her apron pocket and gave it to Nori.

Nori's sobs subsided, and she wiped her eyes. "I knew Daddy might find out and be angry. I thought he might even send me away to finish high school. It seemed worth the risk to keep from losing Danny like I was, but I never thought he'd do something like this. Mr. Tolentino's an old man, and he has heart trouble. He'll never make it out in the pineapple fields, Aunt Mitsy. It could kill him." The tears came again, and Nori buried her head in Mitsy's side.

Mitsy let Nori cry for a few moments before she spoke. "Nori, you're in no condition to face your father tonight. He said he might be late for dinner, but I don't know how late. I don't want him to come in and find you like this. I'll bring a tray to you in your room. Try to eat something, and then just stay in there tonight and give me a chance to talk to him."

When Hiromi finally arrived home, nearly an hour later, the dinner table was set for two. Mitsy could tell from his flushed face that he had been drinking again. "Where's Nori?" he asked.

"She was sick to her stomach," Mitsy said simply. "I gave her some tea and sent her to her room to rest."

Hiromi started for Nori's room. "I want to talk to her," he said.

"She's ill!" Mitsy said emphatically. "This is not the time to talk to her!"

To her surprise, Hiromi relented and sat down at the table. They ate in silence for a few minutes, then Hiromi looked around and spoke again. "Where's Annie? Everytime you come to see us, she takes a vacation. I may just look around for another housekeeper."

"You might have a hard time finding one after what you did to Benito Tolentino today. The people on this island think a lot of that little man."

"Don't get involved in this, Mitsy," Hiromi said evenly. "It's none of your concern."

"I'm already involved. I've known about Danny and Nori for quite a while. I think you're making lots too much of this, Hiromi."

Hiromi's eyes flashed. "You knew she'd spent the night at the beach alone with him and didn't tell me?"

"She didn't do anything of the kind. Half the students from Lanai High were there that night. They just went off to find a quiet place to talk. If you weren't so pig-headed, they could have had that talk right here in your own living room."

"Be careful, Mitsy," Hiromi warned.

"Somebody's got to talk to you, and everybody else on this island seems to be afraid of you. Hiromi, you're my favorite brother; everybody in the family knows it, but for the first time in my life, I'm ashamed of you. What have you got against Filipinos anyway? You'd think the racial prejudice we Japanese put up with during the war would have made you sick to death of it. It killed our father and broke our mother's heart. It has embarrassed you and me and our brothers a thousand times. Now you've lost the respect of the people of Lanai. If there's a strike, it could cost you your job. Worse still, you may have lost the love of your only daughter. Is it worth it?"

Hiromi Satō sat for a long time without saying anything. When he finally answered, he spoke very slowly and distinctly, and he looked straight into Mitsy's eyes. "You are my only sister, I love you, and so, this one time, I will overlook your meddling in my affairs. You knew about Danny and Nori; I assume Benito Tolentino knew about it too. It would seem that everyone on this island knew about it but me. I will not be made a fool of. The Filipinos obey me because they know what to expect if they refuse. If I ever show weakness, they'll tear me to pieces. They respect me because I am strong and consistent."

"It's not respect they feel for you, Hiromi, it's fear. You can't lead men with threats and intimidation. You certainly can't control a daughter that way for very long. How are you going to deal with Nori?"

"I'll talk to her when I get back from the beach tomorrow. Leave my daughter to me, Mitsy, and as for the Filipinos, I wouldn't worry about them. Most of their leaders owe me favors. Now, go to bed and forget all this doomsday stuff. I'm going to turn in early myself. I have a lot of fish to spear tomorrow."

Hiromi did turn in, as he said, but he rested little.

Chapter

27

The next two weeks were the worst Danny could remember since his mother's death. Every day his father went off in a bus or the back of a truck to work in the fields. Each night he returned exhausted and covered with a layer of red dust. By direct order from Hiromi Satō he was assigned the most menial tasks available: hoeing, planting, trudging behind the giant conveyors with the picking crews. A mature pineapple is not terribly heavy by itself, but multiplied by the thousands he picked, they became a mountainous burden to the little man. Sometimes he felt he could not lift one more, yet he continued day after day. There were times when he felt pain in his chest, and when the crew stopped to rest, he would dig out his little brown bottle, shake out a tiny white pill, and place it under his tongue. In a few moments, the pain would leave, and he could go on.

With basketball over, Danny came directly home from school. He took over all the household chores, even the cooking, and though he was not as good a cook as his father, Benito never complained.

"You some good boy," Benito said one night after Danny had refused to let him help clean up after dinner. "You take too good care your pop, eh? By 'n' by I come all lazy." He managed a feeble smile, rested his head back in the chair and tried to watch TV, but he was soon asleep.

Danny was standing at the sink, washing dishes. "Some good boy," he said under his breath. "If it weren't for me, you'd still be down at the harbor, working with your friends." Danny looked over his shoulder at his father. He seemed smaller and frailer, even in two weeks. Others had noticed too. "We've got to do something about Benito," they'd say. "It isn't right for him to be sent back to the fields after all these years."

But what was there to do? If they complained too much, they might also find themselves out in the fields, working beside Benito. And whom could they complain to? Hiromi had most of the foremen in his hip pocket. They had good pay and cushy jobs that they owed directly to Hiromi. The workers' only real weapon against Satō and his underlings was their power to call a strike. If they voted to walk off the job and let the pineapples rot in the fields, someone would have to listen to them, but it was a terrible price to pay for a chance to be heard. Strikes hurt everyone.

The last big one had cost Dole Pineapple millions, but it had hurt the workers too. They got a substantial raise in pay, but it took years to get back what they had lost in wages during the strike. Benito's friends agonized about his situation, but they had their families to think about and their own jobs. Maybe Hiromi was just making an example of Benito. Maybe he'd let him sweat it out in the fields for a few weeks and then send him back to the harbor.

Danny stopped seeing Nori outside of school. He was with her in classes they shared and in student council meetings and at no other time. Someone had told Hiromi about them being together at the beach. Whoever that someone was, Danny would make sure they had nothing new to report. On the first day that Benito went to the fields to work, Danny had to conduct a student council meeting after school. Though his mind was not on the business at hand, he got through it somehow. After the meeting was adjourned and everyone had left, Danny sat alone, working over some papers. His mind was so full of thoughts and confusion that he didn't notice when Nori reentered the room. Finally he looked up. "Nori," he said, alarmed.

"Nobody saw me come back," Nori said softly. She closed the door behind her and leaned up against it. For a few moments she was silent, then the words came tumbling out. "I had to talk to you. When I heard about your father—" She started to cry. "I felt so awful. I'd do anything, Danny, anything at all, but I don't know what to do. Daddy won't even talk about it. In fact, we hardly talk at all. It's like living alone." Tears streamed down Nori's cheeks. "If only I hadn't come to you on the beach that night, none of this would have happened. It's my fault, it's all my fault."

Danny took her in his arms. "It's my fault too, Nori. I wanted to come with you that night, wanted it more than I can tell you. I wanted to be with you as much as I could. I still want to, but we can't. Neither of us is really to blame. It's because of your father that everything is a mess. He hates Filipinos, and that's what I am; I can't change, and he won't."

Danny held Nori until she was calm again, then he spoke, "I don't think there's anything to do, except stop seeing each other completely. Maybe he'll decide to let Pop go back to the harbor." Danny looked down into Nori's tear-filled eyes. He felt a tightness in his throat that made speaking difficult. "Please know that I still feel the same way about you as I always have," he said. Nori nodded silently. Then he released her from his arms, and she turned and left the room.

Danny felt himself sinking into a depression. The sight of his father coming in the door each night after work was a soul-wrenching experience. He had hoped that Hiromi would relent after a couple of weeks; it had now been three, and there was no indication that his attitude had changed.

Benito never went down to the bowling alley to visit with his friends in the evening anymore. He took a shower, had some dinner, dropped into his chair in front of the TV, and soon fell asleep. On the weekends, he seemed to recover a little, but by Monday night he was going downhill again. By Friday night he could barely make it home from the park where the bus dropped the field workers off.

"How did it go today?" Danny asked as he opened the door for his father. It was Friday night, and he had heard Benito kicking off his boots and dropping them on the back porch.

"Not so too bad today, Danny," Benito croaked. "I t'ink maybe so I come used to dis hard work, eh?" He smiled up at Danny, and Danny smiled back. The relatively dust-free areas of his face, where his goggles and mask fit, emphasized his mouth and eyes and turned his warm smile into a clown's grin.

"Why don't you take off your clothes right here in the kitchen," Danny suggested. "I'll put them in the hamper and wash them all tomorrow. You have a shower and get ready for dinner, okay?"

Benito chuckled under his breath as he struggled out of his clothing. "You make me remember Rosvena, jus' den. When I first bring her Lanai, I every day work in da field, come home like dis, all over dust. She say jus' like you, 'Benito, take off clothes, no make mess, eh? Try hurry, clean up quick; by 'n' by dinner all burn up.' I no tired den, not like now. Sometime we go dance Saturday night at da Federation Hall. You mama some plenty good dancer, you bet; me too! All kind taxi dancer like dance wid me. Taxi dancer come from Maui on Saturday night. Dey dance wid any kind Pilipino bachelor for money, but sometime dey say, 'Hey you, Benito Tolentino, you too much good dancer! You like dance wid me? No need pay me, eh? I dance for fun.' "

"Would Mom let you dance with the taxi dancers?" Danny asked.

"Oh no! Holy smokes, her face come all red!" Benito was laughing impishly. Then in the midst of his laughing, he began to cough. At first it was like part of the laughter, but it persisted until his eyes streamed and he dropped exhausted into a chair. Danny brought him a glass of water, and he drank it down in gulps. "Dat red dust no mo' good in here," he said, pointing to his chest.

"I'm worried about you, Pop," Danny said earnestly as he mopped his father's face with a cool cloth. "We've got to do something. Maybe I should move away for a while. If I was gone, maybe Satō would let you go back to the harbor."

Benito sat up straight in the chair. "No talk like dat, Danny. You go school, graduate, give speech in graduation, make your pop proud. No talk go away. Dat Hiromi push push everybody, not jus' me. He go too far, I t'ink so. We get meeting Saturday night at da Federation Hall. Some guys like have a strike. Dey say, 'Come talk at da meeting, Benito. You say strike, everybody strike.' I don't know, Danny. Too easy call strike, not so easy call strike off. Nobody work, pineapple rot, some big mess dis one."

"A big mess caused by one man," Danny said bitterly. How he hated Hiromi Satō. Why did God allow such a man to live? Rosvena Tolentino, who never did anything but good, died of a burst appendix; his father had a bad heart. Why couldn't Hiromi have appendicitis or heart trouble? Why was it the innocent who always suffered?

Chapter
28

Hiromi Satō sat alone in the saimin shop on that Friday evening, drinking beer and looking out the window at the park. He saw the buses stop in front of Akagi's Dry Goods to drop off the workers from the fields. The wind had been blowing all day, so they were dustier than usual. Most of them were in good spirits at the end of the week, and some of the younger ones trotted off toward their homes apparently with energy to spare.

One small figure moved very slowly indeed, and Hiromi recognized him immediately by the blue cap he wore. Most of the workers at the harbor wore blue caps like that. They were all close friends and liked being identified as a group. Benito's cap was only barely recognizable because of the thick coating of red dust that covered it, but that was him all right. As he watched Benito trudge up the street toward his home, Hiromi felt some guilt pangs, but he took a long pull at the bottle in his hand and shook them off.

He glanced at the stack of papers on the table in front of him. They were the production reports for the past three months, and they were very impressive. Included with them was a letter from the home office congratulating him for managing the most efficient plantation in the Dole system during that period. The letter was signed by the chairman of the board of directors. It's working, he thought. They can't help but notice numbers like these, and it's just the beginning. Wait till they see our production for the next three months.

The front door swung open, ringing the little bell attached to it, and Teru walked into the shop. Hiromi waved him over to his table and then turned in the direction of the kitchen. "Hey Sammy, bring us a couple more beers."

"Cold beer sound good to me," Teru said as he sat down. Sammy soon appeared with two bottles, which he opened and set before them, then he disappeared back into the kitchen. Teru took a drink, staring out the window at the workers walking to their homes. Hiromi made a couple of attempts at small talk, but Teru only nodded, sipped at his drink, and continued looking out the window. Plainly, he had something on his mind.

When his beer was gone, Teru finally turned to Hiromi and spoke, pointing with his empty bottle in the direction of two young men passing in front of the shop. "In da old days, I look same like dem, Hiromi. Your papa too. We work every day in da pine field, from early in da morning to late at night, dust in da ear, dust in da nose, dust in da mout'. We no squawk, we young strong boys. Work all day, play all night, nothing to us, eh? One day your papa say, 'Teru, dis life jus' fine for young fella, but by 'n' by we come old. When we come old, dis life kill us dead, eh? We gotta climb up in dis company, so when we old, we can take litty bit easy. When you papa was boss here on Lanai, he remember da old days in da field. He no send old man out to pick pineapple, eh?"

Hiromi stiffened in his chair. "Look, Teru, I know what you're driving at. It's Benito Tolentino, isn't it? Well, he crossed me, and I can't let him get away with it. His boy was messing around with my daughter behind my back. Benito knew about it, and so did half the town. He made a fool out of me, and I can't let it pass. You get the most out of Filipinos just like you get the most out of mules—you dangle a carrot in front of them, and you carry a big stick. Benito's been eating carrots down at the harbor for years. Maybe he thought I wouldn't use the stick on him, maybe a lot of people thought that. Well, they're wrong, and now they know they're wrong. Oh, I might send him back to the harbor sometime, but not now, and not soon. Every time he crawls on that bus, goes out to the field, and comes back covered with dust, somebody sees him and learns an important lesson: don't cross Hiromi Satō!" His fist came down hard on the table, and Sammy Lee peeked out from the kitchen to see what was wrong.

"Maybe dey learn somet'ing else too," Teru said grimly. "Maybe dey learn you not fair. Maybe dey learn you no care nothing 'bout people."

"Well, it's working," Hiromi said. He picked up the sheaf of papers and shook them at Teru. "These are the production figures for the past three months. They're good, and they're going to get better."

"Maybe dey stop altogether, you no change da way you treat people, work for you," Teru warned.

"You mean a strike? Look, if I got scared everytime somebody mentioned the word *strike,* I'd never get anything done. They're not going to strike over one old Filipino getting dusty; they're too busy worrying about themselves. They feel bad for Benito, sure, but not bad enough to cut off their paychecks."

"Hiromi, I t'ink your papa make one big mistake. He never let you work out in da field. He wait so long for son dat he come soft in da head when he finally get one. He take you wid him everywhere, teach you all kind stuff about da plantation, but he no teach you how da worker feel, eh?"

Hiromi bristled. "I work harder than any of them! I'm up in the morning before they are, and I work later, sometimes past midnight. When they get off that bus and go home, they're free until they get on it again in the morning. I'm never free, never done, I never stop working."

Teru didn't answer, he just looked at Hiromi with sad eyes and slowly shook his head. Finally he stood up to leave. "T'anks for da beer, eh?" he said and turned to go.

"Are you going down to Manele with me tomorrow? I've got a new spear gun I want to try out." Hiromi flushed involuntarily as he heard himself speak the words. He suddenly felt like a child trying to deflect a parent's disapproval by bringing up something pleasant in the middle of a disagreeable conversation.

"Not tomorrow," Teru said, without looking back. "My boat need some work, eh? Maybe another day we go." He left the shop, got into his pickup, and drove away.

Hiromi felt empty. Teru was his oldest and best friend and had been his father's best friend too, a friend whose loyalty neither of them had ever doubted. He had always been there when Hiromi needed him, a quiet, firm support that he could count on. Now Teru was ashamed of him, ashamed of his preoccupation with production figures and quotas, ashamed of his callousness in dealing with personnel. The Benito Tolentino affair had been the last straw. Benito was Teru's friend too.

Hiromi looked at his watch; it was almost dinner time. He remembered that Mitsy would be at the house when he got there, over from Maui for the weekend. She came almost every weekend now and spent hours alone with Nori while he worked. He had always loved having her visit, but lately he had begun to resent her too. She was against him in this Benito Tolentino thing. She had never said anything more after that first night, but her unspoken disapproval almost shouted at him from her eyes. And Nori, Nori was like a shadow, a ghost who haunted the home they shared together. She was respectful and obedient, but distant and aloof. She responded when he asked her questions, but she never volunteered anything, never shared her life with him.

Hiromi felt a strange, unfamiliar feeling coming over him, and it frightened and confused him. He had been in tight situations before but had always felt secure in his resolve and confident of the outcome. He thought of the long swim across the Maui Channel, those many hours in the water, stroking endlessly, rhythmically, feeling no progress. He had closed his mind to thoughts of the depths that he passed over and the teeming life beneath him that he could not see. Once he had seen a dorsal fin out of the corner of his eye, and then another, and another, but soon they were chasing each other over and through the waves, looking more like a long sea serpent than a school of porpoises. He had remembered the old fisherman's saying, "Where you see porpoises, you never see sharks." It had comforted him as he swam on. He couldn't see how far he had come, and he couldn't see how far he had to go, but he could see Teru rowing ahead of him in the boat, and he could hear his voice.

"Dat's good, Hiromi, nice an' easy, eh? You come long ways, boy, too good! Not so far to go now, take easy, eh?"

Hiromi had wanted to quit many times, but Teru's voice urged him on, and the thought of Mitsy and the rest of the family waiting in Lahaina, straining to see Teru's boat, hoping and praying for him, sustained him. And he had finally walked ashore, unaided, and given them all wet hugs, and his name had been repeated over and over in the cheers and shouts of the onlookers.

Now he felt alone, abandoned by Mitsy, Teru, even his own daughter, swimming alone in a dark sea of doubt. His goals, once so clear and distinct, now seemed murky and shapeless. He sat for several minutes leafing through the production reports, pretending to read them. Then, all at once, he shook off the gloomy feelings, sat up straight in his chair, drained the dregs of the last bottle, and shouted at Sammy, "Sammy, come and get your money before I leave without paying and make you sue me for it."

Sammy hurried in and started to count the bottles. Hiromi pulled a large bill out of his wallet and handed it to him. "This ought to cover it. Keep the change." Sammy smiled broadly and pocketed the bill. He stood by respectfully as Hiromi pushed himself up from the table and left the shop. "Well, there's one guy on Lanai who doesn't hate me tonight," Hiromi said under his breath as he crawled into his jeep and started up the road to his house.

The drive home seemed to clear Hiromi's mind and strengthen his resolve. He talked to himself as he drove. "I'm doing what I have to do. If Teru and Mitsy and Nori don't understand, I can't help it. The problem of finding someone to watch the boat while I spearfish is a small one. I think I know someone who would be thrilled to join me for a day's fishing, and he's Filipino!" He laughed sarcastically. "That ought to quiet the people who say I'm prejudiced against them."

Chapter

29

Danny went to bed early that night, but he didn't sleep much. He kept seeing his father standing by the kitchen door, undressing. He looked so thin and vulnerable, like an undernourished child. Somehow, Danny had been sure that when his father came home that night he would have news of his transfer back to the harbor, but it hadn't happened. How long would Hiromi keep him there, another week, another month? Sleep finally came sometime after one o'clock, but about dawn, Danny woke and realized that he would sleep no more that night.

He decided to go down to the beach, alone, without Podogi and Bernard. He needed time to think. Being near the ocean always calmed him and made him feel more secure. The sight of the swells rolling in toward the shore on a windless day, one by one, unhurried, dependable, and neverending, was comforting to him. He needed their soothing influence now more than anytime in his life.

The dark was just starting to give way to light when Danny slipped out of the house carrying his spearfishing gear. He left a short note for his father: "I'm going to the beach. I won't be late. Don't worry. Love, Danny."

When he reached the edge of town, he began to jog toward the road leading to Manele Beach. It was cool, and dew covered the pineapple fields that lined the road. The fields through which he was running were old growth, and the fruit that remained was overripe and beginning to ferment. In the heat of the day, flies swarmed over the decaying pineapples. A heavy, sickish sweet odor filled Danny's nostrils as he ran. Soon the tractors, with their huge disc plows dragging behind, would roll over those fields, turning the thousands of pineapple plants into mulch. Maybe Satō thinks of Pop like an old-growth pineapple plant, Danny mused. Something to use and then plow under and forget.

He ran past a field of immature plants that had not yet begun to bear fruit. A field of mature-bearing plants in the distance bristled with fruit ready for picking. Danny thought about how the young plants were like the kids his age, too young and weak to take seriously, how only the producers mattered, like those in the other field. A picking machine with its long conveyor had been left in the field, ready to begin harvesting the field on Monday. After three or four pickings, those plants would pass their prime and be sprinkled with rotten fruit and flies. Then it would be time for them to be destroyed.

Danny ran on without stopping. The grade began to increase, and he felt his lungs burning. Got to hurry, he thought. Hurry to get to the beach, hurry to kill the fish with your spear, hurry back to Pop, hurry to break Nori's heart, hurry to break your own, hurry to grow up, bear your fruit, and be turned under like a field of rotten pineapples.

A night's sleep had not cooled his desire to strike back at Satō, but what could he do that would not make matters worse? He ran on and on, finally stopping to rest at the top of the hill overlooking the winding road to the beach. He was tired of thinking about Satō and tried to turn his thoughts to other things, but every part of his life was affected by the man. Every direction he turned seemed to lead into a stone wall, and the name of that wall was Hiromi Satō.

Danny stopped briefly at the white sand beach and watched the waves, but they seemed to have lost their calming influence on him. He continued past the beach to the rocks and around the point to the other side, near where he and Nori had spent the evening talking. Thoughts of that night made his heart swell within him. He remembered Nori's warm kiss on his lips, the taste of her salty tears, the hours of talking, and the joy of understanding and acceptance.

He put on his gear and slowly worked his way into the water. Pushing off the rocks, he launched out into the bay. He cleared his snorkle and paddled slowly along the surface, conscious of the cool water, the sound of his own breathing, and the faint salty taste in his mouth. The small fish who lived near the surface moved quickly away as he approached. Deeper down, the larger fish swam lazily along, paying no attention to him at all. His spear gun was loaded, the surgical tubing stretched tight, ready to send its projectile hissing through the water, but Danny was not really thinking about spearing fish at the moment. He moved resolutely toward the rock. He wanted to be alone, and the rock had always served him well as a place of solitude. Once there, Danny could position himself where he could look out to sea and be hidden from the view of anyone on the beach.

Danny didn't sit in his favorite spot by the pool this time. He climbed up into a small niche that shielded him from the bay and gave him something to lean against. He unloaded his spear gun, laid his equipment aside, and stared off to the southeast over Kahoolawe at the misty shape of towering Mauna Kea, a hundred miles away on the Big Island. The waves crashed below him, and the white foam seemed to hang in the air briefly before falling on the black lava rock and running back into the sea. The sun was getting hot, but the breeze from the ocean cooled him as he leaned back against the warm rock. He felt tired, so very, very tired. Finally, he fell into a troubled sleep.

Danny's sleep was disturbed by the sound of a motorboat coming toward the rock. He shifted his position and drifted off again, the throbbing of the motor blending with the sound of the surf. When the motor stopped directly behind the rock, Danny came up with a start. Sleeping in the sun had left him sluggish and confused. Instinctively he knew he didn't want to see or talk to anyone, but for a few moments he forgot why. His perch on the rock was about twenty feet above the water, and the boat was behind the rock, so Danny was hidden from view. He decided to see who was there. As he peeped over the edge, he felt the blood leave his face and pool in his stomach. In the boat was Hiromi Satō and someone else who looked familiar but whom Danny couldn't immediately identify. The other man was fully clothed and wore a broad straw hat. They were directly below Danny, and he could hear their conversation.

"Hey, Presa, drop the anchor, eh?" Hiromi said gruffly. "I'll show you how to poke lots of fish in a short time."

Nita's father, Danny realized. He had seen him at several of the games, sitting near Nita and her friends. What he was doing out in a boat with Hiromi, when he obviously didn't know how to spearfish? Satō did take men from the plantation fishing with him some times, even Filipinos. It was like an initiation into Hiromi's inner circle. After one of these sessions they might find themselves with a job at the maintenance shop instead of working out in the field. The workers on the plantation joked about it. When someone was promoted, they would ask the lucky man, "Hey, you been poke fish wid Satō lately?"

Suddenly it all became clear. Presa had done Satō a great service. The look Nita had given Nori on the day of the award assembly made sense now, as well as Nita's parting threat on that Monday morning after the big game when he had broken up with her. She had seen Nori and Danny leave together that night at the beach and had used her father to get the word to Satō.

Danny felt trapped. He wondered what to do. I can't just go poke fish with him like nothing has happened, he thought. I guess I could swim back across the bay and go home. Satō's underwater, and Mr. Presa is so busy thinking about a promotion that he probably wouldn't even notice. He shook his head and mumbled to himself, "Satō doesn't own this rock, or this bay, or the fish that live here. He doesn't own this island, and he doesn't own me. It looks like he owns the Presa family, but what do I care, they just climbed out of the trees last week."

Finally, Danny decided to stay right where he was. He rehearsed in his mind what he would say if he were discovered. If he comes up here, I'll ask him why he sent Pop back to the fields. If he says anything about Nori, I'll tell him what I think about that too. Danny was nervous; he was even a little afraid, but he was not going to cut and run, not from someone like Hiromi Satō.

Danny watched from the rock as Hiromi dove time after time. He would hang on to the side of the boat and take several deep breaths, then pull himself down toward the bottom of the bay with the anchor rope. Mr. Presa would watch the water intently until he reappeared at the surface, sometimes with a fish wriggling at the end of his spear. He'd hold up the spear, and Presa would remove the fish and reload the spear gun while Hiromi rested. After some more deep breaths, Satō would return to the bottom.

In spite of himself, Danny had to admire the catch that began to pile up in the boat and the length of time Satō could stay underwater. No mahnini or black mamo for Hiromi Satō; he liked the blue uhu and similar sized fish. Danny knew the skill required to bag these fish, and he was impressed. He began to count the number of seconds that Hiromi stayed underwater. He had heard that he could stay under for a full minute. It was never quite that long, but thirty to forty seconds was common for a round trip to the bottom.

After a while, Mr. Presa helped him into the boat for a rest and was almost pulled overboard himself. Satō laughed and splashed water on the fully dressed man. "Sure you don't want to try this, Presa? It's easy, as you can see." Presa shook his head, picked up the last fish, and put it into the gunny sack they were using instead of a creel. He dipped the sack of fish in the ocean to cool them and then dropped them back in the bottom of the boat. "Don't drop those fish overboard, Presa, or I'll make you swim after them." Satō laughed again in a derisive way. Presa said little except to compliment Satō on his skill.

I'd rather work in the fields my whole life than lick Satō's boots like that, Danny thought with disgust. He makes me ashamed to be a Filipino! His mind filled with pictures that tortured him: of Benito working out in the fields, of Nori crying with shame at what her father had done, of the self-satisfied smirk that must be on Nita's face when she saw him avoiding Nori at school. The knot in his stomach grew tighter and tighter.

He heard a splash below him and looked down to see Hiromi back in the water beside the boat. Satō took his deep breaths again and disappeared into the blue depths surrounding the anchor rope. Danny counted the seconds slowly to forty-five, fifty-five, a full minute. Presa was on his hands and knees, trying to look down along the rope to see if Satō was surfacing. When his count reached seventy seconds, Danny knew Satō was in trouble.

Immediately Danny pulled on his goggles and fins and hurled himself out from the overhanging rock to clear a shelf of coral directly below him. He landed right by the boat. The nearly hysterical Presa nearly toppled over. Danny paid no attention. He hung onto the boat as Satō had done, filled his lungs with air as deeply as he could, and using the anchor rope, pulled himself down, hand over hand, toward the bottom of the bay. The first thing he saw as he approached the anchor were the bottoms of Satō's swim fins facing upward. Mr. Satō seemed to be grasping a rock. There was no movement other than that caused by the current. It was as if he had gone to sleep holding on to the rock and had forgotten to let go.

Danny held his nose and blew, equalizing the pressure inside his ears that threatened to burst his eardrums. He forced himself to go deeper, and as he did, he saw a puff of scarlet emit from the wrist of the hand clutching the rock. The hand was deep in a hole in the rock. As Danny watched, a Moray eel the size of a man's thigh slipped out of the hole, its jaws locked firmly on the hand. It immediately withdrew again, slamming Hiromi's seemingly lifeless body against the sharp rock. Blood oozed from gashes on his forehead and shoulder.

Danny knew there was no use trying to pull Hiromi free; the eel would only pull back harder. He grabbed hold of a rock near the hole, drew his knife, and waited. His mind buzzed with questions and doubts. How long can I stay down? I held my breath for a minute and twenty seconds once, but that was lying on the beach, knowing that all I had to do was open my mouth and breathe when I couldn't stand it any longer. How long have I been down here now? Maybe Hiromi's already dead. Maybe I should go to the surface and get a fresh breath; it won't help him if we both drown.

The blood was beginning to flow freely from the arm, billowing out of the hole as the current gently rolled Satō's body back and forth. As he watched his enemy turning and twisting helplessly in the current, the blood staining the water around them both, Danny felt his hatred diminish and finally die out. He choked down the urge to release the air he held trapped in his lungs. It would bring him momentary relief, he knew, but after that would come the demand for air that could not be denied. He forced himself to wait a few seconds longer. Then, all at once, the eel came out again, its neck pulsating slowly. Danny saw the mangled hand locked in its needlelike teeth. Danny slashed at the neck with his knife. The ghastly mouth opened, releasing Satō's hand, and the moray drew back into its hole. Danny clawed for the surface, dragging the unconscious Satō behind him.

Presa helped him get Satō into the boat. Danny scrambled in after him and threw off his fins and goggles. He tore a strip of cloth from a shirt he found in the boat and applied a tourniquet to the arm, above Satō's bleeding hand. Then he tried every technique he had learned in Scouting to revive an unconscious man. Finally with a shudder and a gasp, Satō began to disgorge sea water. He coughed and gagged, but at last he started to breath.

By the time Satō began to revive, Presa had already pulled up the anchor and started the motor. They headed toward Black Sand Beach as fast as the boat would go. The sight of Satō's mangled hand seemed to unnerve Mr. Presa. He looked away as Danny wrapped it tightly in a towel and released the tourniquet. Hiromi's eyes were open, but he made no attempt to move or speak. He seemed to know it was best for him to remain calm and allow himself to be cared for.

"Lucky you come, Danny," Mr. Presa shouted. "I no good swim. I no good for save life too. Mr. Satō, he be okay?"

"I hope so. We have to get him to the hospital as soon as possible. Did you come in Satō's jeep?"

Presa nodded and pointed toward the beach where a jeep was parked.

"Beach the boat as close to the jeep as you can. Every minute counts!"

Presa took Danny at his word and followed the surf into the shore. Gravel and sand grated against the bottom of the boat as they came to a jolting halt.

"Don't worry about the boat. Help me get him into the jeep. Are the keys inside?"

"I t'ink so he leave 'em," Presa answered, jumping into the shallow water and pulling the boat higher up on the beach. They dragged and carried Satō to the jeep and lifted him into the back seat. Presa climbed in the back and put Hiromi's head in his lap.

Danny drove at high speed up the curving road to the crest of the Palawai crater, then on through the pineapple fields to Lanai City and the plantation hospital. When Satō was safely under the care of the nurses, and Dr. Chuck had been called for, Danny left without a word, leaving Mr. Presa to make the explanations.

Chapter

30

"Wake up, Danny," he heard his father call from the other side of the door. "Japanee girl come for see you. She long time wait for you wake up. You pau sleep yet, you finish sleep already?"

Danny looked at the window through half-closed eyes. "It's still dark outside," he said to himself. "But I can't sleep in; I have to get up early this morning. I'm going to the beach to poke fish." He felt confused and fuzzy. He closed his eyes and dozed off... He was at the beach, out on the rock asleep. Something kept waking him up—it was the sound of a motorboat behind the rock. The sound finally stopped, and he went back to sleep. He was falling off the rock; no, he was jumping off the rock, with his fins and goggles on. The bottom of a boat was between him and the sun. He was looking up through thirty feet of water. He looked down and saw Hiromi Satō's swimfins floating up toward him. There was an eel, a big one with puffs of scarlet billowing from its mouth. "Too late, too late for Satō," he heard himself saying. Then a sound from far away, a rapping on wood, a muffled knock, perhaps from up there in the boat.

Benito was knocking insistently on his bedroom door. "Danny? Girl wait long time. You wake up now, Danny, okay?"

He sat up in bed, still confused, the nightmarish dream still vivid in his mind. Slowly he remembered—the crimson cloud spreading out from the injured hand; the knife slashing at the eel; the interminable trip to the surface, dragging the unconscious Satō, seeing the surface like a wavy mirror so far above him; the little convulsive reflex actions of his lungs trying to breath underwater; his legs feeling like stone; the sweet relief as his head burst free from the water and air filled his lungs; the effort of hoisting Satō up toward Mr. Presa as they worked to load him into the boat.

The door opened and light flooded the room. "Too much sleep you get, Danny. How you gonna sleep nighttime?"

Beyond his father's silhouette, Danny could see Nori sitting with an open book in her lap. "I'll get up," Danny said. He stood up and walked to the doorway.

"I'm sorry your father woke you, Danny," Nori said softly. "I asked him not to. I could have waited longer."

"Seem like you feeling fine, eh, Danny? I get Federation meeting in clubhouse; I late already." Benito walked to the door and stopped. He turned to his son. "You make you pop plenty proud. You too good boy. Satō no like Tolentinos, but you betcha, Danny Tolentino save his life." He stepped forward and hugged his bewildered son. Then he hurried out the door.

"I told him, Danny," Nori said. "He wanted to know what was going on."

Danny nodded. He felt close to tears. "I still don't believe it myself. Is your father all right?"

"He's slept most of the afternoon. I stayed with him and fed him an early supper of broth and crackers after he woke up. They'll probably keep him in the hospital for a few days— he's lost a lot of blood, and there's a chance of infection. Later, they'll have him go to Honolulu for an operation to repair his hand, but he's safe, and he's alive, and you're the one who saved him." Nori took Danny's hand and hugged his arm. "If it hadn't been for you—" She began to cry.

"Oh Danny, I was looking over our yearbooks while I waited for you to wake up. We've been together a long time. It's going to be hard for me to leave next fall. Mostly it will be hard to leave you, maybe harder than I can stand. I love you, Danny. I owe you so much. You're the reason my life here has been so wonderful. Now I owe you even more. You've given my father back to me. You saved his life, you really did!"

"Nori, I feel a little guilty hearing you talk like this. I hated your father for what he did to Pop. I was so angry, I felt like killing him, not saving his life, but when I saw him down in the water so helpless, my anger left me. All I could think about was trying to help him."

"When I heard about Daddy sending Benito back to the fields, I was angry too. Maybe a little anger is good for me. It helped me make a decision that I've been trying to make for a long time."

"What's that?"

"To live my own life. I've been so afraid of what Daddy would think that I've been hiding my feelings and my actions from him. I even made you part of my dishonesty. What happened to your father is really my fault."

"Don't blame yourself," Danny said. "Hiromi Satō is a scary guy. Nobody wants to take him on."

"I made up my mind to talk to him, to tell him the truth and to stand my ground."

The grave, determined look on Nori's face seemed strangely out of place. A picture of this petite young woman confronting her powerful father flashed through Danny's mind, and he felt admiration and dread at the thought. "Have you decided when to talk to him?"

"I already have," Nori said. "After I gave him his supper, I told him how happy I was to see him feeling better. 'When you're strong enough,' I said, 'I need to talk to you about something.'

"He smiled at me and said, 'I'm not doing anything right now. Why don't you go ahead and tell me what's on your mind?' Then he waited for me to speak. I've never seen him so calm and open-minded. It was like what I had to say was the most important thing in the world.

"I started very carefully to talk to him, and soon it all came flooding out: my concern for what he was becoming, my fears about his drinking, my feelings for you." Tears ran freely down Nori's cheeks, but she continued. "I told him that I didn't want to forget my mother. I want to remember her and talk about her and think about how wonderful she was. I told him that I've been painting a portrait of Aunty Mitsy and that when it is done, I want to paint one of Mother from the picture that he keeps in his drawer and hang it on the wall in my room. I expected him to explode, but he just nodded and let me talk. I told him that I'm tired of hiding my life from him, that I want to stop being afraid of him, that I want to love him and have him love me. Oh, Danny, I told him everything, and he listened to me!"

There were tears in Danny's eyes too when she finished. He took her two hands in his and held them. "What did he say?" he asked.

"He said I could use our spare bedroom for a studio and bring mother's easel down from the attic. He told me to use her paints if they were still good and buy whatever else I needed. I know it may not last, this new openness, once he gets well and starts to work again, but maybe it will be better than it was, and maybe it will improve. He wants to see you. He told me to come and get you and not to come back without you. Will you come?"

For a long moment they just looked at each other. "Yes, I'll go with you," Danny finally said.

By the time they got to the hospital, Danny was wondering if he had made the right choice. The words from Satō Danny had overheard in the saimin shop kept coming to mind. What if Satō would humiliate him in front of Nori?

Nori took hold of Danny's hand as they walked into Hiromi's hospital room and led him right up to the bed. Hiromi was sleeping, but he woke up when he heard their footsteps. He was groggy from his medication but made an effort to be alert. He extended his good hand; the other was swathed in bandages. Danny took the hand and was surprised at the firmness of the grip of this man who had come so close to dying.

"Hello, Danny," Hiromi said.

"Hello, Mr. Satō," Danny answered.

Hiromi gestured toward the glass of water on the stand near his table. Nori helped him take a drink. He cleared his throat and began to speak. "You saved my life, Danny. I'm grateful."

"Anyone would have done what I did, Mr. Satō," Danny said.

"I wonder. And I was down pretty deep. There aren't many on the island who could have done what you did. I thought my life was over." He looked down at his bandaged hand and said nothing for a moment, then as if reliving the experience in his mind, he began to speak slowly. "At first, everything seemed to happen so fast. The eel grabbed my hand, and I lost my knife. I jerked and strained to get loose, then things slowed down. My hand sort of went numb; I couldn't feel the teeth anymore. It sounds strange, but I stopped being afraid of that ugly monster, and I remember thinking 'what comes next?' "

"Were you still conscious when I came down?" Danny asked.

"I heard the sound when you hit the water and saw you pull yourself down past me with the anchor rope, then I blacked out. I probably looked as though I was already dead. There are plenty of men on this island who would have been glad to leave me there. You had some pretty good reasons yourself to do just that. I woke up in the boat while you were wrapping my hand." Hiromi's eyes misted slightly, and his voice became husky. "I still wondered if I'd make it, but it looks like I'm going to."

Nori sat down on the bed and took his hand. "Tell Danny about your plans for his father."

"Benito goes back to the harbor on Monday morning. When Koizumi retires next month, Benito will take over as a supervisor. He's been doing a supervisor's work anyway; it's about time he got paid for it."

Amazed, Danny could only smile and nod.

"Danny, I've been prejudiced against Filipinos for years. I'm ashamed to admit it, but it's true. Doctor Chuck said my hand will never be the same. I'll be able to use it, but it won't be a pretty thing to look at. Well, every time I look at that hand, I'm going to remember how close I came to death and how a Filipino boy saved me from it."

Danny felt a hand grip his shoulder and turned to see Teru smiling his ragged smile at him. "Some lucky, you stay down by da rock poking fish today. Almost Hiromi finish, I t'ink so." He drew his thumb across his throat. "How you feel, Hiromi?"

"Much better, but I'm afraid you'll have to fish alone tomorrow." Hiromi said.

"You tell Danny about Benito?" Teru asked.

"I just told him."

Teru chuckled. "Some good! Maybe Danny like go fish with Teru sometimes, make extra money for college. Teru get too old for fish alone all time, and my partner get hand all smash up." He gestured at Hiromi.

A thin smile crossed Hiromi's lips. "If the workers strike, I may need that job, Teru."

"Are they going to strike?" Danny asked.

"Da Filipino workers meet tonight at da Federation clubhouse. Maybe so dey like have strike, eh?" Teru said.

"It's because of Pop, isn't it?"

Teru nodded.

"Do they know about Mr. Satō's plan for Pop?"

"Hiromi say no tell 'em. He say he no give job Benito for stop strike; he give 'cause Benito deserve dis promotion."

"Don't worry," Hiromi said. "The promotion will stick, strike or no strike. I'll see to that."

A nurse walked by and heard them talking. "What's going on here?" she asked. "Mr. Satō, Dr. Chuck said one visitor at a time."

"We're just leaving," Nori said. "Bye, Daddy. I'll come by in the morning." She kissed him on the cheek, and the three of them left the room.

When they were outside, Danny turned to Teru and spoke, "Why not tell the union about Pop's new job. It might head off the strike."

"Hiromi some proud man. He say tell nobody till after da meeting."

"But that might be too late! Teru, will you go with me to the meeting?"

"Da Federation for Filipino only. I t'ink so dey not so much like Japanese fella bust in on dem, eh? Anyways, Federation no call strike, union call strike."

"But the Filipinos have a majority in the union. If the Filipinos vote for a strike, there'll be a strike."

Teru shook his head sadly. "I no can do nothing, Danny. I promise Hiromi."

"Well, come with me anyway. We'll wait until after the meeting and then tell them. Maybe they'll change their minds. We have to do something."

Teru agreed. Nori made Danny promise to call her later and left them. They hurried to the hall and stood outside one of the open windows. Benito was speaking to the group.

" . . . you too much good friends," he said, his voice heavy with emotion. "You like call strike for help one old Pilipino man get back his job, but how many people dis strike gonna hurt? Some o' you young fella no remember da big strike we get years ago. Dis island stink wid rotting pine, and da fields all over weeds. Okimoto store get nobody for buy grocery. Some people lose dere houses, go way from Lanai, never come back. No call strike for help Benito; Benito old man, only got two maybe three year more for work, eh?"

One of the other men stood up. "It not just you, Benito. Dat Satō hurt any kind guys and keep everybody scared all da time. Maybe tomorrow it come my turn for pick pine in da field. Dis Hiromi Satō some crazy guy; nobody know what he t'inkin', eh? He come lolo dis last little while, push, push everybody, no care for nothing. I say we strike!"

Shouts came from different voices in the room: "Who dis Satō t'ink he is anyways!" "If Benito job not safe, who got safe job, eh?" "Satō hate Pilipino, everybody know dat!" The rumble of discontent began to grow.

An older man stood and waited for the crowd to quiet down. "I come Lanai plenty years ago when Hiromi father run da plantation. Dat Matsuo Satō one fine fella, you bet. He no send old man out to da field. If worker come old, come sick, still gotta work, he find some kind job he can do. Sometime he make job, sweep da shed, pick up da mail, guard da plantation office nighttime. Old man can do somet'ing, make litty bit money, no be shame. Dis Hiromi got no more nothing in here." He patted his chest and sat down.

One after another, men stood and voiced their complaints. Some sounded angry, some just discouraged. Plainly the group was moving in the direction of striking.

Danny started to walk up the steps of the building toward the entrance, but Teru grasped him by the arm. "Waste time, you try talk," Teru whispered, shaking his head sadly. "Even you go inside and tell dem 'bout Benito new job, help nothing."

The secretary of the Federation shouted for quiet, and the president asked for any other comments before they took a vote.

"I like say somet'ing," called a voice from the back of the room." It was a strangely familiar voice, but Danny could not identify the man.

"Salvadore, what you like say?"

"It's Mr. Presa," Danny said under his breath.

"Dis come hard for me," he began. "My family so new to Lanai. We like make friend, not make trouble." He cleared his throat and continued. "My young daughter, Nita, only a sophomore at Lanai High. She like grow up quick, be popular, be famous like her big sister, have any kind boyfriend. I tell her try wait; you get plenty time, but she no listen. Den she get date wid Danny Tolentino, go senior prom, all time talk Danny, Danny, Danny. After da big game wid Wailuku, I drive her down to Manele Beach to be wid Danny at da big party. She act kinda funny dat weekend, an' when she come home from school da next Monday, she no want nobody ask 'bout Danny to her. She say she hate Danny Tolentino."

"What you say about my Danny?" Benito shouted. "You try tell lies about Danny? You t'ink I old man, no can do nothing?" There were footsteps and the sound of chairs being pushed out of the way.

"Whoa, Benito, no huhu! Try wait liddy bit. Danny plenty fine boy. I no talk nothing bad 'bout Danny. Try wait, eh? I too much like him; I like have boy like dis for my own son!"

Benito became quiet, and so did the rest of the crowd. Salvadore Presa continued with his story. Nita had told her father that Danny had given her a lot of attention and then tried to take advantage of her at the beach on the night of the party. When she refused his advances, he had turned to Nori Satō. They had gone off around the point and stayed for a long time alone. She herself had seen them go and return hours later. After that they were always together. One of Nita's friends had seen them coming back from Mahana one Sunday afternoon looking very guilty. Hiromi's prejudice against Filipinos was well known. She wondered what he would say if he knew Nori was spending so much time alone with a Filipino boy.

"I believe everyt'ing; Nita, my baby girl," Presa said sadly. "I t'ink dis Danny some kind big romeo, student-body president, captain of da basketball team, who like hurt nice little girl like my Nita an' Nori Satō. I no like him too. By 'n' by I feel guilty dat Satō know no more nothing about dis problem."

He had finally gone to Satō's office when he was alone and told him. Satō had called him a liar, grabbed him by his jacket, and slammed him up against the wall. Presa had pleaded with him to ask his daughter about what had happened at the beach, and he had let Presa go. As he was leaving, Presa had seen Hiromi take a bottle out of a cabinet and pour himself a drink. That was the day when Benito was sent home early from the harbor.

"But what about my Danny?" Benito demanded. Danny still had not been shown to be innocent.

"I never know Danny," Presa said. "I see him play basketball, dats all. Today he jump down from da rock, dive deep, and save Hiromi Satō life. He save da man who send his papa back to da fields to get sick or maybe die. I say to myself, 'Salvadore, somet'ing wrong here. Dis Danny some fine boy. He no like Nita say. He no hurt little girl; he no hurt nobody.'

"I go home, take Nita to her room, and sit her down on da bed. Den I pull up chair real close so my nose almost touch her nose. I look in her eyes so she know I mean business and say real slow, 'Tell you papa da truth about Danny Tolentino.' She tell me everyt'ing. She come all huhu when Danny go back wid Nori. She like make trouble for him, so she tell me any kind stuffs an' hope I tell Hiromi." Salvadore shook his head sadly. "I come all shame dat my Nita make so much trouble.

"I go back to hospital, and Hiromi is feeling litty bit better so I can talk to him. I tell him same like I tell you. He just sit dere an' listen; he no say nothing. When I leave, Nori come inside room for try feed him somet'ing."

He took a deep breath and began again. "I just like ask one little small question before you take vote. If you lose your wife and get only one little girl left, and somebody tell you what I tell Hiromi, maybe so you come litty bit crazy too, eh? I say, give him chance. If nothing change, we strike. But maybe so dis man learn somet'ing from almost die. Give him chance, eh?"

They decided not to vote just then. They would wait for one month and see if there was a change in Hiromi. As they filed out of the Federation Hall, Danny and Teru told them the good news about Benito's new job. It didn't quiet all their concerns, but it was a good first step. Benito's friends crowded around Danny's father, congratulating him.

Chapter

31

Danny sat on his front steps and blinked in the bright sunlight filtering down through the two large Norfolk Island pine trees in his front yard. He had slept in that Saturday morning, and it felt good to be lazy. The sound of pans banging in the kitchen reminded him that his father was busy cooking breakfast. Benito was singing in his thin, high-pitched voice, and Danny laughed as he recognized the tune and realized that his father was putting his own words to the music, some in Pidgin and some in Tagalog. Danny caught the smell of bacon frying and knew that eggs would soon be cooking in the same pan. Benito loved eggs cooked in bacon grease. Danny also knew that he would soon hear an anxious call to breakfast. Benito liked his eggs over easy, and any delay on Danny's part would ruin them.

"Danny, Danny, come quick! Eggs almost come hard; try hurry, eh?"

Danny rushed into the house, pretending to be out of breath from the exertion. He dropped into his chair and wiped imaginary perspiration from his forehead. "Did I make it in time, Pop?"

Benito looked up from the stove and, realizing that he was being teased, played along. "Sorry, too much slow you come.

Eggs no mo' good now. Only good throw away. Mo' better you come back lunchtime."

Conversation over breakfast centered around Benito's upcoming promotion.

"Some good dis one new job fo' me! I work not so hard, make plenty money. By 'n' by I retire, get good pension, all time sleep late, all time go fishing Keomuku, all time raise chicken for fight. Too good dis life!"

"You deserve it, Pop. You're the best man they have down at the Harbor."

Benito beamed. "You like more eggs, Danny? More bacon? When you brag on your Pop, he give you any kind stuffs!"

"Don't feed me too much, Pop. Nori and I are going on a picnic with the elders and the kids from the branch. I have to eat again in two or three hours."

"Some big trouble you get, eh, Danny? Eat, eat, all time eat. Maybe so I come along on picnic, help you wid dis big problem. If Nori make dat good coconut haupia for dessert, no stuff yourself, eh? Bring home to Benito; he eat for you, eh?"

Danny and Nori lagged behind as the group hiked up Keomuku Road to the place where the Munro Trail began.

"Remember the last time we went hiking?" Danny asked. "We were both nervous for fear your father would find out we were together."

"Daddy's so much different now. He's going to Honolulu to see the doctors about his hand next week. He told me to hang some of Mother's pictures on the walls while he's gone. I've started painting her portrait, and he thinks it's pretty good. I've been asking him questions about her, and he's telling me things I never knew. It's hard for him to talk about her, but he's trying."

"I always feel a little nervous when I come to your house, Nori. I guess I'm afraid he'll go back to the way he was."

"He likes you, Danny. Maybe when his hand heals, you two can go spearfishing together."

"I'll have to practice holding my breath. Nobody can stay down as long as Hiromi Satō."

"Are you going to work for the plantation this summer?"

"I hope to. I may even fish part-time with Teru. Pop wants to give me some money for school, but I wouldn't feel good about it. He retires in a few years. My plan is to work for a year before starting college. If I save everything I make and work summers, I think I can get through at least two years of school without having to stop to work again."

"I'll hurry and get through and get a job; then I can help you," Nori said determinedly.

"Maybe you'll find some handsome guy with lots of money and forget all about me," Danny teased. Nori punched him in the ribs.

"You've got to stop hitting me like that," Danny said, pretending great pain. "I bruise easily. Come on, let's catch up with the group. I'm anxious to see what delicious things you have in that basket."

After lunch, Bernard led the elders and the branch kids on up the trail. Danny and Nori let them go on ahead and sat for a long time looking out at the blue water that separated them from Maui and Molokai.

"The channel looks like a lake today. You should have seen it from Teru's fishing boat that night when we went over to play Lahainaluna!" Danny stood and took in the whole panorama. "Look! You can see Oahu. It doesn't look like much from here, but that must be it." Danny pointed off to the northwest beyond the tip of Molokai. "I'll come here sometimes when you're away at school. I'll borrow some binoculars and see if I can see you."

Nori laughed. "Everytime there's a clear day like this, I'll climb up to the top of Diamond Head and wave a white scarf." She stood on tiptoe and waved her napkin feverishly. Suddenly she stopped laughing and looked up at Danny. "I've never been away from you for more than a few days, Danny. How will I stand it?"

Danny put his arms around her. "We've got all summer to be together. Don't start talking about saying good-bye." He kissed her softly as tears began to fill her eyes. "Come on now, Nori," he warned. "If you keep this up you'll have me crying too." He held her out at arm's length and feigned great concern. "Have you ever seen Pilipino cry? Oh! da terrible sight, boy. Face come all twist up. Eyes get swollen, all red and scary. And oh! da noise! Scare any kind birds and animals away, even fish swim out to sea!" He grabbed her by the hand and ran up the trail to catch the others.

They came upon Elder Opi walking slowly up the trail by himself. "Those kids move too fast for me," he said as they joined him. "I want to enjoy this hike. They act like they want to hurry and get it over with."

"You're right," Nori said. "The days go by fast enough without running through them."

"It's beautiful here, but there's one thing missing," Elder Opi said, "running water. It makes me kind of homesick. Back home, when you find a place this green and leafy, there's usually a river or creek running through it, especially in the spring when the snow is melting up on the mountains. You don't see that many streams in Hawaii unless it's raining. I miss the sound of those mountain streams."

"Have you been homesick a lot?" Nori asked.

"Not a lot, just once in a while." Elder Opi answered. "Hawaii is beautiful, but home is home, and nothing quite replaces it. You'll see what I mean when you go away to school next fall."

"I'm homesick already," Nori said looking up at Danny.

"I thought we weren't going to talk about you leaving," Danny said. "That's months away."

"But the time is going by so fast! We'll be graduating in a month, and then you'll be working every day. Before you know it, the summer will be gone."

"Time does pass quickly when you're enjoying your life," Elder Opi said. "I'm going to be homesick for Lanai when I leave."

"That won't be for a long time," Danny said reassuringly. "Maybe they'll just leave you here like they did Elder Ihunui."

"I'm afraid not. When the mission president was here for branch conference last weekend, he told me to get ready for a move."

"But you've been here such a short time!" Danny said.

"They're going to make me mission secretary," Elder Opi said. "I can't imagine why. The Maui District report is always late because of me. Maybe they think I need the training."

Danny felt an emptiness at the thought of leaving. "First, you. Then I lose Nori in September," he said. "I guess I'd better get used to saying good-bye. Bernard is almost sure to get a full scholarship at the University of Hawaii, so he'll be leaving with Nori. If I work a year for the plantation, I can probably go to school after that, but I don't know for how long. I may have to stop every few quarters and work some more."

"Maybe not," Elder Opi said. "Can you keep a secret?" Danny and Nori nodded. "When the mission president went to Salt Lake City for general conference a few weeks ago, he had an interview with President McKay. The Church is planning to build a college on Oahu to serve the islands of the Pacific. They'll make the official announcement sometime this summer. The tuition will be low, and there'll be scholarships and part-time jobs for students who need them. Students will come from Samoa, New Zealand, Tonga, Fiji, Tahiti—all over the Pacific. It will be a good school, with a full program of activities. They might even have a basketball team. Do you know any good players?" Danny's mouth had dropped open, and Elder Opi smiled at his excitement.

"Is it really a secret?" Danny asked.

"He said to keep it quiet until the announcement, but you two were looking so forlorn, I couldn't resist sharing the good news. Think of it, Danny. The school will open in the fall of 1955, just when you were planning to start. You'll be a charter member! Now enjoy the rest of the school year and the summer. You'll be separated for a few months, but maybe that will do you good. It won't be as long as I'm being separated from my girl."

"I didn't know you had a girl waiting for you back home," Danny said.

"I think she's waiting for about three missionaries now, but I have an advantage."

"You're the favorite, right?" Nori said with a smile.

"No. I'll be the first one to get home. I get released on the first of March next year. The competition gets back in April and May. Also, the other guys will be coming from snow country, so they'll be pale and unhealthy looking. When she sees

244

my tan, handsome face, she'll just melt into my arms, don't you think?"

"I'm sure of it," Nori said, laughing.

"I'd better get back to the group," Elder Opi said finally. "Elder Global will be looking for me. You know what a little worrier he is. Did I say little?" They all laughed. "Now remember, you've got some secrets to keep. Not a word about the new school, my transfer, or my girlfriend, okay?" He walked away.

"I wish the new school were starting this fall," Nori said.

"So do I, but a year isn't forever. You'll be back next spring, and when you see my tan, handsome face, you'll probably just melt into my arms."

She smiled and took his hand as they walked through the Norfolk pines that lined the Munro Trail.

Lee G. Cantwell served a mission in Hawaii from 1953 to 1955 and spent eight months on the island of Lanai. The setting for the novel and many of the characters are based on his experiences there and on subsequent visits to the Islands. The author is a practicing dentist; he received his D.M.D. from the University of Oregon. He and his wife, Karen Hansen, reside in Smithfield, Utah. They have two sons and two daughters. *Crosscurrents* is Lee Cantwell's first published novel.